THE LEGACY

THE LEGACY

DIANE AMOS

FIVE STAR
A part of Gale, Cengage Learning

GALE
CENGAGE Learning

Detroit • New York • San Francisco • New Haven, Conn • Waterville, Maine • London

GALE
CENGAGE Learning

LIBRARY OF CONGRESS CATALOGING-IN-PUBLICATION DATA

Amos, Diane.
   The legacy / Diane Amos. — 1st ed.
   p. cm.
   ISBN-13: 978-1-59414-815-6 (alk. paper)
   ISBN-10: 1-59414-815-5 (alk. paper)
   1. Inheritance and succession—Fiction. 2. Texas—History—
   1846–1950—Fiction. I. Title.
   PS3601.M67L44 2009
   813'.6—dc22   2009027508

First Edition. First Printing: November 2009.
Published in 2009 in conjunction with Tekno Books.

Printed in the United States of America
1 2 3 4 5 6 7 13 12 11 10 09

THE LEGACY

CHAPTER 1

June 2, 1887

You cold-hearted varmint,

Was it up to me, I wouldn't send this letter.

But your paw needs to see you one last time.

Hurry. One more thing, if you arrive before he dies, the ranch will be yours.

A.

Bitterness crept up the back of Jeremiah T. Dalton's throat as he reread the words filled with contempt. He slipped the letter back in its envelope and dabbed the perspiration from his brow with the silk handkerchief normally tucked in his suit pocket just for show. Lowdown, Texas was hot as hell, which seemed fitting, considering he was about to meet the devil himself.

An old cowpoke, sitting in the stagecoach on the seat opposite him, gave Jeremiah a slow perusal. "You ain't from round these parts."

"No, I'm not."

"What brings you out this way?"

He noted the old geezer's grin with missing front teeth and the wide black hat that shadowed his face. Jeremiah straightened his Derby on the seat beside him and smiled politely.

"Family business."

"That so." The old man scratched his whiskered jaw, then reached out. "Buck Ridley, here."

Jeremiah shook his hand. "Jeremiah T. Dalton."

7

"Can tell from your accent you're from back East a ways."

Jeremiah nodded.

Buck pulled out a crushed box of *Battle Ax Plug* tobacco from his shirt pocket, bit off a chunk and offered Jeremiah what remained. "Do you chew?"

"No, thanks. It's not one of my vices."

Buck stuck the additional wad in his cheek and seemed content to ride in silence.

Jeremiah leaned back against the seat, closed his eyes and thought back to his childhood. Not once had his mother uttered a kind word about the man responsible for his birth. According to her, his father was a conniving, fast-talking good-for-nothing. One fact was indisputable; his old man had never given a damn about him. As a boy, Jeremiah wrote countless letters that went unanswered. Finally, he gave up hope of ever seeing his father again.

As an adult, Jeremiah wanted nothing to do with his father, although he preferred the term *sensible* to *cold-hearted* as the letter had indicated.

"Wedding or funeral?"

Jeremiah glanced up. "Huh?"

"Wedding or funeral brung you here?"

"Someone's taken ill."

"Didya say Dalton? Wouldn't happen to be related to N.H. Dalton?"

"My father," he replied, the words sticking in his throat like a sharp bone.

"Well, I'll be diggered. Didn't know N.H. had himself a son."

Realizing his father had kept his existence a secret, Jeremiah's gut coiled with anger. He was grateful when Buck turned his attention to the view from the window.

As the stagecoach rolled into town, Jeremiah studied each building and tried to recall something from his past. Ridley's

Livery, a large wooden structure, stood off by itself, and though Jeremiah could imagine himself as a small boy admiring the horses, nothing about the livery looked familiar.

Several stores came next, among them Fred's Barbershop, The Dressmaker, and Bufford's Mercantile. From the opened double doors of the general store, he saw packed shelves and narrow aisles. Its overflowing merchandise spilled onto the crooked boardwalk where two men sat on a crude wooden bench, playing checkers, surrounded by shovels, brooms, baskets, and barrels. A surprising thought surfaced. Bufford's sold the best candy for miles around. Was this a memory or merely his sweet tooth on the trail of licorice whips and lemon drops?

An hour later Jeremiah sat on a bench outside the Lowdown Federal Bank, his patience in no better shape than the white shirt plastered to his body. He'd telegraphed his time of arrival and had received a response that someone would meet his stagecoach.

The rumble of wagon wheels and an approaching dust cloud interrupted his thoughts. He stood, cupping a hand over his eyes, and spotted a rickety wagon heading toward him. He was about to jump aside when the driver, a tall boy, pulled back on the brake.

"Whoa," he shouted in a high-pitched voice.

Beside him sat a little girl with probing eyes and a mean frown.

The slightly built driver hopped down from the wagon. "You Jeremiah Dalton?"

"Yes, what took you so long?"

"Had things to do."

"That's it? No explanation?"

A satisfied grin surfaced beneath the rim of the western-style hat.

Jeremiah plunked his Derby on his head. Salvaging what remained of his manners, he smiled tolerantly, grabbed his heavy bag, and gestured for the lad to take the other. Much to his amazement, the youngster climbed onto the wagon without lifting a finger.

"Young man, might I remind you that in time you'll be working for me?" He mimicked the tone his future father-in-law used effectively with the servants.

The youngster hopped down and stood inches from his chest. "I'll work for you when rattlers sprout legs!"

The raised voice was clear, defiant, and definitely not masculine. Caught off guard, he bent to look under the brim of the hat.

Cold green eyes glared back at him. He studied the heart-shaped face and the small nose splattered with rusty freckles. As he straightened, he noticed the wilted daisy sticking from the hatband.

Big mistake, he realized, feeling like a fool. What would possess a woman to wear men's trousers and a shapeless shirt?

She yanked her hat off her head and slapped it against her thigh, raising dust and setting free a riot of bright curls the color of carrots, a vegetable he detested.

Eyes the color of polished pewter held Abigail Wilcox captive. Her heart skipped a beat as she studied the features much like his father's. The similarities ended there, however, for N. H. Dalton was a kind and loving man.

Determined to make Jeremiah Dalton's ride to the ranch as miserable as possible, Abigail had chosen this small wagon with broken springs and a front seat barely wide enough for her and Clarissa. Her daughter had kicked up a fuss about coming, but Abigail had insisted, which explained the child's sour mood.

Standing with her back to the wagon, Abigail gazed into the

flint-gray eyes filled with disbelief. She pushed aside unruly curls that had tumbled over her forehead and, sucking in her breath, thrust out small breasts. Why had Jeremiah Dalton's mistake hurt so much?

The tension stretched between them until Clarissa leaned over Abigail's shoulder. "Maw, how long you two gonna gawk at each other?"

Clearly uncomfortable, Jeremiah ran a finger inside the stiff collar of his stained white shirt. "I apologize for the error, Mrs . . ."

Abigail straightened her shoulders. "It's Miss and don't worry none about the mistake."

Shock flickered over his features before she turned and hopped onto the wagon.

She didn't care diddly what he thought.

If only that were true.

Shame had carved a crater the size of Texas in her heart. At first she'd hidden her secret behind a cheap gold band, but word got around.

People looked down their noses at her. So instead of prolonging the inevitable, she preferred to set the record straight from the start.

Jeremiah walked to the back of the wagon, heaved his bags onto the planks, and hopped aboard. He pushed aside the hay with his shoe before sitting down. Abigail released the brake and flicked the reins. She expected him to grumble.

He dug in his pocket and produced a crumpled paper bag. "Lemon drops, anybody?"

Lemon drops were Abigail's favorite, but taking one seemed traitorous.

Clarissa had no such qualms. "Thanks," she said, grabbing two.

Abigail bit her lip and concentrated on hitting the pothole in the middle of the road.

For the next hour, Jeremiah tried unsuccessfully to cushion his rattling bones. Each time the wagon struck a hole, the loose boards beneath him separated just enough to pinch his backside.

For years he'd heard tales of his father's ranch, a sprawling twelve thousand-acre spread with a large hacienda-style house staffed with servants. As Jeremiah bounced along in the rickety wagon, he wondered if these reports were more of his mother's exaggerations. If this chariot was an indication of the condition of the Dalton ranch, Jeremiah would be on the next train heading East.

As he reached up and rubbed his hand along the back of his aching neck, he spotted a familiar cluster of four cacti resembling the silhouette of a cowboy with Stetson and pipe.

If he hadn't seen the large sign swaying from the top of a stone archway, he'd have voiced his suspicions; they'd been traveling in circles.

He read the words, *Dalton Ranch.* The gold lettering above the carved image of a steer spoke of wealth and power. Stone walls bordered either side of the winding road that led to an adobe-colored two-story building. From the recesses of his mind came the vision of a small boy rocking on a wooden porch swing. Before he could question his rambling thoughts, the wagon entered a courtyard, and that same porch swing appeared.

An unexpected shiver raced down his spine as Jeremiah spotted a man sitting in the shadows on an oversized rocker. He didn't realize the wagon had stopped until the young girl dashed toward the old man and kissed his cheek.

"How ya feeling, Grandpa Dalton?"

Until now, Jeremiah's memories had been dim, but those of

his father were vivid.

And painful.

Jeremiah unclenched his fists and breathed in deeply. For years he'd promised himself if this day ever came, he'd greet his father with aloofness.

He unfolded his stiff frame from the wagon and reluctantly strolled toward the porch. Jeremiah couldn't make out his father's face, but he felt his penetrating gaze.

Though he'd told himself he wouldn't so much as shake hands with this man, as he neared the porch, Noah stretched out trembling arms. This wasn't the person Jeremiah remembered, but a frail old man. For a moment Jeremiah stood there staring down at the gnarled fingers covered with parchment-like flesh, and his resolve crumbled.

In a moment of weakness, he clasped his father's hands.

CHAPTER 2

Abigail watched the scene with mixed emotions.

When Noah's fingers slipped from Jeremiah's grasp, she leaned forward and brushed a strand of silver hair from his forehead. "Noah, what are you doing up?"

"I was damn tired of rotting away in bed. Got up to see my son."

Jeremiah didn't deserve to be called Noah's son. Unwilling to hurt Noah's feelings, she kept her opinion to herself. She blinked back tears and trailed her fingers against his cheek. For years Noah had been there for her, and she for him. She dreaded the day when he'd no longer be around.

Refusing to dwell on the inevitable, she forced a smile. "You look tired. Shouldn't you rest?"

Noah inhaled a shuddering breath. "Maybe, just a small nap. Jeremiah and I have lots of catching up to do."

Noah cupped the arms of the chair and pushed himself up. The veins on his shaking hands bulged. Getting out of bed had taken its toll. Though Abigail knew she was thinking irrationally, she blamed Jeremiah Dalton for Noah's deteriorating condition.

Noah stepped forward on wobbly legs. Abigail wanted to help him, but he'd only push her away as he always had in the past. She walked beside him and prayed he wouldn't stumble.

Noah wrapped unsteady fingers around Jeremiah's arm and leaned against his unyielding frame. "I'm glad you came."

The old man stared into his son's face, waiting for some re-action.

Jeremiah stood stiff as a fence post, his hands by his side, indecision playing across his face. Finally, with what looked like great effort, a strained smile surfaced.

Noah exhaled deeply. The feeble smile he directed toward Abigail broke her heart and reminded her of his numbered days.

"Before I go get myself a little shuteye, tell me what you think of our gal? Don't you agree she's a special lady?"

Jeremiah Dalton's cool gaze swept over her. "Yes."

"I knew you two would hit it off." Noah's sharp mind was way off track, which Abigail attributed to his failing health.

Noah waved her over. "Give me a hug, then go fetch the sur-rey. While I'm dozing, take Jeremiah on a tour of the property."

After a sandwich, a bath and some clean clothes, Jeremiah felt like himself again. He blamed his emotional reaction to seeing his father on the jarring ride that had scrambled his brain. He called himself a fool for even wanting to believe he cared for his old man.

But no matter how hard he tried, instead of hatred, he was gripped by a deep sense of loss that caused him to grieve for what might have been.

He glanced around his poorly ventilated attic room and wondered whether Miss Wilcox was responsible for his accom-modations. The narrow bed, though adequate, barely held his long frame. If he forgot to duck when he rose in the morning, he'd strike his head on the slanting ceiling.

He strode across the room and peered at his reflection in the cracked mirror above the dresser. He ran a comb through his hair to tame the lock over his forehead that no pomade could keep in place. Not wanting to appear overdressed but determined to maintain an air of civility, he omitted the tie but still wore his favorite green silk vest. He rolled the sleeves of his crisp white shirt to his elbows.

After brushing the lint from the crease of his linen pants, he straightened, popped a lemon drop in his mouth, and slipped the bag of candy into the back pocket before descending the stairs.

He saw Abigail sitting in the parlor with her back to him, one hand holding a glass of water, the other tapping a handkerchief to the corner of her eye. Although Jeremiah didn't understand her, he understood tears. Evelyn, his fiancée, had drenched his shirt on several occasions over trivial matters. He was willing to lend a shoulder to Miss Abigail Wilcox. As she patted her eyes, he rounded the settee and rested a compassionate hand on her arm.

Startled, Abigail Wilcox leaped to her feet and bumped into him. The glass flew. Its contents spilled down the front of his silk vest. To keep her from falling, he tried to wrap his arm around her waist, but she shoved him away.

She heaved an exasperated sigh. "Don't you know better than to sneak up behind someone?"

"Sorry, Miss Wilcox." He withdrew a white handkerchief from his pant pocket and mopped the water from his soaked vest.

She turned, marched across the room and glanced over her shoulder. "Call me, Abigail. It'll make your father happy."

"In that case, call me Jeremiah."

"Won't be easy, but I'll do it for Noah's sake." Her curt reply set his teeth on edge.

"Excuse me a minute." He hurried outside and laid his vest over the porch railing to dry. When he went back into the parlor, he discovered Abigail was gone. He found her heading toward a large barn that stood about two hundred feet from the house.

As he caught up with her, he was aware of something bumping his leg. He spun around and looked down at an immense hog.

"What's it doing?"

A glint of humor brightened Abigail's eyes. "Looking for food."

"Why isn't this creature in a pen? Why isn't it bacon?"

The pig butted him, and for one insane moment, he considered the possibility it understood what he'd said.

"It's Clarissa's pet." Abigail folded her arms across her chest.

After jabbing its snout against Jeremiah's pant leg, the pig snorted before lowering its bulk to the ground.

Abigail rubbed its head. "Good boy, Hamlet."

"Have you ever considered a puppy instead?" He thought the comment might elicit a smile, but he was wrong.

"I bet you have food in your pocket."

He'd forgotten about his lemon drops.

Though he hated to give that damn pig a lemon drop, he watched the hairy snout lift expectantly as he tossed a piece of candy that never hit the ground.

Hamlet crunched down on the hard treat and seemed to beam. Jeremiah laughed at its comical expression. The sound died in his throat when Abigail speared him with an angry glance.

She abruptly stalked away.

He caught up with her and grabbed her shoulder. "What's the matter with you?"

She spun around and met his gaze, her intense dislike of him evident in her scowl. "I don't think you want to know."

When she tried to pull away, he tightened his grip. "I never was one to run from the truth."

"You're a cold-hearted varmint."

The familiar salutation nudged his memory. "You sent the letter?"

"Sure did, but I didn't want to."

Jeremiah let go of her shoulder.

Abigail made no move to leave.

"If you felt that way, then why did you bother sending the letter at all?"

"I did it for Noah. I knew how much he wanted to see you. And I know what part of that letter got your attention." She blew a curl from her forehead. "That little scene earlier turned my stomach."

"What are you talking about?"

"You may be able to fool a frail old man who's grasping at every small shred of attention you so lovingly dole out. But I see clear through you, Jeremiah Dalton."

"And just what is it you see?"

"A hawk coming in for the kill."

"You sure don't believe in giving a guy a chance, do you?"

"I'm too smart for that." As if rethinking her position, she studied him a moment. "You want a chance? Then answer this. If I hadn't mentioned you'd be inheriting your father's ranch, would you have come?"

Unable to defend himself, he glanced away.

They walked to the barn in silence, and as Jeremiah contemplated what she'd said, he spotted a goat dashing toward them with a green rag in its mouth.

Too late, he recognized what remained of his favorite silk vest.

In a brief lapse of control, he cursed aloud.

Abigail gazed down at her legs covered by men's loose-fitting britches. She could easily understand why the ranch hands treated her like one of them.

Jeremiah brushed a lock of hair from his forehead. "I want to apologize for cussing in your presence. There was no call for such language."

He couldn't have surprised her more if he'd pulled a rattlesnake from his hip pocket. No one had ever given thought to what they said in front of Abigail Wilcox. She waved her hand in a gesture that indicated it hadn't meant a thing when all the time her heart was thumping so hard she could barely hear herself say, "Doesn't matter none."

"It does to me. And I'll try to do better from now on."

She shrugged. Given the chance she could grow to like this man.

She tucked a curl beneath her hat. "I told Whip to get the surrey ready. And don't worry none about the vest. I'll buy you another at Bufford's next time I'm in town."

He seemed pleased and genuinely surprised. "That isn't necessary. I have others."

"That goat belongs to my daughter, and I won't be indebted to any man."

He took her hand and rested her fingers around his elbow. When they reached the surrey, he made sure she got her footing and assisted her onto the seat, which was nonsense because Abigail could have easily hopped on without help. But she enjoyed the attention. Once she was seated, he reached down and handed her the reins. The simple courtesy meant the world to her.

When Jeremiah Dalton climbed aboard the wagon, Abigail smiled and discovered the simple gesture came naturally.

Jeremiah noticed the tall man with black handlebar mustache, leaning against the entryway to the barn. The scowl he directed at Jeremiah spoke volumes.

Jeremiah motioned with his chin. "Who's the charming individual?"

Abigail waved the man over. "Whip, there's someone I'd like you to meet."

Whip sauntered toward them and stopped beside the carriage. He wore faded, snug-fitting Levis and a light blue shirt with a neckerchief. He hesitated a few seconds before reaching up.

Jeremiah shook his hand. "Pleased to make your acquaintance. I'm Jeremiah Dalton."

"Figured as much." Whip turned his head to one side and spat on the ground. "You staying on long?"

"I haven't decided yet."

"I reckon Noah was mighty glad to see you."

"He seemed to be."

"Good thing you arrived in time. It would have been a damn shame for you to travel all this way for nothing."

Jeremiah got his meaning loud and clear. Whip knew he was here for only one reason.

His inheritance.

When Whip turned and disappeared inside the barn, Jeremiah speared Abigail with a hard look. "Did you tell everyone my reason for coming, or does it just seem that way?"

Her chin inched upward. "You needn't use that tone with me, Jeremiah Dalton."

"I'll use any tone I want. I've had it up to here." He ran his finger across his neck. "Ever since I arrived, you've done nothing but give me dirty looks. On the trip from town your daughter kept stealing glances over her shoulder as if she expected me to knife her in the back."

He inhaled a long deep breath, which did nothing to soothe him. "This brings me to another point of contention. Why did you pick me up in a wagon not fit for swine when you had this surrey at your disposal?"

She laughed softly. "I thought you'd enjoy seeing the countryside from the back of the wagon."

"Yeah, I bet."

She dipped the brim of her hat down, but not before he caught the glint of satisfaction in her eyes. "If a little hay is too tough for you, then you'll never survive in Texas."

Jeremiah had always considered himself the sort of man who possessed a great deal of self-control. What did it matter that she thought him a coldhearted son of a bitch?

But she slid him a sidelong glance that did him in.

He cast a pointed look at her. "When the will is read, my first duty as owner of this ranch will be to send you packing."

A brief flicker of despair zipped over her features before she raised cutting eyes to his. "I don't care diddly what you do. I'd leave now except Noah needs me."

She turned her head to the side and spat next to the wagon.

Jeremiah had never seen a woman spit in public. Come to think of it, he'd never seen a woman spit. Certain that the shock registered on his face, he met her gaze and watched in amazement as she lifted her head at a haughty angle that dared him to say anything.

Despite the hard edge to her eyes, he saw vulnerability in their depths. For a moment, he wanted to wrap his arm around Abigail's shoulder and shelter her from the storm brewing in her heart.

He quickly regained his senses when she hopped down from the wagon at a clip that would have rivaled any man. "This was a mistake. I'll find someone else to show you around."

Peace at last, Jeremiah thought.

CHAPTER 3

A Mexican waving a large sombrero ran out of the house. "Señorita Wilcox, come quickly!"

Abigail stopped abruptly. "Pedro, what's wrong?"

Jeremiah heard the tremor in her voice. Her hands shook. She seemed unable to move.

He hurried to her side and held her arm in a firm grip. "Abigail, let me help you."

"Huh?" A shuddering breath racked her body. She yanked her arm free and ran toward the house with Jeremiah at her heels.

They rushed into Noah's bedroom; several people lifted tear-filled eyes at Jeremiah before gazing helplessly at Abigail. For several seconds she stared at Noah's still form beneath the white sheet.

Thinking Abigail might collapse from shock, Jeremiah stayed by her side, taking in her pale features and sad eyes. He expected her to weep or possibly to scream out in anguish.

Pedro pulled a wrinkled handkerchief from his pants pocket and sobbed uncontrollably. Abigail moved next to him and placed her hands on his shoulders.

"Noah wouldn't want you to carry on this way. You were there for him when he needed you. That's all that matters."

Jeremiah's chest tightened. He had never been there for his father. He didn't even know the man who'd called himself his father.

And now, it was too late.

The following day whenever Jeremiah turned around, he'd catch Whip or Pedro eyeing him as if he'd crawled out from under a rock. Though Jeremiah had never expected to stay in Texas long enough to make lasting friendships, he hadn't anticipated the animosity aimed at him, either. To her credit, Abigail no longer glared when he walked by but instead completely ignored him.

Looking forlorn, Clarissa spent most of her spare time next to her mother. Clearly, the child had loved Noah. Jeremiah felt a pang of regret whenever he thought of Clarissa's relationship with his father. As a boy, he'd yearned for some sign that his father cared.

Tomorrow after the funeral, Sam Burns, Noah's lawyer, would read the will. Jeremiah would finish his business and leave Texas. And he'd never return.

Blaming the feelings roiling inside on restlessness, Jeremiah decided to escape into town and send Evelyn a telegraph. While there, he'd visit Bufford's to buy more lemon drops.

When he gazed at his reflection in the mirror, he noticed that the same blasted strand of hair had fallen over his forehead. He located the pomatum on the bureau, unwrapped the foil and, holding his hair in place, stroked the waxy stick against the stubborn lock. He grabbed his waistcoat and Derby and headed downstairs.

Just knowing he was leaving the ranch for a few hours lifted his spirits. Even when Jeremiah spotted Pedro glaring at him from the kitchen door, he found it easy to smile.

"I'm going into Lowdown for a while. I was hoping you'd give me directions."

"Si, Señor, I will show you."

Jeremiah followed the man to the front porch. Expecting a set of complicated directions, he was shocked when Pedro pointed to the small rise in the distance.

"Señor, if you go over the hill, you will find Lowdown."

Jeremiah gazed in the direction the Mexican had pointed. "Once I go over the hill, how many miles is it to town?"

Pedro looked at him as if he were mentally incompetent. "Over the hill, you will see Lowdown."

Jeremiah shrugged. Leaving Pedro staring at his back, he marched toward the barn. Once he found the cacti shaped like a cowboy, he'd rely on his sharp memory.

When he entered the barn, Whip greeted him. "You going someplace?"

"As a matter of fact, I am. I'd like you to recommend a docile animal."

"Zeb would be perfect," came the drawl from behind him.

Jeremiah turned and tipped his hat to Abigail. She wore men's Levis rolled to her ankles with a three-corner tear in the seat of her pants. On her head sat a tan western-style hat with two fresh daisies in its band. Fiery orange curls dangled along the side of her face.

Noah's death had been rough on her, and Jeremiah wanted to ease some of her pain. He smiled cordially. "I'm surprised to see you out and about."

"The chores won't get done by themselves."

"I'm going into Lowdown. I'd be honored if you'd escort me," he said out of courtesy.

She cleared her throat. "I have too much to do."

He was relieved. "That's a shame."

"Sure," she replied with sarcasm.

He lifted a shoulder. "Suit yourself."

She turned to Whip. "Mr. Dalton doesn't have all day. Get Zeb ready, pronto."

Whip chuckled as he headed toward the last stall. It wouldn't have surprised Jeremiah if a saddled bull charged from around the corner.

"Have you ridden much?" Abigail asked, tipping her head.

"Some." It had been years since Jeremiah had sat atop a horse.

"Exactly the type of answer I'd expect from a greenhorn."

"And you're an expert about greenhorns?"

"I've seen enough of them to know what they're like."

"Meaning?"

"They say one thing and mean another."

He cocked an eyebrow. "That so."

She nodded.

"If you'd give this greenhorn a chance, you might be surprised to learn I'm really a nice guy."

"There's no time for that. Tomorrow, after the will is read, I'll be packing, remember?"

"Oh, that. You caught me at a bad moment. I didn't mean what I said."

She gave him an I-told-you so look that he ignored.

"When I sell the ranch, I figure you'll help the new owner get settled in. Whether he wants you to stay will be up to him."

He hadn't expected to see her mouth lift in a coy smile, but when he followed the direction of her gaze, he understood.

"Miss Wilcox, when you and Whip are through amusing yourselves, remove the saddle from that poor jackass and get me a real horse."

The following day, several hours after the funeral, Jeremiah entered his father's study. Heads turned toward him. He popped a lemon drop in his mouth and tried not to frown. The sweet candy didn't lessen the bad taste he got whenever he saw the disgruntled looks on people's faces. He crossed the room and leaned a hip against the bookcase.

Sam Burns, Noah's attorney, cleared his throat. "If everyone is ready, we can proceed with the reading of the will."

Jeremiah noticed Abigail first. She wore a pale-blue dress that accented her trim waist. Though faded, the soft cotton material contrasted with the orange of her hair highlighted by the sun streaming through the window. Its color reminded Jeremiah of flames dancing in a fireplace. He wondered what Abigail would look like in fine silk and found he couldn't picture such a thing.

Everyone from miles around had turned out for the funeral, making it clear his father had loyal friends and might not have been as bad a person as Jeremiah had been led to believe. He tried to remember the names of those present.

Hank and Jillian Bufford, owners of the mercantile, sat together on the settee facing the desk. Beside them on a straight-back chair, Pedro dabbed at his eyes every few seconds and took loud shuddering breaths. Her face buried in her mother's lap, Clarissa sobbed. The soft sound carried across the room. Abigail ran her fingers along the child's shoulders and bent down to whisper in her daughter's ear.

To Abigail's right, Whip tried unsuccessfully to calm the woman bawling on his other side. Jeremiah had noticed the woman at the funeral and because of her distress assumed she had been one of Noah's closest friends. As he studied her jet-black hair pulled back in a severe bun, he noticed that Whip's hair was the same striking shade. The eight chairs brought in from other parts of the house were all occupied, and at least another dozen people, some of them ranch hands, stood around the perimeter of the room.

The lawyer angled his glasses over his nose. "Over the course of his illness Noah Dalton conferred with me on numerous occasions about the distribution of his estate. And though I don't agree with some of the provisions in this document, let me assure you this will is valid. Of sound mind until he drew his last breath, Noah had definite ideas of what he wanted done with his ranch."

The attorney lifted the water glass from the desk and took a deep swallow.

The fine hairs at the base of Jeremiah's skull prickled with apprehension.

Sam Burns set the glass down. "To my good friend Hank Bufford, I cancel his debt and leave him two hundred dollars."

The people in the room issued a collective sigh.

Looking pleased, Jillian Bufford squeezed her husband's hand as he smiled down at her.

"To my maid of many years . . ."

Jeremiah could tell these proceedings were going to take some time. It seemed that Noah had a flair for theatrics.

". . . and a train ticket to California to see her daughter and grandchild, plus one hundred dollars for living expenses."

Noah was definitely a generous man. A warm feeling crept into Jeremiah's chest.

"To Adele Diaz . . ."

The woman seated beside Whip lifted her head and tapped at the corners of her eyes. Whip wrapped his arm over her shoulder.

The lawyer reached behind him and lifted a carved wooden box, then directed his comments to the black-haired woman. "There are papers and some things in here that Noah wanted you to have."

Whip stood, walked across the room, and took the box from the attorney. He returned to the couch and set it on Mrs. Diaz's lap. As she glanced down, plump tears splashed against the smooth mahogany surface. Her fingers gently traced the wood engravings.

"To my cook and good friend, Pedro . . ."

Forty minutes later the only ones not addressed in the will were Abigail, Whip, and Jeremiah, who popped another lemon drop in his mouth and rolled the candy over and under his tongue before tucking it against his left cheek.

"To Alfonso Diaz . . ."

"Where the hell is everybody?" The booming voice preceded the ruddy-faced man who rushed into the room a moment later. He slapped his thigh. "Well, I'll be damned. You folks having a shindig without me?"

The attorney eyed the man skeptically. "Sir, do you have business with Noah Dalton?"

The man's wide grin revealed several missing teeth. His tangled hair hung to his shoulders and a week's worth of trail dust clung to his clothes. "Sure do. I'm kin, Noah's baby brother."

Several in the room gasped.

Sam Burns turned his attention to the document on the desk. "And what is your name?"

"Mortimer Dalton, but you can call me Mort."

The attorney's brow furrowed. "I thought you were incarcerated."

"Ain't no more."

Mr. Burns stepped forward. "I'm afraid I have some bad news. Your brother passed on two days ago."

Mort glanced around the room. "Looks like Noah done good fer hisself. Probably jest as well he's already kicked the bucket, 'cause seeing me woulda finished him off fer sure." His gruff laugh followed.

The lawyer's face flushed. "Your name's here, and Noah's made provision for you in his will. If you'll have a seat or stand over there." He jerked his chin toward the bookcase.

The stocky man made his way across the room and planted himself next to Jeremiah. The smells of smoke, horse, and sweat penetrated Jeremiah's nostrils. He tried to inch away, but the ranch hand to his left made escape impossible. Jeremiah studied the face that could make a grown man wince. Mort's right eye, surrounded by puckered flesh, seemed only able to squint. Thick bushy eyebrows met at the bridge of a bulbous nose, which crooked first one direction, then another. A wide scar ran along the side of his face and disappeared in a thick gray beard.

Sam Burns shuffled through the papers on the desk. "Where was I? Oh yes, here it is . . . Alfonso Diaz, my trusted ranch hand, I give ten Mustangs and three hundred dollars."

Mrs. Diaz tapped Whip's hand at about the same instant Abigail turned to him and smiled. Jeremiah concluded that Alfonso and Whip were one and the same.

"To Mortimer Dalton, my only brother, who's never done an honest day's work, I give you a job on this ranch for the next six months. If you prove yourself to be a decent law-abiding citizen, my estate will provide you with enough cash to start your own small spread. Otherwise, you get nothing."

Mort muttered under his breath.

Jeremiah wondered what Noah had in store for him.

The lawyer straightened and looked at Abigail for several seconds before turning his gaze toward Jeremiah. Jeremiah rolled the hard candy from one cheek to the other and tried not to worry about the attorney's pensive expression.

"Before I read the last of this document, I'd like everyone to leave the room except for Pedro, Mortimer, Alfonso, Abigail, and Jeremiah."

A low murmur followed the retreating crowd. Jeremiah's gut tightened when the attorney shut the door and nodded for him to sit down. "Have a seat. This may take awhile."

Abigail stepped forward. "Is something wrong?"

"No, not at all, but I saw no need to have the others present."

Jeremiah waited for Abigail to sit before settling down beside her on the settee. Behind him, he heard the scrape of a chair and the creak of the couch springs.

Sam sipped more water, then glanced at Abigail. "Noah loved you. He said you were his daughter in every sense."

The words unsettled Jeremiah. Abigail had achieved what he couldn't; she'd won his father's love.

The attorney leaned forward. "Abigail, Noah wanted you to have the land you two discussed along with an additional five hundred acres. That's if you agree to the terms of the will."

"What terms are those?"

"We'll discuss them shortly."

She sighed softly.

The lawyer turned to Jeremiah. "Your father left you the remainder of his estate."

Relieved, Jeremiah let out a slow breath.

"However, there are stipulations."

"Stipulations?" Jeremiah pushed the word through clenched teeth.

Sam nodded. "I don't want to bore you with the fine details so I'll give you the abbreviated version. Your father didn't want his ranch sold to the highest bidder. Noah hoped you'd grow to love this place as much as he did. In order for you to inherit his estate, you have to live on this ranch for six months. You need to learn every aspect of ranching, including roping and riding."

Abigail covered her mouth with her hand; a soft laugh escaped.

The lawyer turned to her. "According to the provisions of Noah's will, for the next six months you'll be helping Jeremiah to achieve his goals."

At the news, Jeremiah sucked in a deep breath. The lemon drop flew down his throat and stuck in his windpipe.

He covered his mouth and coughed hard.

Abigail slammed a fist against his back, dislodging the candy and nearly splintering bone.

It was going to be one hell of a long six months.

Jeremiah stared at Sam Burns. "Tell me you're not serious?"

"Everything I said is written here in black and white."

"I've a mind to pack my bags and leave first thing tomorrow."

The lawyer pushed his glasses up his nose. "Of course, you have every right to do just that, but if you go, you'll lose your inheritance. You've come a long way to leave empty-handed."

Jeremiah wanted to shout that he didn't care about his father's lousy money. He wanted to tell the attorney where he could shove the paperwork. He wanted to turn to everyone in the room and tell them he was heading East, but his future with Evelyn depended on his wealth. He needed to give the matter more thought before reaching a final decision.

Abigail leaped to her feet. "What if I refuse to help Jeremiah?"

The attorney frowned. "You'll lose everything promised to you in the will."

"Hell's bells, I'll likely strangle the man if I have to nursemaid him for six months."

Jeremiah cursed under his breath. "Last thing I need is a bossy cowgirl telling me what to do."

Sam Burns gave a disgruntled sigh. "No need to worry about it. I'm expecting you two will kill each other before the end of the week."

Jeremiah's heated gaze traveled over Abigail's seething features. "I'm bigger and stronger. Chances are I'd survive a confrontation between the two of us."

She shoved a curl from her forehead. "I'm smarter than you any day so I'd likely win."

Mort cleared his throat. "Mr. Big Shot Lawyer, can I say somethin'?"

"No!"

"I can git through to these two fools better 'n you." Ignoring the lethal look on Sam's face, Mort strode to the front of the room and plunked himself in front of Abigail and Jeremiah.

"If you two don't learn to git along, you both lose. Now stick that where the sun don't shine."

Jeremiah slid a brief glance toward Abigail and saw that Mort's words of wisdom had sunk in.

Mort dusted his hands against his filthy pants and grinned at the lawyer. "I'll let yer take over now."

Jeremiah turned to Sam. "What happens if Abigail refuses to help me with the ranch?"

"Whip will be put in charge of showing you the ropes. And when the six months are up, you'll also inherit her share of the property, which I might add is a choice parcel."

Abigail elbowed Jeremiah aside. "What if he skedaddles before the time is up?"

"As long as you've done your part, you're all set."

"I wouldn't want to lose my land because this greenhorn can't hack the work."

Jeremiah speared Abigail with a disgruntled look she chose to ignore. "Don't worry, I can do the work."

She grabbed Jeremiah's hand and ran her fingers along his palm. When she glanced up, he lost himself in her deep emerald eyes. His chest constricted. The craziest thing happened. He couldn't decide whether he wanted to wring Abigail Wilcox's neck or kiss her.

Her upturned face held him captive. He studied the healthy glow of her complexion dotted with freckles. Not a single trace of powder marred Abigail's skin. Had she painted her mouth, or were her lips naturally tinted? Their color reminded him of fresh strawberries. Did they taste as sweet?

Fortunately, someone in the room coughed, bringing Jeremiah to his senses. He pulled his hand free.

He wondered what Abigail was up to when she smiled. "Your hands are as soft as a babe's bottom. I can hardly wait to slam a shovel into them."

Behind him, Whip and Mort chuckled.

"Señor Burns."

All heads turned toward Pedro. "What happens to the ranch if Señor Dalton does not last six months?"

Jeremiah frowned at Pedro. "Thanks for the vote of confidence."

Whip grinned. "Damn good question if you ask me."

Sam Burns shuffled the paperwork on the desk. "That's why I asked you gentlemen to stay behind. If for any reason Jeremiah Dalton fails to live up to the terms of this will, half of Jeremiah's share of the estate will go to Abigail. The other half of the property will be split between you three men."

Mort slapped his hands together. "If I hadn't sworn off killing, I'd shoot you myself."

Mort's gruff laughter hinted he was joking.

The look on his face said otherwise.

Later that night someone pulled a journal and pen from the bedside table and scrawled these words.

If I didn't write down my thoughts, I'd go mad. Maybe I've already lost my mind. When the will was read, something inside me snapped. Life sure isn't fair. Jeremiah had better leave soon, or he'll make the trip back to Boston in a pine box!

CHAPTER 4

Jeremiah had all night to gather his wits. Around three o'clock the next morning he decided his mother had been right. She'd told him hundreds of times that Noah was a conniving, low down snake in the grass. As a child, he didn't understand. But now he did.

His old man was a controlling bastard.

Like a criminal serving out his sentence, Jeremiah was stuck in Texas. If he didn't make the best of this difficult situation, he'd lose his inheritance and maybe Evelyn too.

He didn't fault his fiancée for wanting nice things. Besides, he enjoyed seeing the fairer sex in fine silks and jewelry.

A Parisian couturier made all of Evelyn's clothes. Pearls adorned her dainty earlobes and slender neck. Emeralds, sapphires and diamonds weighted down her fingers. Indulged by her parents since birth, Evelyn assumed money miraculously grew in Jeremiah's pockets. Without his inheritance, he could never provide for her in a suitable fashion.

Evelyn was spoiled.

One other flaw marred her character.

Patience—Evelyn had none.

Jeremiah had accepted her imperfections.

After all, he had faults, too. Quick to anger, he often said things he later regretted. Though he prided himself on being a gentleman, he'd been known to cuss in the presence of ladies. On one such occasion, poor Evelyn had fainted dead away.

Jeremiah only had to take one glance at Evelyn's angelic face with skin the color of cream and lips painted a deep shade of red to feel desire for the raven-haired beauty. He enjoyed wrapping his hands around her tiny waist and pulling her to him. He loved to nuzzle her neck and inhale her flowery fragrance.

Unfortunately, those times were few. Concerned he'd muss her long tresses piled high on her head or wrinkle her garments, Evelyn had pushed him away with a smile, a kiss and a promise of things to come. Those promises would have to be postponed. To Evelyn ten minutes was an excruciating wait, six months a lifetime. Luckily, he wouldn't be around when she received his telegram.

Jeremiah was a man of reason. What were six months in the scheme of things? He'd do his time. Six months to the day he'd sell his father's ranch and leave Texas, never to return.

Accepting his fate, he decided to take control of his father's ranch. First on his agenda was finding a bedroom with several windows for cross ventilation and a bed large enough for him to stretch. Finally, his tense muscles began to relax, and Jeremiah had just dozed off when a loud rumble of thunder awakened him.

Startled, he jerked his head off the pillow and peered out the window. He was surprised to see a star-studded sky. Thinking he'd been dreaming, he laid his head down and closed his eyes when he heard the same noise, which he recognized as pounding on his door.

Expecting an emergency, he leaped from his bed, stumbled across the room and yanked the door open. Fist raised, Abigail looked ready to punch him.

"Let's get going." Her irritating drawl drilled into his tired brain.

He yawned. "What's wrong?"

"Time to rise and shine."

Through the hall window, he glanced at the night sky. "If this is your idea of a joke, it isn't funny." A slight breeze stirred the hair on his legs. He'd forgotten he was clad only in his underwear.

"It's no joke. Cows need milking."

"Shit."

"While we're on that subject, the stalls in the barn need cleaning, too."

He almost swore but caught himself in time.

In the semi-darkness the silhouette of Abigail's unruly curls piled high on her head reminded him of a bunch of broccoli. His anger at being awakened at this ungodly hour lessened considerably when the subtle fragrance of roses distracted him. Taking a deep breath, he indulged himself for a moment. He found the smell strangely erotic. His body reacted instantly, and he dropped his hands to conceal his arousal.

"Mucking out stalls sounds like a job for the hired help." To his chagrin, his voice was deeper than usual.

"You coming down with a cold?"

"No, why?"

"Your voice doesn't sound right."

"I'm fine."

She shrugged. "According to Noah's will, you have to learn everything. On day one of your six months' stay, you are the hired help."

"Why so early? The stalls will still be there in a few hours."

"Look, greenhorn, I don't have all day to hold your hand. Now get."

"I won't be bossed by a woman."

"I'm a fore*man*," she said, stressing the last syllable. "I got a mere six months to whip your sorry ass into shape. I'm not about to lose my land because of your laziness."

"I'm a quick learner. It'll probably only take six weeks."

"More than likely six years, but we don't have that long."

"What time is it, anyway?"

"Four."

He ran his hand over his forehead and pushed back his hair. "You always start this early?"

As she nodded, her brassy curls bounced around her head. So unlike Evelyn's lacquered creations. He found himself fascinated by the soft locks.

"Well, you going to get dressed, or do you need help with that, too?"

Though the idea piqued his interest, he didn't press his luck. "I'll be ready in ten minutes."

"Make it five."

He saluted. "Yes, boss."

Jeremiah lit the lantern in his bedroom and rummaged though his suitcases for his clothes. He hadn't bothered to unpack because he figured he'd only be here several days. Nothing in his luggage was suitable for farm chores. When he got the chance, he'd go into Lowdown and buy work clothes.

He slipped his legs into tan linen pants and pulled his arms through the sleeves of a crisp white shirt. Jeremiah swore under his breath. He had to put his life on hold. After shoving his feet into his favorite alligator shoes, he ran a finger along his mustache, combed his hair, and slicked back a stubborn lock before hurrying down the stairs.

When he reached the hall, he saw Abigail tapping her foot and pointing to the clock.

"What took you so long?"

"I had to get dressed."

"That should take ten seconds. What did you do with the rest of the time?"

Ignoring her, he hurried to the door and was tempted to let it slam in her face. He remembered his manners. "Ma'am," he said and waved his arm for her to go through.

She sashayed by without so much as a nod. Too damn tired to say anything, he followed her across the yard and into the barn where the pungent odor of hay and animal feces turned his stomach and reminded him of the long days ahead.

"Six months," he muttered under his breath.

"What?"

"Nothing, boss."

Abigail took a lantern from inside the door and instructed him to do the same.

While Jeremiah carefully picked his way across the dung-covered floor, Abigail stomped over everything in her path. It amazed him that she didn't gag at the smells around them. He was so involved in watching her that he forgot to look down. Something soft squished beneath his right sole. He lowered the lantern and blinked at the massive mound of manure encrusting his shoe. He lifted his leg, his shoe plopping free. He'd smell no better than the barn for the rest of the day. Something told him he'd probably smell like this for the duration of his stay.

"Well, what now?"

When he lifted his lantern, he saw Abigail with her arms crossed. "I've never seen anyone drag their feet the way you do. What's taking so long?"

Not about to confess his problem, he gritted his teeth and strode toward her with long confident steps. Twice more he heard the familiar squishing and plopping sounds. Silently he cursed, but he did so with a smile. He'd be damned if he'd let Abigail know how miserable he felt.

"This is Belle, Betsey and Beulah."

He gazed at the soulful expressions on the cows' faces and could see in their eyes they didn't want him messing with their private parts.

Jeremiah decided to impress Abigail. "Nice looking bovine you got here."

"Talk like that in front of the men, and they'll laugh you out of the state. They're cows."

She swung the door to the stall open and hung her lantern over the nail. She pulled a stool across the floor with her booted foot and sat down. "Pay attention. Grab hold of two teats and gently squeeze. That's a good girl, Belle. You're doing fine."

He watched for a moment, mesmerized by the rhythmic pinging of milk striking the metal bucket. "How hard are you pulling?"

"It's not so much a pull as working your fingers from top to bottom. Here, you try it," she said, and vacated the three-legged stool.

Jeremiah tried to hide his concerns as he sat and found himself at eye level with the cow's distended belly. Slowly, because he had no choice and because Abigail was watching, he wrapped his fingers around two teats and was reminded of a couple crude jokes he'd traded with friends.

He squeezed, but nothing came out. When the cow mooed, he jumped and almost fell off the stool.

"Don't let her see you're nervous. And for heaven's sake talk to her. She likes that."

He heaved a ragged breath. "Belle, trust me, I don't like this any better than you do." Feeling like a fool for talking to a cow, he waited for Abigail to laugh.

She gave his shoulder a reassuring pat. "That's good. Belle likes to hear a voice when she's being milked."

Jeremiah squeezed and gave a gentle pull, but no milk came out. When he heard a ping in his metal pail a minute later, he almost shouted for joy. "Hot damn, Belle, we're really cooking now."

Abigail moved to the other side of the stall and sat beside one of the other cows. "How you doing today, Beulah?"

Within seconds Jeremiah could hear the continual pinging of milk in her pail. Occasionally, he succeeded in extracting milk from the cow's udders, but even then, the milk didn't always hit his bucket, evident by the growing wet spot on the leg of his pants. Just when he thought he was finally getting the hang of it, Belle swished her smelly tail over his face, smearing a residue along the side of his head that turned his stomach.

"Shit!" he shouted.

Abigail glanced at him and broke into a raucous laugh. "I forgot to tell you to tie the tail to her leg."

"I bet you forgot. I just hope I get to return the favor."

CHAPTER 5

Abigail had lost her mind. There sat Jeremiah with a scowl and cow poop on his face, and she couldn't stop thinking he had to be the sexiest man alive.

She'd gotten a kick out of watching him tiptoe around each cow patty, scared to death of messing his fancy shoes. His shocked expression when he wrapped his fingers around Belle's teats would forever be imprinted in her mind.

As she watched him trying to wring milk from the frustrated cow, she remembered the feel of his palm against her fingertips yesterday. She'd expected a sissy's touch but instead had found a powerful, masculine hand. Her breath had wedged in her throat like a fishbone. When she finally regained her senses, she'd spoken to him in anger.

During the night she dreamed of his fingers tracing the sides of her face, her neckline, and the contours of her breasts, the mere thought pebbling her nipples. Infuriated with herself, she leaped out of bed and went to wake the man who had turned her life upside-down.

There he stood half naked, setting her head spinning like a top. He had a smell all his own, like a meadow in springtime after a fresh spring rain. Her throat had thickened. Tempted to run her fingers through the coarse hair that matted his chest, she barked out orders, hoping to disguise her attraction.

Jeremiah was an Easterner through and through, from the toes of his foolish-looking shoes right up to the cowlick on his

41

forehead. Why did she continually have to fight the urge to push the hair from his brow? Why did he affect her so? Being near him made her ornery as a bear with a blistered paw. She'd had it with Easterners.

All Easterners.

When she caught him glancing in her direction, she spat on the ground. "You don't have time to be gawking around." She recognized the disgust in his eyes and prided herself on a job well done.

He grunted and returned to his task.

When they finished milking the cows, Abigail stood. "What say we go get us some chow?"

Jeremiah straightened and rolled his head from side to side. "First good thing you've said this morning." He reached for her bucket. "Let me carry this for you."

His offer made her so lightheaded she could have giggled like a schoolgirl. Her foolish reaction to his kindness got her dander up. "I'm strong as most men, better than some. I'll carry my own milk."

He took her pail anyway. "I didn't mean it as an insult."

She spat on the barn floor, then glanced up.

Instead of disgust, mischief twinkled in his eyes. "Worst spitting I ever seen."

"What?"

"I said you don't spit worth a damn. You have to give it your all. Like this." He puckered up and let one zing. "See," he continued, cocking an eyebrow and waiting for her to say something.

At a complete loss for words, she wheeled around and stormed from the barn, his deep laughter ringing in her ears.

Once Abigail showed Jeremiah where to store the milk, she made a quick getaway. She called herself a dimwit as her

42

stomach twisted at the mere thought of him. Each time he glanced her way, her heart pitter-pattered like rain on a tin roof. In his presence her cheeks had turned crimson. If that didn't beat all—her blushing like a maiden who didn't know the ways of men and women. Abigail knew all she cared to know. The act of coupling was painful, brief and the *consequences lifelong*.

Far too often, she'd heard the crude term for a child born out of wedlock. The word wounded and wedged itself in her heart like a bullet. Though she held her head high, it pained her to know her daughter would pay for her mistake.

When she entered the kitchen a few minutes later, she noticed Jeremiah seated in Noah's chair. Though he had every right to sit at the head of the table, it irked her to see him there. Bold as can be, he patted the chair next to him.

"Boss, I saved you a seat."

"Thanks," she said, continuing past him and plunking herself down beside Mort, whose sinister grin made her skin crawl. Every fiber of her being told her Mort was dangerous. Later this morning she planned on heading into Lowdown to see what information Sheriff Clark could dig up about Mort. She needed to know since he was sleeping under the same roof as Clarissa.

Thankfully, Mort had washed, and he didn't smell nearly as bad as he had yesterday. Just being this close to him peppered her arms with gooseflesh. Yet she preferred sitting beside the disgusting man than next to Jeremiah.

Whip made a point of seeking Jeremiah out. "Greenhorn, how did you and the ladies get along this morning?"

"Huh?"

Abigail saw the confusion on Jeremiah's face. "Whip means the bovines."

Whip's forehead wrinkled in confusion. "The what?"

"Bovine's the highfalutin' word Easterners use for cows."

Whip and Mort, along with hired hands Hank, Blue and Will, almost busted their guts.

When Jeremiah frowned at her, she nodded and gave him a satisfied grin.

"That's two I owe you," he muttered under his breath, then chuckled along with the men.

Though he seemed unaffected by her callous comment, she'd seen a flicker of pain cross his face. Deep inside Abigail regretted making a fool of him. She knew what it meant to be an outsider, to be the brunt of everyone's jokes, to be the target of everyone's cruelty. Right then, she decided to lighten up on Jeremiah, at least when others were around.

Pedro stuck his head out the kitchen door. "Señor Dalton, would you like some of my Mexicali special?"

Jeremiah poured himself a cup of coffee and glanced toward Abigail.

"You better say no," she said.

He hesitated before his face took on a knowing look. "Pedro, that sounds fine to me. Thank you."

Abigail was surprised he'd ignored her warning.

Jeremiah winked. "We Easterners are a smart lot. Common sense dictates I do the opposite of whatever you suggest."

She added a little molasses to her coffee. "Suit yourself."

"I plan to."

A few minutes later, Pedro stuck his head out the door. "Blue, give me a hand, pronto."

"Hold yer horses," he replied with an impatient wave of his hand.

"Loco, estupido." Pedro rolled his eyes and slammed the kitchen door.

Grumbling under his breath, Blue pushed himself to his feet. As the old cowpoke limped across the room, Abigail was reminded of Noah's kindheartedness. Blue had shown up at the ranch two years earlier with no place to stay, a broken shell of a man, pleading for a chance to work. Noah had given him more than a job, he'd given him back his pride.

A few minutes later Pedro delivered a plate brimming with his Mexicali special to Jeremiah. "Enjoy, Señor."

From across the table Abigail saw numerous green flecks in the scrambled eggs. She waited for Jeremiah to take a large bite, anxious to see his eyes water.

When he didn't grab his fork and dive right in right away, she wondered if he suspected. "You'll hurt Pedro's feelings if you don't eat your breakfast."

His warm smile turned her limbs to mush. She considered warning him again.

"Rest assured there's no chance of my hurting Pedro's feelings. As you Texans would probably say, I'm so hungry I could eat horses."

She shook her head. "I never heard a single Texan say that. Sounds like more greenhorn talk to me."

Before he could reply, Pedro and Blue returned with trays laden with biscuits, fried potatoes, eggs, and ham. They placed breakfast in the center of the table and sat down. As everyone started filling their plates, Abigail kept a watchful eye on Jeremiah.

The men around her dove for the food. Knives clinked. Forks scrapped. Lips smacked and Mort belched. To an outsider their morning meal might resemble hogs slopping up swill. Though she'd grown accustomed to the lack of decorum, an uneasy feeling crept up her spine as she watched Jeremiah witnessing the crude display.

Much to Abigail's surprise, her appetite faded. She grabbed a piece of biscuit and a small serving of eggs, figuring if she didn't eat now, she'd be starving later. As she nibbled on the biscuit, she found herself watching Jeremiah's every move.

He was a fussy son of a gun. Buttered his toast, then leaned back in his chair as if he had all day to shoot the breeze. He cut his ham into cubes before taking a bite. Not one bit of grease coated his mouth as it did with the other men at the table, yet he still dabbed at his lips with a white handkerchief he pulled from his pocket.

When Jeremiah finally lifted a large bite of Mexicali special into his mouth, everyone at the table stole glances in his direction.

Jeremiah blinked twice, then nodded toward Whip. "What were you saying about the price of beef?"

Abigail saw the shimmer in Jeremiah's eyes but was shocked to see him take another bite.

Unable to restrain herself, she asked, "How's breakfast?"

He swallowed and turned to Pedro. "This is really good. What are the little green things I see in the eggs?"

"Jalapeño peppers, Señor. I hope it is not too hot."

Jeremiah's cheeks turned pink. "No, it's perfect."

He was lying through his teeth. Abigail could almost see flames shooting from his mouth. His lips curved into a phony smile as he lifted his coffee mug. Instead of draining the cup as she expected, he took a sip. When Abigail had first arrived at the ranch, Pedro had made his specialty for her, too. She hadn't fared nearly as well as Jeremiah. Tears had streamed down her face, and she'd gulped water for hours afterwards.

"Can I get you something to drink?" she offered, suddenly feeling sorry for him.

"No thanks, coffee's fine."

How Jeremiah managed to clean his plate was a mystery to Abigail. The fact that he didn't run from the room first chance he got amazed her. She watched him take in several short puffs of air and knew his mouth was ablaze. If he left before the other men, he'd be the laughingstock of the ranch. And though in a way the thought pleased her, she couldn't let that happen.

"I'm fixin' to go into town and pick up some supplies. Jeremiah, if you're through lollygagging, I figured you'd come with me."

"Sure, boss."

"If you'll meet me in the barn in a few minutes, I'll help you with the horses."

He stood and sauntered across the room as if he had all the time in the world.

Once he left, Abigail rose, walked across the kitchen, and took her hat off the peg. When she glanced out the door, she couldn't see Jeremiah anywhere. She suspected he was behind the barn, draining the well.

As Abigail approached the barn, she spotted Jeremiah coming from around back. "What have you been up to?"

"I've been checking this structure for repairs."

She wanted to ask him about the wet spots on his shirt but decided to let it pass. "Good idea."

When he rewarded her with a wide grin, her heart galloped like a wild stallion. Her idiotic reaction soured her mood.

"Let's get going, we don't have all day."

He saluted. "Yes, boss." Before she realized what was happening, the infuriating man reached for her elbow and escorted her into the barn. By the time she thought to pull away, they were already standing in front of the horse stalls.

She grumbled something about crazy greenhorns under her breath and stomped off. She reached up to yank a saddle down from a wooden bracket and found herself imprisoned by Jeremiah's arms. As he assisted her, she considered slapping his fingers away, but her hands shook so much she couldn't very well make a fuss without him noticing.

Lord almighty, she feared she'd swoon as the heat from his

body penetrated hers. Abigail Wilcox, considered a harlot by many, was ready to faint like an innocent maiden at the mere touch of his muscled arms.

Effortlessly, he lowered the saddle from the peg.

She took a breath to clear her head. "I don't need you mollycoddling me. Treat me like one of the men."

"Sure thing, boss," he said with a wink that hinted he wasn't paying attention.

She blew a curl from her forehead. After glaring at his retreating back, she grabbed another saddle and marched across the barn ready to make him pay—for what, she wasn't certain.

As Abigail approached, she was ready to give him both barrels if he so much as touched her saddle, but fortunately for him, he didn't make a move. "Do you see a horse that appeals to you?"

He hooked his alligator shoe over the lower rung of the stall and glanced around. "Mighty fine-looking animals."

"You're looking at some of the best horseflesh in Texas."

He paused to study the horses, then pointed to the one in its own enclosure. "I really like that albino over there."

"I'll bet my britches you couldn't ride that stallion from here to the door without eating dirt."

His heated gaze meandered along the shapeless pants covering her legs. "Lady, don't go betting your britches unless you're prepared to lose them."

She uttered a nervous laugh. "I doubt I have anything to worry about."

"You're still taking a chance. What if I throw caution to the wind and try riding the albino? What if I make it to the door?"

A wave of heat flushed her body.

Her voice came out an octave too high. "If Moonbeam kills you, you won't be around to collect on that bet." She lifted her chin. "So if you've a mind to ride that horse, sure as shooting you'll be pushing up daisies."

"Put that way, I'll wait until I've had more experience."

"Even Whip can't ride that horse."

"Is Whip the standard the ranch uses to decide whether a horse can be ridden?"

"Whip did the rodeo circuit for a while. He's as good as they come."

"Maybe." Confusion wrinkled his brow. "What's the sense of having an animal no one can ride?"

"That horse will make good breeding stock."

Jeremiah studied albino for a while before turning to Abigail. "Which horse do you suggest I ride?"

"That piebald over there is a good mount. He's strong and predictable."

"How do I know I can trust you? You might be trying to kill me off so you can get your inheritance sooner."

"As tempting as that sounds, I couldn't live with myself if you were injured because of something I did."

Ignoring the skepticism on his face, she chose the palomino for herself, then led the horses from the stall. "If you'll watch, I'll show you what to do."

Before she could stop him, he lifted her saddle onto her mount. Too weary to remind him that she could have done that for herself, she heaved an exasperated sigh. "Once you've got the saddle on straight, lift the stirrup and pull the girth strap tight against the horse's belly."

When Jeremiah heaved the saddle onto his mount, the piebald lifted its head and nickered loudly. Jeremiah jumped back and tried to cover his ungraceful move with a nonchalant wave of his hand. "I think he's a little nervous."

From where she stood the horse didn't look nearly as nervous as Jeremiah. "Don't spook him, or he'll tear you in two."

Concern furrowed his brow. "You're kidding, right?"

"Maybe."

"What's his name?"

"Lancelot."

Jeremiah patted the horse's neck and in a deep timbre said, "Now take it easy, Lancelot. All I want to do is ride you to town. If you do this for me, I'll get you something special at Bufford's."

Lancelot whinnied and playfully nudged Jeremiah's arm.

"That's a good boy." When Jeremiah pulled the girth strap, the black and white horse filled its belly with air.

It took all of Abigail's willpower not to burst out laughing. When the horse let out its breath, the saddle would go slack, sending its rider toppling. She took great satisfaction in the thought. If she made Jeremiah's life miserable enough, he might actually decide to leave.

As Jeremiah led his horse outside, Abigail chuckled under her breath. She was being cruel, she told herself, but seemed unable to stop. It would serve him right for . . . she remembered how he'd ignored his father. For years she'd considered Jeremiah a cold-hearted man, and she'd hated him with every fiber of her being. Disliking a man she'd never met had been easy. But it was a damn sight harder to hold a grudge while captivated by his smoky gray eyes.

He seemed about to swing onto his horse when he hesitated and raised his right hand. "Wait a minute, I almost forgot." He took off at a run and disappeared behind the barn.

The nerve of him, wasting time as if she had any to spare. When he returned, she'd chew him out but good. Though Jeremiah was gone no more than a few seconds, she was in a dither by the time he showed his face, wearing an earth-shattering grin that threatened to melt Abigail's bones. As he strode toward her, she glanced at the bluebonnets in his large hand.

Abigail shook her head in disbelief. He painted quite a picture: Derby cocked at a becoming angle, a silk vest hugging an impressive chest, stained linen trousers, mucked up alligator shoes, and wildflowers.

She was about to tell him to get a move on when he strolled over to where she stood. Reaching for her hat, he stuck the fresh blooms into her hatband.

Eighty-eight degrees outside, and Abigail's tongue froze to the top of her mouth. When she finally set it loose, it wasn't worth a damn anyway. At a loss for words, she gawked at him as if he had two heads. "Why'd you go and do that for?"

"I saw them earlier when . . ." He gave a sheepish smile. "When I was swigging water like there was no tomorrow. I thought they'd look perfect on your hat."

No man had ever given Abigail flowers. She felt all choked up, and if she hadn't turned away, he'd have seen the tears welling in her eyes. She blinked furiously and cleared her throat. "We better skedaddle."

As Jeremiah approached his mount, Abigail made a split-second decision. "You better check the girth strap. That piebald's been known to fill up with air when he sees a saddle."

He reached under the horse's belly and gave the leather strap a tug. "Thanks," he said with a grin that set her stomach to fluttering, making her wish he were leaving today instead of six months from now.

Abigail swung onto her horse. "You got yourself a lady back East?"

Jeremiah's face lit up like fireflies in a jar. "Yes, her name's Evelyn."

Abigail flicked the reins and studied him from the corner of her eyes. "She pretty?"

"Prettiest thing you've ever seen."

Abigail's stomach slammed into her knees. She didn't have to look twice to see he was a goner for Evelyn. She tried to ignore the rush of disappointment swamping her.

Just because he'd stuck a few weeds in her hat didn't give her the right to expect anything more. Surrounded by sophisticated ladies back East, Jeremiah would never take a second look at the likes of her. She'd be a fool to think otherwise.

As they rode together toward town, she figured she'd ask Jeremiah one more question to settle her mind. "Are you fixin' to marry Evelyn?"

"As soon as I get back to Boston."

Gripped by the sudden desire to yank out every hair on Evelyn's head, Abigail reckoned it was time to change the subject.

CHAPTER 6

Because Abigail wanted to show Jeremiah the ranch, it took forty-five minutes to reach town. Jeremiah questioned his ability to walk again. By the end of the short trip, his mount seemed as wide as he was long. Each time the horse took a step, Jeremiah's backside became airborne before slamming down onto a saddle that felt like concrete. As Lancelot reached the hitching post, Jeremiah knew he couldn't show his discomfort.

He'd borne the brunt of everyone's laughter since day one. Determined not to add to anyone's amusement, he took a deep breath and managed to swing a leg over Lancelot without as much as a grimace. Though he'd remained quiet, every muscle screeched in protest.

For Abigail's benefit, he lifted his shoulder in an easygoing shrug. "I feel invigorated after that ride."

"Good," she said without hesitation, " 'cause you're going to be doing lots more riding before your six months are over."

A curse almost tumbled from his lips. Instead he nodded nonchalantly. "I can hardly wait."

"Yeah, I bet. I have some business to attend to with Sheriff Clark. Here's a list of things you can fetch at Bufford's. Meet me back here in an hour."

He took the piece of paper and saluted. "Sure thing, boss."

Abigail stepped toward him, so close that he felt her breath against his chin. "Just you remember that. For now, I am the boss. I get the feeling you say the word but think differently. You need me."

"I know that."

"Good."

In the sweltering Texas heat, droplets of perspiration gathered on her tiny nose, sprinkled with freckles. Something about the woman appealed to him. He wondered how she'd look dressed like a lady with her wild hair restrained by a velvet ribbon at the nape of neck. At first glance some men would mistake Abigail for a growing boy. He studied her clothing with curiosity. A white western-style hat dipped over her forehead and hid breathtaking eyes. Loose-fitting men's denims and an equally loose-fitting shirt disguised the fact she was female.

Even at this close range, it was hard to detect the breasts hidden beneath the shirt pockets. But Jeremiah could tell they were there. Something about the woman drove him to distraction. Maybe it was because she clearly didn't want a man's attention. Maybe it was because Evelyn was far away. Or maybe it was because he'd gone stark raving mad.

Just then, Jeremiah's leg cramped and he reached down to massage the kinks.

"You got yourself a charley horse. Straighten the leg instead of bending it the way you're doing."

He glanced up. "Oh this, this is nothing."

"Chances are there's another part of you that's in worse shape than your legs. I saw the way you were bouncing all over that saddle. Remind me to give you the horse liniment when we get back to the ranch."

"A lady shouldn't be mentioning such things."

She jabbed her finger into his chest. "I've been called lots of things, but a lady isn't one of 'em."

He didn't know how to reply to such a statement so he decided to ignore it.

Her smile looked more like a smirk. "As I said, you'll be mighty sore come sundown."

"I won't be needing any horse liniment," he said through clenched teeth because she aggravated him and he couldn't figure out why.

She laughed. "Just in case you change your mind, I keep a bottle in the kitchen under the sink."

While every muscle in his legs protested, he stood in a relaxed stance. "Trust me, I won't be touching your liniment."

He considered asking her to meet him later to massage his aches. If he had ever said such a thing to Evelyn, she'd have blushed and slapped his face, not hard enough to leave a mark, just enough to protect her reputation.

How would Abigail react? When he glanced at the six-shooter by her side, he figured he wouldn't push his luck.

Abigail was glad when Jeremiah looked away. She's stood her ground, making it clear he didn't intimidate her.

Men were a lot like horses—you had to show them you weren't afraid. Otherwise, they'd trample all over you. She hadn't always felt this way. Just thinking of herself at age sixteen made her shudder. Every bit the lady back then, she'd been gullible. No, stupid. After Clarissa was born, she'd decided the only way to survive in a man's world was to prove her grit. She couldn't do that decked out in ruffles and lace.

She smiled in satisfaction. She'd done a bang up job. The men at the ranch treated her like one of them. As she walked along the boardwalk, she could hear the hollow ring of her boot heels on the wooden planks.

"Hi, Gordy," she said to the strapping cowhand walking toward her.

"Abigail, I want to place my bet."

"What are you talking about?"

"Me and Whip were downing beers at the Rattler last night. He told me you folks were betting on what day the greenhorn would leave."

"Whip's got himself two problems, his big mouth and spending too much time in the saloon. That was supposed to be just a friendly wager between friends."

"Well, I want in."

She glanced across the street and saw Jeremiah disappear into Bufford's mercantile. "Don't reckon there's any harm letting you join our little wager."

Gordy handed her a piece of paper and a leather drawstring purse weighted down with coins.

"What's all this?"

"After Whip left, I told a couple of guys and they wanted in, too. Pretty soon, dern near everyone had given me a golden eagle along with their guess when Noah's kid would turn tail and run back East."

Abigail was against this from the start. She tried to discourage Whip and the others, but they wouldn't be swayed. She unfolded the paper in her hands and stared down in disbelief at the fourteen names written in an uneven scrawl.

Gordy gave a lopsided grin. "You got a lot of loot there."

Abigail sucked on her lower lip. Returning the money and canceling the bets would create a ruckus. She pretty much went along with what the men wanted as long as no one got hurt. And as long as Jeremiah didn't find out, there'd be no harm done. "You make sure you keep your trap shut, you hear?"

"Don't worry about that. My lips are tighter than an old maid's . . ."

Abigail frowned.

"Sorry, sometimes I forget you're a woman."

"That's all right. I jest don't want no gutter talk 'round me." She allowed cursing and had done so herself to gain the men's respect, but she'd drawn the line at vulgar language aimed at a woman's privates. She tied the strings to the drawstring purse around the belt at her waist and stepped away when she heard Gordy calling her.

"Oh, I almost forgot."

She glanced over her shoulder.

"Some of the men couldn't come up with the cash last night. They'll be dropping off their money later this week. That's if the city slicker hasn't already hightailed it out of here."

Abigail hated everything about this wager. Betting on a man's failures didn't set right with her. When she'd first met Jeremiah, she didn't think he'd last a week. Since then, she'd seen the determination on his face. She doubted he'd last six months, but he sure hadn't come all this way to give up without a fight.

As she continued along the walkway, she was surprised to see Pedro walking toward her. "What are you doing in town?"

"I needed a few provisions and figured I'd come in before it got too hot."

"You should have told me what you needed at breakfast."

"Si, Señora, but I did not know I was out of salt until you were gone."

Abigail remembered seeing two boxes of salt in the supply room but decided not to mention the fact. Whatever Pedro was doing in town didn't concern her as long as he got his chores done.

She nodded as he walked past her. "See you later."

Abigail took a few more steps, opened the door to the Lowdown Jailhouse, and tiptoed toward Sheriff Clark, who dozed in a chair with his long legs on top of his wooden desk. His Stetson, pulled down over his face, hid his rugged features. Without making a sound, she picked up the opened handcuffs lying on the desk and was about to clamp one around his wrist when he sprang to his feet and yanked both her arms behind her back.

"You're the shiftiest woman I ever set eyes on, Abigail Wilcox."

Abigail frowned. "You low down, conniving . . ."

"You know better than to speak to a lawman that way. What's to keep me from throwing you in the slammer?"

"You tricked me. You weren't sleeping."

"Course I was awake, and a good thing, too. Wouldn't look good for the townspeople to find their sheriff handcuffed to his desk, now would it?"

"Let go of me."

His eyebrows arched upward. "I've a good mind to lock you up."

"You wouldn't dare."

"Oh, I dare all right. If you have a lick of sense, you'll surrender."

She hesitated only long enough to try to stomp on his foot, but she missed. "All right, I give up, satisfied?"

He chuckled. "Damn right, I'm satisfied. I like getting the upper hand on you."

When he let her go, he bent and grazed her cheek with a light kiss. "How's my favorite gal, today?"

She smiled up at him. The sheriff had been a close friend of Noah's, and he'd spent a lot of time at the ranch. She and the sheriff were always trying to play tricks on each other and today she'd almost won. "I was hoping you'd nose around some and see what you can find out about Mortimer Dalton."

He frowned. "I'm one up on you. I've already done some digging, and it ain't good."

Abigail's gut twisted. "What did you find out?"

"Mort's a hotheaded gambler. He killed a man for cheating at cards several years back. Done his time, and according to the telegram, he's simmered over the years."

"You reckon he's still dangerous?"

"Damned if I know, but you'd best keep a close eye on that scalawag."

"You can bet your boots I will."

Sheriff Clark barked a loud laugh. "Speaking of betting, I've got something for you." He dug a gold coin from his pocket. "Put me down for three weeks."

Abigail was confused for a moment. "Huh?"

"I'm saying Jeremiah Dalton won't last a month."

Abigail pounded her fist on the desk. "This has gone too far."

"What d'ya mean?"

"I didn't cotton to this betting from the start."

The sheriff planted his hand on his hip. "And why do you suppose that is?"

"I don't like it, that's all."

"Have you placed your bet?"

"Absolutely not." She pulled the paper from her pocket and wrote down the sheriff's name.

"Why not? What's gotten under your cap?"

She lifted her chin in disgust. "I just don't think it's right."

"You didn't see nothin' wrong when you bet on that Bible salesman. If my memory serves me right, you cheered right along with the rest of us when he boarded the train."

She couldn't think of one argument in her defense.

A knowing look crossed his face. "Well I'll be, you're smitten with that Easterner, aren't you?"

The air whooshed from her lungs. "Where did you get such a fool idea?"

"Prove it, then. Place your bet."

Abigail picked up the pencil and jotted down her name.

Wide grin on his face, the sheriff craned his neck so he could get a better look at the piece of paper. "Well?"

Five months, two weeks and three days! she wrote behind her name, adding a giant exclamation point for the sheriff's benefit.

Instead of shutting him up as she'd hoped, he slapped his Stetson on the desk. "You're worse off than I thought. That foolhardy bet only proves you can't think straight around that prissy Easterner."

Jeremiah had gumption. He wasn't prissy by a long shot. She considered setting the sheriff straight, but common sense kept her silent.

Jeremiah had picked up the supplies and was admiring the various cowboy hats inside the mercantile when he felt someone's hand on his arm.

"Well I'll be, it's Jeremiah Dalton, ain't it."

Jeremiah recognized the old man he'd met in the stagecoach. "Buck Ridley, right?"

"Yup."

"You work around here?"

"I own the livery. I heard about Noah's will. Seems like you're gonna be staying awhile."

"Looks that way." Jeremiah nodded and tried to hide his annoyance. "Seems word travels fast around these parts."

"Nothing people like better than chewing the fat. Helps pass the time away." He hesitated and his eyes lit with excitement. "Will you be needin' a horse?"

"I got a horse already."

Buck grinned. "You ain't talking about that old gelding you rode into town?"

"It got me here, didn't it?"

"That old horse has so much rheumatism, he can't take three steps without building up a sweat. You're riding an animal that doesn't have enough sense to swish flies away with its tail."

Ignoring Buck's comment, Jeremiah took a gander at the display of hats to his left. He laid his Derby aside and tried on a black Stetson. Once he'd pulled it down so it shielded his eyes, he scowled into the mirror, trying to look as ornery as a Texas cowhand. The hat gave him a different perspective. Since he was stuck here for six months, he might as well look like everyone else. He curled the sides of the hat in, thumbed the brim up, and turned to his companion. "What do you think, Buck?"

The older man ran his fingers over Jeremiah's Derby on the counter. "This is a mighty fine Derby."

"Yes, it is. But I'd like your opinion about this hat." Jeremiah smiled at Buck, who barely glanced in his direction.

"It's all right, but not as grand a hat as this one."

Jeremiah lowered his voice. "Maybe we can make a deal."

"What kind of deal?"

"Can you keep your mouth shut?"

Buck nodded anxiously.

Jeremiah lowered his voice. When he finished explaining what he had in mind, Buck winked. "Well, I'll be diggered."

Jeremiah wasn't sure whether that was bad or good.

"I didn't think you had it in you. Count me in."

This time, Jeremiah understood.

And he was damned pleased with himself.

As Abigail passed the Rattler Saloon, she could make out the silhouette of a man beneath a horse blanket, out cold on the wooden bench in front of the establishment. He stunk of booze and sweat. One leg was bent, the other stretched across the walkway. As Abigail carefully stepped over his long limb, she jumped back in surprise when a snore ripped from his throat.

"Cussed men," she mumbled under her breath, wrinkling her nose in disgust.

Quick as a striking rattler, arms came out of nowhere and yanked her off her feet. She landed against the drunk's chest.

Her hat went flying.

"What's that ya said, lil' lady?"

"Open your eyes, you fool. I ain't no lady."

Glassy eyes squinted open in a flushed face. "You'll do."

Abigail wasn't worried. She'd handled the likes of him before.

"How 'bouts a lit' kiss, sweetie."

As he attempted to pull her head toward him, his fingers worked the combs from her hair. Her mass of unruly curls sprang free. With all her might, she swung back and belted the man in the chin.

"Ouch. Why'd you go and do that for?" A grin exposed rotted teeth. "I git it, you want to play rough. That's okay with me 'cause I like my women wild."

His foul breath gagged her as he twisted his fingers through her hair and pulled so hard she thought she'd be bald before he let go. She pummeled his chest with both hands and tried to knee him good, but he blocked her attempt. When his mouth skimmed hers, she bit down on his lower lip and wondered if he'd crush her to death as vise-like arms squeezed the breath from her lungs.

"Mister, you best let go of the lady, or I'll part your hair with this peacemaker."

The drunk loosened his suffocating grip.

Abigail leaped to her feet and near died on the spot when she eyed the man behind the gun. Beneath the black Stetson was the meanest scowl she'd ever seen. She recognized the rigid jaw and had to take a second glance to be certain it was really Jeremiah. The poor fool was going to get himself killed. All decked out like a cowboy with a Colt in both hands, he'd be mistaken for a professional gunfighter.

Jeremiah waved the gun in his right hand back and forth. "Apologize to the lady."

"That ain't no lady."

"My patience is running mighty thin. If I don't hear an apology in the next three seconds, I just might add a notch to my gun belt."

It was clear to Abigail that the tooled leather belt was new as were the holsters hanging over his hips. His Levis looked so stiff it was a wonder he could bend his knees. Gone were the foolish alligator shoes, replaced with leather boots with thick heels. He looked green behind the ears even in his Texan duds.

The drunk eyed Jeremiah. "Strikes me you probably don't know which end of the gun is which."

"I know I got the right end pointing toward you." Before the drunk could open his mouth, Jeremiah pulled back the hammer on his weapon. The distinct click widened the drunk's eyes.

"I don't see what the fuss is all about. I was just having me some fun."

"Apologize to the lady."

A crowd had gathered, and Abigail's face flushed as she felt the bystanders staring at the back of her head. Jeremiah had called her a lady, and she didn't doubt that many disputed the fact.

She sidled up to Jeremiah and whispered. "No harm's been done. Let's go."

He never spared her a glance but continued to stare ahead. "I'm waiting. Apologize or tell me which side you want your hair parted."

"Was a time a man could have hisself a lil' fun without someone making such a doggoned fuss."

Jeremiah lifted the Colt and aimed.

The drunk turned to Abigail. "Ma'am, I'd be much obliged if you'd forgive me. I didn't mean you no harm."

Jeremiah personally escorted the man to his horse. "Don't come back, you hear?"

Embarrassed, Abigail leaped onto her mount and rode out of town. As they approached the ranch, she turned to Jeremiah.

"You embarrassed me back there."

"How so?"

"I can take care of myself."

"Are you telling me that drunk was your beau?"

Her face flamed. "Of course not."

"If you were in control, then why didn't you put a stop to it?"

"I was about to when you showed up."

His smart-aleck smile should have made her angry, but instead it wiped all reason from her mind.

"I showed up just in the nick of time. Admit it, you aren't as strong as a man even though you dress like one."

"I'll admit no such thing."

"Suit yourself, you know I'm right. And though it galls you, you needed me today." A deep laugh rumbled from his chest. "Imagine that, Abigail Wilcox, damsel in distress."

She flicked the reins so her horse would trot ahead.

Several minutes later she glanced back and was glad to see how miserable Jeremiah looked bouncing on top of Lancelot. "You're going to get yourself killed running around with those guns hanging from your belt. You're lucky you didn't meet your Maker today."

"What makes you think I don't know what I'm doing?"

She didn't even consider the possibility. "Trust me, you have to get rid of those guns, or they'll be the death of you."

He set his jaw at a stubborn angle. "I'll do no such thing."

"In that case, you'd better learn how to shoot."

She couldn't see his eyes beneath the wide brim of his black hat, but she noticed his fleeting grin.

CHAPTER 7

They'd reached the rise overlooking the ranch when Abigail heard a ruckus behind her. When she turned, she spotted Jeremiah and his saddle tumbling toward the ground. She heard the thud when his head struck a large boulder.

She turned her horse around, leaping off as she approached. "You all right?" She held her breath, waiting for him to speak.

Looking dazed, Jeremiah pushed himself onto one elbow and rubbed his forehead where a large egg had begun to form. "I've been better. If this is your idea of a joke, I'm not laughing."

His face was pale and blood dripped from the wound above his eye. She dug in her pocket for her hankie and pressed the delicate material against the cut. "Hold still. And don't go blaming me."

He frowned. "Who else am I going to blame? You're the one who showed me how to saddle the beast. Bet you'll have yourself a good laugh when you relate the story to the others."

She was furious. The nerve of him, thinking she'd do anything as despicable as this. She threw her hankie down. "Hold this yourself. If I stay here much longer, I'm liable to strangle you with it."

She stalked away, mumbling under her breath. As she bent to examine the saddle, she saw that the girth strap had snapped in two, which surprised her because Whip checked all the equipment on a regular basis. It wasn't like Whip to be so careless.

She knelt down, aware of Jeremiah hobbling in her direction.

Though his steps were shaky, she was relieved to see his color had improved. Abigail's heart skipped a beat as his large shadow fell over her.

Trying to ignore his presence, she lifted the broken strap with her right hand. It was an effort to breathe with him this close.

Jeremiah squatted down beside Abigail and slid long fingers along the sharp edges where the leather had snapped apart. He glared at her with accusation in his eyes.

"Looks like someone took a knife to this."

Several days later, when Jeremiah finished mucking out the chicken house and horse stalls, he had blisters on his blisters. But he knew the condition was temporary. In another week his hands would toughen and manual labor would no longer bother him. He'd worked as a longshoreman for some time before buying the business six years ago. Unfortunately, Evelyn persuaded him to learn the ropes in her father's bank. Pushing a pencil for two years had weakened his stamina. And he was paying the price for being out of shape.

He was determined to remedy the situation as soon as possible. He'd done a series of pushups this morning, and each day before the others woke, he ran for an hour. Though that left him feeling as if he were close to death's door, he was more determined than ever to finish what he'd started.

Since he'd fallen off the horse, Abigail had cut him some slack. And though he'd probably never call her *Miss Merry Sunshine*, she'd been more pleasant, keeping her opinions to herself. He'd seen little of Abigail except at the breakfast table when she insisted on sitting next to Mort, who by now probably wondered if Abigail had a thing for him. Jeremiah laughed at the ludicrous thought.

Since Jeremiah's so-called accident, he kept a close eye on everyone. Though he'd struck his head and injured one leg, he

suspected that whoever had done the deed was most likely trying to aggravate him rather than kill him. With Lancelot trudg-
ing along at such a slow pace, Jeremiah would have had ample
time to leap off when the saddle slipped had his mind not been
otherwise preoccupied. From now on, he planned to keep his
train of thought on what he was doing rather than on Abigail
Wilcox's firm behind.

Pushing the bossy woman from his mind, he sighed. From
the corner of his eye, he spotted Clarissa peeking at him over
the stall. He set the shovel aside, pulled his bag of candy from
his back pocket, and popped a lemon drop in his mouth.

"Humm, humm, this has to be the best candy I've tasted
since leaving Boston. It's too bad no one's around to share it
with." As Jeremiah rolled the lemon drop over and under his
tongue, he heard shuffling behind the wall. Expecting Clarissa
to show her face, he was surprised when a goat bolted toward
him.

Protecting himself from its sharp horns, he lifted the shovel
as a shield. "Get away from me, you pesky creature."

"Mister, you touch Caesar, and you'll be sorrier than a
skinned rattlesnake."

Startled by her outburst, Jeremiah stared at the child, who
hadn't uttered a word to him since Noah's death. Her long
braid had come undone, her hair cascading down her back like
silk. She was dressed in clothing similar to her mother's, and
were it not for her beautiful hair, she'd resemble a boy.

A corner of the girl's mouth lifted in a sneer. "What ya doing
staring at me like a fly on horse dung?"

The insolence of the kid got to him. "Where are your manners?"

"My maw says to speak my mind and not let nobody step all
over me."

The child could have benefited from a switch to her behind.

But Jeremiah realized she'd been through a rough time. Besides, it wasn't up to him to try to change the values that Abigail had instilled in the child, or in this case, the lack of values. He reined in his growing agitation and counted slowly to ten. "Your mother's right about that."

Clarissa's grin vanished. "You joshing me?"

"I mean what I say. To my way of thinking, a man's word is worth more than gold."

"My maw says a man's word isn't worth diddly."

"I stand by what I say. I may be a lot of things, but I'm not a liar."

Her eyebrows rose.

"You shouldn't ever let anyone take advantage of you. And speaking your mind is a powerful thing, but . . ."

She rolled her eyes in disgust.

"That doesn't give you the right to hurt people's feelings. You can't go through life tossing out words that inflict pain."

"Maw says I can say anythin' I want."

"Then your maw's wrong."

He thought her smile was adorable until she spoke.

"Your sourpuss could curdle milk."

"If you'd control your mouth, you might even be likable. And I might share my candy with you."

He could tell she was mulling over what he'd said, though he suspected it was the candy rather than his words of wisdom that gave her pause. Abigail was dead wrong to raise her little girl this way. But it was none of his business.

In six months, he'd be gone. Figuring he'd said enough for one day, he stuck the brown paper bag under her nose. "Would you like a lemon drop?"

At first he thought she was going to refuse, but slowly she smiled up at him. Though the child might sound a lot like her mother, she wasn't as stubborn.

"Sure, can Caesar have one, too?"

The goat nudged in closer at the sound of the crinkling paper bag. Clarissa took a piece for herself and one for her pet. Before Jeremiah could put the bag away, a rotund pig hurried around the corner. Its loud snorts and wiggling nose brought a smile to Clarissa's face.

The child's giggle warmed Jeremiah's heart. "Don't you feed your animals?"

"Yes, but Caesar and Hamlet like your lemon drops best. Me, too."

He hurled the candy and watched it disappear midair. Later that afternoon when he left the barn, he figured he'd made two friends in Texas—that's if a goat and a pig could be counted as friends.

At three the next morning, Jeremiah crept from his room and tiptoed down the stairs and outside. As he took a moment to gaze at the star-studded sky, his heart twisted with loneliness. How would he ever survive six long months? So far, except for a pig that followed his every step and squealed whenever Jeremiah made a sound, he didn't have anyone to talk to. Oh, everyone spoke to him all right, but not about anything that really mattered.

He missed Boston. He missed his friends.

Most of all, he missed Evelyn.

He entered the barn and struck a match, lighting the lantern that hung on a wooden peg inside the door. He glanced over his shoulder to make sure he wasn't being followed. Seeing no one, he strode toward the shelves to his left and reached way in the back, pulling out the bottle of Sloan's Horse Liniment he'd purchased at Bufford's. Seems that everyone sang praises for the medicine. And Jeremiah agreed with them.

He slipped out of his Levis and applied a liberal amount to

his aching muscles, taking a moment to knead his legs and feet. The cool liniment seeped into his painful joints, reviving him. Unfortunately, Sloan's smelled like turpentine, and Jeremiah had no intention of letting on that he'd been using the stuff. To disguise the scent, he sprinkled a little bay rum over his arms and legs before pulling on his socks, pants, and boots, and slowly stretched his legs. In a few short days, he'd gained some strength, but he had a damn long way to go.

He then saddled Lancelot and led him through the door, blowing the lantern out. Once they were out of earshot, he swung onto the horse and kneed him forward. Nothing Jeremiah did could make the horse move any faster. Finally reaching Lowdown, Jeremiah steered his mount into the livery. In the flickering light of a nearby lantern, he saw Buck Ridley asleep on several bales of hay.

He dismounted and walked toward the old man.

Buck lifted his head. " 'Bout time you got here. I was getting a little shuteye and must have dozed off." Buck stood and dusted the loose hay off his pants, and plunked the Derby on his head. "Let's get going." He led Jeremiah to a barrel suspended from the rafters by four ropes.

"This here is your bronco."

Jeremiah laughed as he gave the barrel a push and watched it sway back and forth. "You're a kidder, that's for sure. Now, let's get down to some serious business."

The old geezer's brow knit. "I ain't pulling yer leg. This barrel is yer bronco 'til you prove yer ready for the real thing."

Jeremiah heaved a disgruntled sigh. "I don't know what you're trying to prove, but we had an agreement."

"Precisely, and if you want to learn to ride, you'll do as I say."

"Seems to me I'm taking a step backwards. I already ride Lancelot."

"An arthritic blind old lady missing a leg could ride that old nag, so you needn't brag 'bout that."

It dawned on Jeremiah that he didn't have a choice. Feeling like a moron, he lifted the saddle onto the barrel.

Buck rubbed his chin. "If Abigail Wilcox could see you now she'd laugh so hard she'd likely split her britches."

Ignoring the old man's raspy chuckle and the image of Abigail's split . . . "Damn," Jeremiah muttered. He tightened the tie strap, swung onto the barrel, and lost his balance. He twisted his fingers around the ropes, his legs kicking the air and making matters worse. As the barrel swayed, he tightened his hold until the rough rope was imprinted in his palms.

Buck's loud laughter bounced around the quiet interior. He took a handkerchief from his shirt pocket and rubbed his eyes.

"I'll be diggered. If I live to be a hundred, I ain't likely to see nothin' funny as you on this here barrel."

Jeremiah almost jumped off, but he wasn't a quitter. A lot depended on his being able to ride a horse. "I'm glad you're entertained. Now can we get down to business?"

Buck waved his concerns away. "Sure, sure, let me catch my wind." After a shuddering breath his appraising gaze traveled over Jeremiah. "Before we put a real horse between them legs, you gotta learn some basics." The old man dug in his pocket and pulled out a plug of *Battle Ax Tobacco*. He ripped off a piece and offered Jeremiah what was left with a nod.

"No thanks."

"Yer back's as stiff as a new corset. Your legs are diggin' in so cussed hard it's a wonder the barrel don't splinter. Relax, take a breath."

Jeremiah did as he was told. The barrel swung back and forth, and he found himself holding on for dear life.

This time Buck didn't laugh as he ran his hand along Jeremiah's leg. "Close your eyes and concentrate on nothing but your leg. Let it go limp. Forget yer sittin' in a saddle and pretend yer sittin' on a sofa beside a pretty gal."

Jeremiah tried, but he no sooner started to relax than the barrel swayed. He lost his concentration.

"Let me show you how it's done."

Jeremiah was happy to oblige. If he thought getting on the barrel posed a challenge, getting down was worse. He felt like a fool by the time he stood on solid ground.

The old man cocked his hat to one side. "Yer gotta have attitude." He swung onto the barrel and sat up proud and tall, his back straight yet relaxed. "Lookie here, you don't see my knuckles turning white. Pick up the rope with a gentle hand, like this," he said, lifting the reins for him to see. "Pretend your fingers are brushing up 'gainst a woman's leg. Gentle like. Note the stirrups. My boot slips in easily. Now, put your hand on my leg."

Jeremiah hesitated.

"I ain't asking you ta court me. Do what I say."

Feeling self-conscious, Jeremiah wrapped his fingers around Buck's calf.

"Feel that, not a single knot. That's what yer gonna do this week. Each day, yer gonna git up on that useless horse of yours, and pretend yer riding this here barrel. Close yer eyes and loosen every muscle yer got."

Frustration kicked in. Jeremiah scowled. "Don't tell me we're done already?"

"Don't matter none to me, but the sun's 'bout to come up and you said you needed to be back."

Jeremiah glanced out the window and was shocked to see the rosy glow in the east. He couldn't believe he'd been here over ninety minutes. "If it takes me this much time to learn to sit on a barrel, how long do you figure it'll take me to learn to ride a wild stallion?"

Buck chewed for a spell and tucked his wad against his cheek. "Ain't lookin' too promising, I'll tell ya that."

When Jeremiah entered the kitchen, all heads turned toward him.

Abigail wiped her hands on her trousers and glared. "Ain't got time to be sleeping in."

"I've been up since before dawn," he replied without explanation.

He yanked out his chair and cautiously lowered himself onto the oak surface. Between the grueling hours of work, Jeremiah's exercise routine, and his early morning jaunt to the livery, his muscles protested the slightest move. He helped himself to a serving of eggs and toast and motioned Pedro to fill his cup.

"Thanks," he told the cook, reaching for the coffee and taking a refreshing swallow. "Boss, what are your orders for today?"

"I thought you'd finish cleaning the stalls."

"Sorry to disappoint you, but no can do."

"Why not?"

He loved the way Abigail's nose wrinkled when she got angry. He deliberately took a bite of toast and chewed until nothing remained in his mouth. "Already did it."

"The horse stalls, too?"

" 'Fraid so."

"The chicken coop?"

He made an imaginary check mark in the air. "Got it."

"Hamlet's . . ."

"Did that, too." Her wide green eyes held his interest for a moment as he inspected the thick fringe of lashes surrounding them.

"Looks like I've mastered farm shit," he said with a cocky grin and watched a blush claim her cheeks.

Whip and Mort covered their mouths and tried to hide their

laughter behind quaking palms. Blue hooted without concern.

The color of Abigail's eyes deepened. "First thing after breakfast, I'm going to teach you how to shoot."

Whip eyed the Colts by Jeremiah's sides. "Abigail doesn't allow anyone to wear their weapons inside the house."

Jeremiah took a swig of coffee. "That makes sense."

Whip nodded. "Would you like me to hang your gun belt in the hall with the rest of ours?"

"That won't be necessary. No one touches my guns but me."

Abigail whacked her cup down. "That's precisely what I mean. You can't go around with that looks-could-kill snarl, challenging people. Chances are, you can't shoot worth a lick."

Dumbfounded, he returned her frown. "All the facts aren't in yet."

She anchored a hand to her hip. "I'd say we should dig your grave now in case we're too busy later."

Mort spoke with a full mouth. "He's a big son of a gun. I sure don't want to be digging that hole."

Abigail exchanged knowing looks with the others at the table. "No need, I'll show him what to do."

Whip said, "Don't expect he'll catch on any too fast. He's only here for six months."

They nodded collectively.

Jeremiah cleared his throat. "Fries me to hear you talking as though I'm not in the room. I've done some shooting."

He recognized the skepticism on Abigail's face. "Yea, if I recollect, you did some riding, too."

Everyone at the table roared with laughter.

Jeremiah gritted his teeth.

Whip slammed a coin on the table. "I've a twenty-five dollar gold piece that says I can beat you, Jeremiah."

Anger got the best of Jeremiah, and he shot off his mouth before he'd had a chance to think. "Count me in."

Mort eyed him suspiciously. "I sure would like to take both of your money, but I ain't got any cash right now."

Jeremiah spoke in a slow even voice. "I can wait till payday."

Abigail left the room and returned a minute later. "You're on," she said, plunking her money on the table.

He covered her hand with his and watched her green eyes widen. "I sure hate to take everyone's hard-earned cash."

Her smug grin told him how she felt. "You'll be leaving with empty pockets."

When he chuckled beneath his breath, her freckled nose wrinkled in disgust.

"Care to up the wager?" he asked.

"What do you have in mind?"

"When I win, you'll help me with my chores."

Abigail's face took on a determined look. "And when I win, you'll do your chores and most of mine too."

He stood and shook her hand. "You got yourself a deal, boss."

Whip scraped his chair back. "You don't know what you've gotten yourself into. Abigail's the best shot there is, even better than most men, except for me."

Abigail nudged Whip. "Don't be too sure of yourself. Last time, you won only by one point, and I've practiced since then."

Jeremiah cocked an eyebrow. "Sounds like stiff competition."

Whip spared him a glance. "You're out of your league."

Jeremiah grinned.

As Abigail left the room, she turned to Jeremiah. "I bet my britches you can't hit even one of the thirty bottles Pedro sets up on the stone wall."

Flexing his fingers by his side, Jeremiah strode out the door. "Now, that's what I call a mighty interesting bet."

CHAPTER 8

When Jeremiah had a minute to calm down, he realized what he'd done. He'd lost sight of his goal and spoken when he should have remained quiet. An inner sense cautioned him to keep a low profile and not to let others know he was a sharpshooter. Though the wound on his forehead had begun to heal, whenever he looked in the mirror, he was reminded that someone had wanted to harm him. Because of this he figured the element of surprise might come in handy later.

But he wished he hadn't tormented Abigail with his brash talk. Because of his inability to control his tongue, he'd be doing his work along with hers. Despite that, he felt it important not to divulge his secret. He grinned, thinking of the trophies that lined his bookcases back east. He didn't doubt that both Whip and Abigail were good shots, but he was certain he could beat them.

Unfortunately, that would not happen today.

A few minutes later Jeremiah took hold of Abigail's elbow and escorted her to the back pasture where Pedro was setting up empty whiskey bottles as targets. Jeremiah watched Whip pace off the distance with long strides. His black handlebar mustache accented his grimace and chiseled features.

Abigail tried to wiggle free of Jeremiah's grasp. "I'm not one of them lame-brained, highfalutin' females who can't walk without help."

He tightened his fingers and watched a frown spread across

her freckled face.

"That so."

"Yes, now let me go."

"Can't."

Her pale eyebrows darted upward. "Why not?"

"Just making sure you don't back out of our little bet."

"Humph, that'll be the day." She yanked her arm away.

"Maw." Clarissa ran toward them with her goat at her heels. "Maw, can I shoot, too?"

"Not this time, sweetie."

"Don't seem fair. Why can't I?"

Abigail's brow furrowed. "Because I said."

"Just a couple shots, pleeeease."

"I don't have the time. I'm fixing to teach Mr. Dalton a thing or two about shooting."

Clarissa rolled her eyes. "It ain't fair."

Abigail planted her hand on her hip. "What did I tell you about that word?"

"Sorry, Maw, I forgot. It isn't fair."

Abigail hugged her daughter to her side. "That's much better. You can't go through life talking like an ignorant farm girl."

"Yes, Maw."

Caesar sidled up to Jeremiah and gently butted his leg. Jeremiah absently stroked the goat's head and offered him a piece of crust he'd tucked in his pocket. As the goat nibbled on the bread, Jeremiah spotted the silhouette of a rider astride a yellow horse galloping in their direction.

"Whip," the man shouted, flapping his hat in the air. "Am I too late to place my bet?"

"Word sure travels fast around here," Jeremiah said to Abigail, unable to understand how anyone would know about their shooting match.

With a look of guilt in her eyes, Abigail nodded to Whip.

"Take care of the matter, pronto."

Whip led the man about a hundred feet away and spoke in a low tone. After taking a quick glance at Jeremiah, the stranger handed Whip a coin, and Whip jotted some information on a piece of paper. Within minutes, both rider and horse disappeared over the rise.

As Whip sauntered toward them, Jeremiah studied the satisfied look in the granite-colored eyes. "What was that about?"

"Nothing that concerns you."

Mortimer's laugh said otherwise.

Abigail cleared her throat. "You going to gab all day?"

Jeremiah thumbed his Stetson back. "No, boss."

"I wish you wouldn't call me that."

"Why?"

"I don't like the way you say it."

"But you are the boss. Aren't you?" Jeremiah paused. "Though it would be a hell of a lot easier if you weren't. What should I call you, then?"

"Miss Wilcox will do."

"That's too formal a greeting for close friends like us."

"We aren't close friends."

A tortured look claimed his features. "You're breaking this Easterner's heart, boss . . . er, Abby."

Her scowl indicated she didn't approve of the familiarity. "We've wasted enough time. Don't have all day to be lollygagging. Take your weapon out of its holster," she commanded in a voice fit for a drill sergeant.

"Which one?"

Her lower lip pursed. "I don't care diddly. Grab a gun before I'm tempted to shoot you with mine."

"What kind of way is that for the gentler sex to speak in front of her impressionable daughter?"

"Clarissa, leave now," she ordered in a voice that defied argument.

When the child was out of ear range, she poked her finger into Jeremiah's chest. "Don't ever spout off such dribble in front of Clarissa again. I've raised my daughter to believe women can do whatever they want."

"I wasn't going to say anything because I didn't think it was any of my business, but since you brought up the subject . . ." He inhaled a deep breath and tried to figure how best to voice his opinion. "Under your tutorage, your young daughter is well on her way to being a fouled-mouth brat."

Whip gave Abigail's firing arm a light push. "Go ahead. Shoot him now. I'll say he was attacked by coyotes. No one will be any the wiser."

Around them the gathering ranch hands exchanged nervous laughs.

Abigail was angry. She didn't cotton to having a know-it-all Easterner telling her how to raise her daughter, but that wasn't what really got her dander up.

Jeremiah was right.

But she'd lie naked on a cactus before confessing such a thing. Ever since that first time she'd held her baby in her arms, Abigail had vowed that her child would not repeat her mistakes; Clarissa would never be a meek little girl. Clarissa would not tremble in her shoes when confronted by boys. Clarissa would never let a man sweet talk her and leave her for a fool.

Over the years Abigail had kept her promise, encouraging her daughter's sometimes outrageous conduct, even when it meant overlooking rudeness. In her zeal, Abigail had overcompensated. And though even she at times found her daughter's outspoken behavior intolerable, she figured it was the lesser of two evils.

As Abigail marched to where the men were standing, she saw Clarissa creeping in the tall grass by the fence. The child could outshoot most men. But there wasn't time to indulge her daughter right now. Abigail's heart swelled with pride and love as she thought of her offspring, so much like her and yet so different. When unexpected tears flooded her eyes, Abigail blamed the wave of emotions on her monthly curse, a time when even she could not deny what she was—a woman, the weaker sex.

"Hell and damnation," she mumbled, kicking a loose stone in her path.

"Well, if it isn't Miss Sunshine herself," Jeremiah said with a taunting grin.

She wanted to slap that smile from his face. As she gazed into pewter eyes shadowed by the wide brim of his black hat, fire curled through her middle and settled where it shouldn't, sending shock waves to her arms and legs.

My, the man was a handsome devil. With the scar on his forehead and the stubble on his chin, he looked rugged, dangerous. *And kissable.* She licked her lower lip. Her breath lodged in her throat like a half-chewed chunk of beef.

"Who goes first," someone shouted, breaking into her thoughts.

"Doesn't make any difference to me," she replied in a harsh tone, trying to mask the confusion welling inside.

Half an hour later, Abigail and Jeremiah were still waiting for their turns.

When Whip aimed and fired, another bottle exploded. He directed his gaze at Jeremiah. "That's twenty-seven out of thirty. Hotshot, see if you can beat that."

If Whip's sarcastic tone bothered Jeremiah, he didn't let on.

Abigail chewed her lower lip and frowned. She desperately wanted to win the shooting match to prove to her daughter women were every bit as good as men. When she turned, she caught Jeremiah gawking at her. Before she could wipe the scowl from her face, his gaze locked with hers. His charcoal eyes had more effect on her than the sweltering Texas sun.

As he smiled, she detected a lemony scent on his breath. From out of nowhere a ridiculous thought took hold—were his lips as sweet as her favorite candy? Her mind spun out of control.

He whispered, "Your sourpuss could curdle milk." A deep laugh rumbled from his chest.

How often had she said the same thing to Clarissa? "It's your turn," she said, doing her best not to return his smile.

With unsteady hands, he fumbled with the guns in his holsters. When he finally freed both weapons, Jeremiah lifted and pointed both Colt 45's at Whip. "Am I holding them right?"

Whip ducked down. "Holy shit. Don't you know nothing? Never point a gun at anyone."

Abigail yanked on Jeremiah's arms. "You damn fool, you're going to kill someone for sure."

He cocked an eyebrow. "Why's that?"

Realization dawned. For all his big talk, he didn't have a clue what he was doing. "You don't know how to shoot, do you? You're just like most men. Letting pride get in the way of common sense."

"You think so?"

"Why else would you bet all that money when you don't stand a chance of winning."

He shrugged. "I see what you mean."

"You could have killed Whip."

The thought brought a smile to Jeremiah's face. "Now, that would have been a crying shame. But I don't think there was any chance of my killing him. This gun isn't loaded."

Whip sighed. "You took a year off my life. Be more careful next time."

"Will do." Jeremiah slid bullets in the chambers of both guns and looked blankly at Abigail. "Now what?"

"Put one of those Colts away. Trust me, you aren't ready to

81

shoot with both."

He slid a gun into his left holster, then pointed to the bottles. "Aren't the targets too far away?"

As she gave him an encouraging tap on the back, she caught of whiff of turpentine and bay rum. Before she could question the strange combination, he smiled down at her, and she shook her head, trying to get back on track.

"Try not to worry about the distance. It looks worse than it really is. Just aim and fire."

He stood rigid as a fence post, legs glued together and pointed the gun in the general direction of the targets.

"Not like that," came her bossy voice in spite of her best intentions. "Your stance is all wrong."

"What do you mean, boss?"

"Spread your legs."

He slid one foot a measly two inches away from the other.

"Here, let me help you." She bent and wrapped her fingers around his right knee, pulling his leg over a good eighteen inches.

"I'd like you to do that again," he muttered with a wink.

Panic twisted her insides. She leaped back and hooked her thumbs in her back pocket to steady her trembling hands. "You're joshing 'cause you're nervous. You feel like a fool 'cause you're afraid you won't measure up."

"You think so?"

She nodded. "Definitely. You're covering up your fear with humor."

"I see what you mean."

Surprised that he was being so agreeable, she smiled. "Now aim and fire, but keep your legs the way you have them."

Jeremiah lifted his arm, sighted down the barrel, and fired. A branch from an oak tree some one hundred feet away fell to the ground.

"What do you think?" he asked, worry etching his handsome face.

Abigail had never seen a worse shot. "Not bad, but you were off a little."

He seemed oblivious to the snickers and jeers all around them.

His brow wrinkled. "I thought for sure I'd hit a bottle. Guess this is harder than it looks."

Abigail squeezed his arm, hoping to encourage him, but got waylaid by the definition of muscles beneath her fingertips.

"Don't let it get you down. It'll come. You have to be patient."

All around them knee-slapping laughter ensued.

From twenty feet away came Clarissa's giggle. "I coulda done better with my eyes closed. You're either blind or dumber than a tree stump."

Abigail gave her daughter a stern look. "Enough. Now you go finish your chores."

As Abigail started to glance away, she saw Clarissa sticking her tongue out at Jeremiah. Abigail was beside herself. She'd always encouraged the girl to say whatever she wanted, but she'd gone too far.

Abigail stepped up to the firing line. "Let me show you how it's done. You'll have to practice a little each day, and in time, you'll get better."

She blasted the first three bottles. "See," she said, "it's all in the way you stand. Oh, and you have to concentrate on the target instead of the gun barrel."

He nodded, appreciation for her skills in his eyes. "Mighty fancy shooting, Abby."

Her name on his lips, like a soft caress, sent a shiver down her spine. She basked in his compliment and his warm smile as the men behind her clapped and hooted. "Way to go, Abigail."

She missed bottle four because her mind was on Jeremiah

instead of her shooting, because she couldn't focus with him watching her. She wanted to cuss but didn't. Training her eyes on the targets, she hit five, six, and seven. With the men cheering her on, she blasted the next fifteen bottles, the sound of splintering glass ringing in the air. Unfortunately, she felt Jeremiah's gaze at her back and missed again. Her heart took a sudden dip.

Whip stepped closer. "If you miss another, we tie, miss more and I win."

She didn't need to be reminded. "Everyone gawking at the back of my head isn't helping any."

"In that case, me and the boys will look the other way. You'll have no excuse if you lose."

Once Whip went to lean against the barn with the ranch hands, she took a calming breath and was about to fire when Clarissa called to her in a muffled voice.

"Maw."

Abigail's bullet ricocheted off a rock.

The men stood around Whip clapping and making a fuss.

"Darn it!" Abigail swung around, ready to give her daughter a piece of her mind, but found herself unable to utter one word. Perched on the top rung of the fence, the child stared helplessly at her mother. At Clarissa's feet, poised ready to attack, was a huge rattlesnake.

If Clarissa moved, she'd die.

Abigail's hands shook so much she didn't dare fire her weapon. She cursed her weakness. If that had been a stranger, Abigail could have handled this emergency, but seeing Clarissa had rendered her useless. Whip and the others seemed unaware of their dilemma.

"Stay very still, Clarissa," Jeremiah told the child.

Sweat beaded Abigail's forehead and nose. From a distance a longhorn mooed, chickens clucked. How could she be aware of such nonsense while her daughter's life hung by a thread? Abigail had never experienced such fear and hopelessness, not even when she was alone, unwed, and ready to give birth. If she lost her daughter . . .

Filled with panic, she debated whether she should chance trying to shoot the snake.

What if she missed?

Did she dare shout to Whip?

Would the added noise make grave matters worse?

Clarissa teetered on the fence. "Maw, I bet I can jump down and run faster than that snake can bite."

"Don't even consider that." Jeremiah said, a tremor in his voice.

Abigail recognized the look of defiance on her daughter's face.

Clarissa's wide smirk was directed at Jeremiah when she leaped down, her heels kicking up dirt.

In the blink of an eye, the giant snake snapped forward.

Abigail screamed.

Jeremiah hands flew to his holsters. Both guns fired at once, riddling the rattler with bullets.

Seemingly unaware of how close she'd come to losing her life, Clarissa ran to her mother. Abigail held her tight, sobbing with relief. "You have to learn to listen."

"I told you I could outrun the critter."

"By not listening to Jeremiah you almost got yourself killed." Abigail pulled a lace hanky from her pocket and dabbed at the corners of her eyes.

Looking confused, her daughter lifted her head. "You said to pay no mind to fancy-talking Easterners."

"You're right, I did, but this was different." Guilt clawed at Abigail. She couldn't blame the child for misunderstanding. "From now on, I want you to listen. And no more wise-mouthing, either."

"But . . ."

Abigail lifted her daughter's jaw. "No ands, ifs, or buts. You be a good girl and go apologize to Mr. Dalton for the mean things you said earlier."

"You said not to fib, and I'm not sorry."

Abigail had her work cut out for her. "Just 'cause something is true doesn't give you the right to say it."

The child's chin rose in defiance. "I'll say what I want, when I want."

Abigail heaved an exasperated sigh. "We'll discuss this again later. Mr. Dalton saved your life. Now, you should shake his hand and thank him."

Shuffling slowly, Clarissa made her way to Jeremiah. "Thank you," she whispered, never glancing up. "Bet I coulda outrun that mean old snake."

Jeremiah hunkered down, until he was eye level with the child. "I don't think so, sweetheart. From my way of thinking, you either have to start listening to warnings or you have to learn to run much faster."

She stole a glance, her impish face sporting a grin. "I was thinking of doing a little of both."

He patted her shoulder. "I think that's wise."

Now that the danger had passed, Abigail shifted her attention to Jeremiah. Never in her life had she seen anyone draw guns as fast as he had. Never had she seen such accuracy.

Once Clarissa sauntered away, Abigail took a moment to watch the men who'd gathered around Jeremiah.

"Ain't seen shooting like that in a coon's age."

"Me neither," another said.

"Lightning doesn't strike any faster than you did, Mr. Dalton."

Jeremiah shrugged. "Call me Jeremiah."

Even Whip, grudging admiration in his eyes, said, "Way to go, greenhorn."

Jeremiah seemed to be taking all the comments in stride.

When the last man walked away, Abigail stepped toward Jeremiah. The thick lump in her throat warned of impending tears. "I can't thank you enough."

Jeremiah took her small hand in his, surprised to find calluses and a firm grip that spoke of hard work, strength, and determination.

"I'm only glad I could help." The gentle breeze carried the scent of roses, a smell that would forever remind him of her. She'd removed her hat, and beneath the carrot-colored curls dangling over her forehead were green eyes with flecks of gold. He'd heard of men sacrificing everything they owned in search of the precious metal. He'd never understood the obsession until now.

"I don't think I'd want to live if anything happened to Clarissa." Her fingers lingered in his

Her voice reminded Jeremiah of New England maple syrup, sugary and sweet. He smiled down, wanting to trace her upper lip with his finger.

She blinked away tears, her sad eyes pulling at his heartstrings. Tough Abigail Wilcox had never looked more vulnerable.

Or more lovable.

As she leaned into him, he was drawn to her fragile side. He wanted to wrap her in his arms and protect her from harm. Their relationship had crossed an invisible barrier. The near accident had started to forge a strong friendship.

Slowly she pulled away, dropped her hands to her sides. The softened features took on a stubborn look. Her chin jutted upward.

"Something wrong?"

"You knew how to shoot all along."

He grinned. "I guess it slipped my mind."

"You're a lying scoundrel, Jeremiah Dalton."

"I was merely following your instructions. You're one hell of a teacher, Abby."

"You, Jeremiah Dalton, are full of bull."

Were it not for her tone, he'd have concluded he'd been wrong about their budding friendship.

CHAPTER 9

Clarissa rolled her eyes and pursed her lips.

Abigail was so glad her daughter was all right that even seeing her pouting mouth didn't upset her. Trying to appear angry, Abigail planted an ornery look on her face. "What in tarnation got into you? You know better than to fuss with a rattler."

Clarissa's chin rose in defiance. "I was gonna outrun it. Besides, I wasn't 'bout to listen to that fancy-pants know-it-all Easterner. You said he was a cold-hearted varmint. You said you'd rather shoot yourself in the foot than believe one word from his mouth. You said he was so low his belly scraped the ground when he moved. You said . . ."

Abigail raised her hand. "Whoa." Though the words sounded darn familiar, she was flabbergasted to hear her daughter repeating such things. "Where'd you hear all this?"

"The night before Mr. Dalton got here, I heard you talking to Whip and Pedro."

"I said all that?"

Clarissa nodded. "You said everyone should ignore his slick talk, and that only a ninny would believe such dribble." She blinked back tears and took a shaky breath. "I sure didn't want you to think I was dumb. So I decided to do the opposite of everything Mr. Dalton said."

When Abigail thought how close she'd come to losing Clarissa, she had difficulty breathing. Gathering her daughter in her arms, Abigail rested her chin against the silken hair on top of her head. Abigail didn't rightly know how she'd survive if anything ever happened to Clarissa. "I reckon I exaggerated some. You know I blow off a lot of steam, but . . ."

But what? For years, hatred had festered inside Abigail until she couldn't look at a man without remembering her shame and her stupidity. Not only had Frank Myers taken her innocence, he'd robbed her of her ability to trust. Abigail lifted Clarissa's chin until she squarely met her blue eyes. "Don't you ever do anything as foolhardy again, or I swear, I'll lock you in your bedroom until . . ."

Recognizing the familiar threat, Clarissa's tear-streaked face lit with amusement. "Until I'm twenty years old, right?"

Abigail tweaked her nose. "That was before this happened. Thirty years old sounds better to me."

"That's pretty old, right, Maw?"

"Not as old as I feel right now. Seeing you leap from that fence likely aged me fifty years." With her arm wrapped around her daughter's shoulders, Abigail strolled into the house. When they entered the bedroom, she nodded toward the rolltop desk in the corner and patted her daughter's behind, giving her a slight shove. "Be a good girl and show me what you learnt yesterday."

"Aw Maw, can't we skip that foolishness for one day."

"Reading and writing is too important. You're going to grow up to be someone special, and that isn't likely to happen without proper learning."

"Aw, Maw, I don't see why I need to count beans in a jar. Beans make me gag." To illustrate her point she stuck her finger in her mouth and made a face.

Abigail hid her smile. "You don't have to eat the beans, just count them."

Feet dragging, Clarissa made her way to the desk, pushed up the rolltop and scooted onto the stack of books piled high on the chair so she could reach the desktop. Her thin shoulders drooped as she lifted the container of dried beans, dumped some out, and arranged them in rows of ten. "I don't see why I gotta do this."

"My tongue gets tired of repeating the same old thing."

Clarissa folded her arms across her chest. "I don't need to be able to count beans to earn me a living roping and breeding longhorns."

"There's more to running a ranch than taking care of livestock. You need to keep books, you need to know how to read and count, otherwise some fast-talking thief is going to rob you blind. You need to practice counting beans now so you'll know how to count more important things later."

After one final, "Aw, Maw," she turned to the desk. "Ten rows, each with ten beans makes one hundred gagging beans. Take one row away, that still leaves ninety sickening beans." She peeked at her mother, but Abigail pretended not to notice.

While her daughter did her arithmetic, Abigail's chest swelled with pride. The girl was real smart. Abigail could read well enough to get by, and she was quick with numbers so no one would dare try to pull a fast one on her. But even though she got along well with just a little learning, Abigail wanted much more for her daughter. She wanted to give her the world, to protect her from harm, and to help her grow into a self-sufficient woman. Abigail was certain a good education was the key.

Several minutes later Clarissa slid the beans into the glass jar. "Can't I stop now, pleeeeease?"

"I'm powerful proud to hear you counting like that. One of these days you'll go to college and show everyone what I already know, that you're about the smartest girl in all of Texas."

"Aw, Maw, I don't want to go to college. I wanna be just like you. I want to own a ranch and raise longhorns, horses, goats, and pigs. Maybe even a few chickens 'cause I like eggs so much."

"I've had it up to here with your backtalk." Abigail ran a finger across her neck. Every day they went through the same thing, and it got on Abigail's nerves, but she figured the price was worth paying. When her daughter grew, she'd be an educated lady with the world at her fingertips. The thought made Abigail smile. "Nothing you say will change my mind, so quit fussing and get on with your reading."

Clarissa rolled her eyes, but didn't voice her objections. "All right," she said with a deep sigh, opening her book and running her index finger under the first line of her reading primer. "The boy ran to the store to buy ffffff . . . what's this word?"

Abigail sounded the word out and hoped she was giving Clarissa the right answer. "Flour," she replied, a hint of doubt in her voice. It shamed Abigail that she couldn't read all the words. She knew the important words that dealt with ranching and such, but there were so many that meant nothing to her.

"Flour and molasses . . ." Clarissa pointed to the last word.

Soon her daughter would read and write better than most folks in these parts. Would Clarissa look down her nose at her mother?

Clarissa quickly stashed the reading book aside and started to work on her penmanship. Several minutes later, biting her lip, she looked up. "What do you think, Maw?"

Abigail stretched her neck to get a closer look at the uneven scribble, which resembled chicken scratch. "It's a little better, but you need to round out your letters a bit more. Here, let me show you."

Abigail took the slate, wrapped her fingers around the thick piece of white chalk, and drew a fat *D*. She enjoyed teaching Clarissa, but the girl was fast approaching the time when Abigail would not be able to help her any more. Once they had their own place, Abigail planned to hire a tutor to teach her child what she couldn't.

"Gee, Maw, I wish I could write like you."

"In no time at all, you'll be writing better than me."

With effort Clarissa wrote the letter *D* three times on the slate. Abigail stood and gave her an encouraging smile. "That's a damn sight better."

Her daughter chewed her lower lip. "How come you cuss and tell me not to?"

The question caught Abigail off guard. "It's not proper for a young girl to swear."

"How old do I have to be before I can cuss, too?"

Abigail glanced into Clarissa's innocent face. "Never. I don't ever want you to swear."

"But you do."

"Yes, but I shouldn't. No one should." Abigail realized she had to change her ways. She was sending her daughter mixed messages. But after deliberately copying some of the ranch hands' bad habits and mannerisms for years, she wasn't sure whether she could stop.

"Then why do you do it?"

"Damn if I know." Abigail's face grew red. "I mean . . . I don't rightly know, but I'll tell you what. From now on, you're going to start listening to what all adults tell you to do, and I'm going start talking like a lady should. How's that?"

"I still won't listen to that Easterner."

"Jeremiah Dalton isn't just any Easterner. He's Noah's son. Don't you think Noah would want you to treat his son with respect?"

Clarissa lowered her head. "I guess so . . . I miss Grandpa real bad," she said, gripping her lower lip with her teeth.

Abigail hugged her daughter. "So do I." She looked away so that Clarissa wouldn't see the moisture clouding her vision. Noah's death had left a gaping hole in Abigail's life, and not a day went by without her shedding tears for the man who'd taken her in when no one else had.

Abigail led her daughter outside. After drawing a shaky breath, she managed to say, "We were lucky to have Noah with us as long as we did. He loved us both, and our lives are better for it. You're a lucky girl to have found such a special grandfather."

"He wasn't really my Grandpa, was he?"

"No, but in the ways that mattered most, he was."

"Jeremiah Dalton is nothing like his paw."

"Maybe you need to give him a chance." The words startled Abigail but left her more convinced than ever that she would never follow her own advice. "Sweetheart, if you look really hard, I bet you'll find some of the same fine traits you loved in Noah. You need to listen to Jeremiah if he says not to do something. He'll recognize danger when he sees it."

"But I thought only a ninny would believe his slick talk."

"That wasn't what I meant by slick talk. If he tells you not to do something, you better listen, or I'll take a switch to your behind."

"Tell me again about my paw. Tell me the part about how he saved the town from a hundred rustlers. He was a hero, right, Maw?"

Abigail didn't like lying to her daughter, but she didn't have the heart to tell her the truth about the man who'd fathered her, a man who ran out the second he learned Abigail was with child. Years back she'd made up a story that had stopped Clarissa's incessant questions. As her daughter grew older, Abigail feared she'd hear the rumors that had grown worse with time.

"I wish my paw hadn't been so wonderful," Clarissa said with a dreamy look on her face. "If he hadn't been a hero, he might still be alive."

Guilt gnawed at Abigail's conscience. "No sense wishing for what can't be changed."

Clarissa nodded. "I know that, but I only wish I'd gotten the chance to meet my paw is all."

Jeremiah had walked in on the last of the conversation. Seemingly deep in thought, Abigail didn't acknowledge his presence. Once Clarissa disappeared into the barn, he stepped behind Abigail. "Sometimes, it's better to have no father at all than one who doesn't give a darn."

Abigail jerked around. "Do you always listen in on other people's conversations?"

"Only when I hear my name mentioned." He was pleased to see she hadn't thrown out the black-eyed Susan he'd slid into her hatband earlier that morning.

"You're wrong about Noah. He loved you."

"Yeah, I bet."

She yanked her hat from her head. Her orange curls bounced around freely.

Surprisingly, the brassy color didn't seem as hard on the eyes as he remembered. The rich tone reminding him of burnished copper. Only the softest hair could be ruffled by such a gentle breeze. His fingers itched to find out for themselves. To keep from doing something he'd regret, he hooked his thumbs behind his belt buckle.

Abigail jabbed her finger in his chest. "You come with me, Mr. Know-It-All." She spun around and marched into the house.

"I don't care much for your sassy mouth, Abigail Wilcox," he replied as he watched her retreating back, fearing she hadn't heard one blasted word.

He followed her into his father's study, a room he'd deliberately avoided because it represented his old man. As he entered, he took in the massive room with floor-to-ceiling bookcases, the mounted trophy of a twelve-point buck and the oil painting of longhorns herded by cowboys on horseback. It was a man's room with thick sturdy furniture.

Abigail waved him toward the desk. The sunrays from the opened window ignited the mane around her head into a flaming halo.

"I don't care much for your sassy mouth," he repeated, because she left him unable to think of anything else to say. The statement lost its strength as he stared into deep emerald eyes that reminded him of the lush evergreens back East.

Ignoring his statement, she turned on her heels and reached down to remove a box from the lower drawer of the mahogany desk standing before a stone fireplace.

"You can call me sassy all you want, but I happen to be right. So put that where the sun don't shine."

No woman had ever spoken to him in such a manner. Anger curled inside as he blinked in disbelief. Before he could reply, he glanced down at the box she'd just shoved in his hands and noticed his name written in black ink in the corner. He set the container on the desk and because his legs seemed unable to support his weight, he lowered himself into the same leather chair where his father had sat countless times.

He didn't know how long he studied the closed box or when Abigail left the room, but when he glanced up, he realized he was alone.

Jeremiah removed the cardboard lid and stared down at a photograph of himself as a small boy, riding on his father's lap atop a black stallion. The air in the room grew stale, and his breath caught in the back of his throat as he studied Noah's wide smile and the large arms he kept tight around Jeremiah's tiny waist. He examined several other photographs, each more telling than the other—though Noah had not shown interest when Jeremiah was growing up, he certainly seemed to care for the youngster in his arms.

In a tattered envelope that bore his name he found a lock of dark hair tied with a blue ribbon. As he stroked the fine wisps of baby hair, he wondered how many times his father had done this same thing.

When Jeremiah removed the photographs from the box, he spotted what was hidden underneath. His pulse drummed in his ears as he lifted a pair of leather boots that fit in his palm, the same pair he'd worn in the pictures. He ran his fingertips over the soft, tooled leather, and the scars inside his heart began to heal. He'd thought his father an unfeeling man, but now he knew the truth. Only a person who cared deeply would have kept these mementos. A wave of emotions flooded over him. Jeremiah reached into his pocket and withdrew his handkerchief to wipe the moisture from his eyes.

CHAPTER 10

Eyes closed, Jeremiah concentrated on his breathing and his form. All week he'd practiced what Buck Ridley had told him. The old man was right. Jeremiah felt in control as he sat on the massive animal.

"Lancelot," he said to familiarize the beast with his voice. "You're a fine specimen."

The horse lifted its head and nickered softly.

According to Buck, it was imperative that Jeremiah speak to his horse. It was all part of the bonding process between animal and rider. According to Buck, horses sensed a rider's nervousness. The feistier the mount, the more important it was to appear relaxed.

Jeremiah discovered that keeping his eyes shut was easy, staying awake more difficult. Each day before dawn, he crept from his room, tiptoed down the stairs, and made his way to the barn where under dim lantern light he rode Lancelot for at least thirty minutes. Even Moonbeam, the stallion no one had yet ridden, seemed to look forward to his morning treat, either a sliver of fruit or a bite of dessert left over from the evening meal. Jeremiah believed in setting goals for himself. And though he did not intend to let anyone know his plans, before he returned to Boston, he'd ride Moonbeam and he'd do it with ease.

Jeremiah inhaled and filled his lungs with the sweet smell of the hay. The pungent odors that had at one time repulsed him no longer aggravated his nostrils. He was surprised how quickly he'd grown accustomed to his surroundings.

As he slid his fingers along the smooth leather reins, he rehashed the conversation he'd had with Whip the night before. *Greenhorn, you better get your act together. It's damn near roundup time, and I can hardly wait to take charge of your sorry ass.*

Jeremiah had nodded nonchalantly, though deep inside his stomach knotted. If only he had more time to prepare, but he didn't.

He'd gazed into Whip's granite eyes and grinned, ignoring the hatred directed at him. Jeremiah couldn't understand why the man held such animosity toward him, but he didn't plan to waste any time worrying about it either. If push came to shove, Jeremiah could hold his own. He'd returned Whip's icy stare before glancing away.

No doubt, Whip would select another horse for him to ride on the roundup. That mount would not be as docile as the creature beneath him now. Jeremiah exerted slight pressure with his knees, and Lancelot hobbled ahead. Jeremiah was delighted with his progress. As the horse plodded along, Jeremiah sat straight and tall, taking slow but confident breaths, pleased that his behind wasn't slamming against the saddle as it once had. While continuing to keep his eyes shut, he allowed Lancelot to lead the way in wide circles inside the barn.

Trust yourself.

Trust your horse.

Jeremiah silently repeated the two phrases. According to Buck, without trust Jeremiah would never be a good rider. And Jeremiah would not settle for simply "good." He wouldn't rest until he'd mastered this skill.

Not having spoken to the horse for several minutes, Jeremiah reached forward and patted the animal's mane. "You're a fine piece of horse flesh, Lancelot." He chuckled. He was sounding more like a Texan each day.

The horse shook its head and snorted, yet Jeremiah remained firmly planted in the saddle. The toughest part of horseback riding, he decided, was making conversation with the animal because he felt like a fool. Jeremiah pulled on the reins. "Whoa, Lancelot, whoa."

The horse took two leisurely steps before stopping to sniff the ground.

Jeremiah opened his eyes and swung his leg over the saddle. He realized that he'd enjoyed the short morning ride. With a satisfied smile, he led Lancelot back to his stall.

He unsaddled the horse and wiped him down before reaching in the back of the cabinet for the horse liniment. Only the liniment wasn't for Lancelot. Jeremiah dropped his pants and applied a liberal amount to both legs. Though he grew stronger each day, his muscles still protested every move. Jeremiah praised Sloan's Horse Liniment as a miracle cure, and he doused himself liberally both morning and night, taking care not to be discovered. The only down side was the smell that he disguised by splashing bay rum over his legs.

He yanked his jeans up and buttoned the fly, then sauntered across the dimly lit interior. The hum low in his throat died when he spotted the silhouette of a slight figure with wild curls on top of her head, leaning against the doorframe.

How much had she observed?

He plunked his black Stetson low on his head and ran two fingers along the felt brim.

Abigail shifted her weight to the other foot. "What are you doing in here?"

"I couldn't sleep so I figured I'd check the animals."

"And how are they?"

"Fine."

She sniffed and wiggled her nose. "What's that smell?"

He gave a nonchalant shrug. "What smell?"

She took a deep whiff. "Can't quite put my finger on it. It's a cross between bay rum and something else." She eyed him suspiciously.

He cleared his throat and gave an innocent smile. "It's the newest scent in men's cologne."

Her face creased in doubt.

"Very popular back in Boston."

"I see."

He took a deep breath. "Since we're on the subject, you smell good, like roses." Good was the least of it. The truth was she smelled wonderful. As lusty thoughts of Abigail flickered through his mind, he reminded himself that Evelyn was the woman for him.

Abigail's eyelids drifted downward; her long lashes swept her freckled cheeks.

How could a woman who'd borne a child blush at such a simple compliment?

In the lantern light, he caught a glimpse of terror in her eyes and wondered what had caused such a stir. The confusion in the pupils turned to disgust.

"Keep your fancy words for someone who'll lap them up like a starving kitten."

She started to swing around, but he wrapped his fingers over her shoulder and forced her to face him.

He saw the fear, indecision, and the look of a hunted animal, ready to bolt. Someone had hurt her deeply, and God help him, he wanted to undo that pain. "Abby, you do smell good, like roses. By your reaction, you'd think I'd insulted you."

She blew a strand of fiery hair from her forehead.

"You need to learn to take a compliment a bit more gracefully."

He waited for her to tell him off, but instead, she did

something he'd never expected.

She agreed with him.

For over a week Jeremiah had planned to move his things into one of the downstairs bedrooms, but by the time evening arrived, he'd had barely enough energy to drag his aching body up the stairs. But tonight after supper, he found he wasn't nearly as tired. As he sauntered down the hallway, he felt eyes watching him. He turned and found Clarissa peeking from behind a chair.

She made a face, which he ignored.

He ambled toward what had been his father's bedroom and opened the door. Hearing footsteps, he spotted Clarissa at his side.

"I don't think you should do that."

"Why not?"

"Maw says to stay out of Noah's bedroom."

"Then you'd better wait out here while I have a look around." Jeremiah sauntered inside.

Clarissa inched into the room. "Maw says it ain't fit for anyone to poke their noses into Noah's possessions."

He gave her a pointed look. "I'll keep that in mind."

"Maw would have our hides if she caught either of us in here."

Jeremiah reached in his back pocket for the small bag of lemon drops. "Here, suck on one of these. Maybe it'll keep you quiet for a while."

She took the candy and tucked a spare piece in the pocket of her pants.

"Is that for Caesar or Hamlet?" he asked, popping a lemon drop in his mouth and enjoying the sweet taste.

"This one's for Maw. I'm gonna put it on her pillow as a special treat. These are her favorite."

"They are?"

"She loves them."

"Whenever I offer her one, she's always said no."

"Maybe that's 'cause you're an Easterner. Maw doesn't like Easterners, you know."

Something about the child's expression struck him funny. He laughed. "That's news to me."

"Maw says I should be nice to you 'cause you're Noah's son."

That surprised him. "Really?"

She nodded. "Maw says if I look really hard, I can find some of Noah in you."

He wasn't sure how he felt about that. Most boys strove to be like their fathers, but he'd never entertained the thought. He pressed his hand onto the mattress of a large bed, thinking how comfortable he'd be stretched out. He sat down and glanced at Clarissa out of the corner of his eye. "And have you found any similarities yet?"

"Not yet, but I'm looking really hard."

He laughed and was joined by a childish giggle. "No one will ever accuse you of throwing around pretty words."

He stood, crossed the room, opened the large wardrobe, and took inventory of Noah's possessions. A leather vest caught his eyes. He took it down from the wooden peg and slipped his arms into the holes. It was a tight fit. The soft hide hugged his chest, making him feel a little closer to his father.

"You shouldn't do that."

He scowled. "I can see that candy didn't shut you up very long," he said, shrugging out of the vest.

"I still have it in my mouth. See." She puckered yellow lips with the lemon drop in between. "I just tuck it in my cheek when I want to talk."

He rolled his eyes. "Now you tell me."

She giggled again. "You know, I think I just found something."
He lost the train of thought. "Found what?"

"Your paw used to make me laugh. He was funny, like you."

"Oh." Somehow, he'd never thought of his father as being anything but mean. And heartless. He'd certainly never thought of him as being funny. Until arriving in Texas, Jeremiah had overlooked the fact that his father was a flesh and blood man who laughed and cried. "Noah made you laugh?"

She nodded. "Don't seem right for you to call your paw Noah. If I ever called my maw Abigail, she'd take a switch to my behind."

He wondered how his life would have turned out if his mother had stayed in Texas. Would he have loved the old man? Swamped with a feeling of great loss, Jeremiah walked across the room and examined the items on top of the bureau. "Unlike you, I don't feel close to Noah because I don't even know him."

"I didn't know my paw either, but I'm sure glad I got the chance to meet yours."

As Jeremiah glanced into the wide blue eyes filled with love for his father, his heart gave a sudden lurch. He reached down and patted the child's head. "You miss Noah, don't you?"

She nodded and blinked away tears. She was a tough little girl, a lot like her mother.

He moved toward the bureau and picked up a thick leather belt with an engraved steer on the buckle.

Clarissa reached out and ran her fingers along the tarnished metal. "Grandpa wore this every day. He said it brought him good luck."

"Would you like to have this?"

She yanked her hand away. "I don't know what Maw would say."

"If this buckle is lucky, I'd bet Noah would want you have it."

"It's not gonna fit."

"It will if I cut it down."

Jeremiah ran a finger along the worn leather, trying to feel a connection to his father. He was no longer sure how he felt about Noah. He'd gone from downright hatred to a state of total confusion. He handed Clarissa the belt. "Here, I know Noah would be pleased. I'll shorten it after I get my stuff moved in here."

"I don't think you should move in here. I don't think Maw will like it."

"Regardless, that's exactly what I aim to do."

He strolled across the room to have a look behind the only door he hadn't opened.

"I don't think you should open that," she warned as he reached for the doorknob. Childish grin on her face, Clarissa raced across the room and disappeared into the hallway.

Ignoring the warning, he swung the door open and came face to face with Abigail. He caught the fire in her eyes. His gaze settled on the lacy camisole hugging her slim curves. His heart slammed into his ribs.

She jumped back, grabbed her shirt from the bed, and held it in front of her like a shield. "Don't you know better than to enter someone's bedroom without knocking?"

Startled, he spotted a vase of wildflowers by the window. Her gun belt and six-shooter hung over the back of a nearby chair, but his gaze returned to the lacy undergarment before flicking away.

He ran a finger inside the collar of his shirt, leaned into the door casing, and gave her a wide grin. "Looks like we're going to be neighbors."

Clearly, his good upbringing had deteriorated in the Texas heat. Jeremiah cursed his lack of manners and turned away so that Abigail could finish buttoning her shirt.

"What in tarnation you doing in here?" came the agitated tone.

When he looked at Abigail again, she was buttoned to her chin, her cheeks a delicate pink.

"I've found myself some better accommodations." He nodded behind him. "I'm moving in."

"You can't."

"Just watch me."

"It isn't decent. These rooms have adjoining doors."

He chuckled. "I noticed that."

If looks could maim, Jeremiah knew he'd be writhing in pain.

Worry streaked across her face. "Noah used both rooms until he got too sick. I moved in here because he needed someone to care for him. I'd leave the door open at night in case he cried out in pain. You'll have to find another bedroom."

That irked him. "You're the bossiest woman I know."

She folded her arms, took a stance that riled the hell out of him.

He stepped back and looked at the bed that would allow him to sprawl. Barely giving her a glance, he strolled across the room. "Be warned. I'm moving in here tonight."

Her stubborn jaw dropped a fraction. "But the door."

He winked. "You can keep it open if you'd like."

Jeremiah dodged the shoe aimed at his head.

When Abigail entered her bedroom later that night, she could hear Jeremiah rummaging around in the next room. It infuriated her that he'd moved into Noah's room. She considered taking her things to another part of the house, but she couldn't.

Propriety warranted that she find another bedroom. Her past warranted that she stay put. Never again would she allow any man to influence her decisions, to make her bend to his words like a spindly limb in a hurricane. But how would it look to the others if she remained in a room that clearly connected to Jeremiah's? Need be, she'd deal with that later, but for now, she wasn't going anywhere.

Abigail sat with the hairbrush in her hands glancing at her reflection in the mirror. She'd been cursed with her grandmother's brassy curls, hair the color of pumpkins. The only thing worse was the freckles that dotted her complexion like rust spots on a wagon wheel. And the Texas sun had multiplied the brown specks until they were all Abigail could see. No wonder Clarissa's father had bolted.

Abigail didn't like this train of thought. Sounded too much like self-pity to suit her. Yet her mind tumbled through the past, and she remembered her father's parting words. "You've shamed us, child. You'll not bring a bastard into this house."

Shoulders down, tears streaking her cheeks, she'd left, but only after pleading with her father to let her stay. She'd had no pride back then, only fear for herself and her unborn child. Abigail had survived, and in the process, had developed an inner strength.

As she ran the brush through her hair, she was aware of a sound coming from Jeremiah's bedroom. She listened a moment and decided it made her edgy to hear Jeremiah's deep-timbred voice singing a tune she could not quite make out through the thick walls.

"Damn him," she said, taking a few steps and putting her ear to the door.

"Oh Susannah, don't you cry for me, I come from . . ."

Straightening, Abigail called herself a jackass. Didn't she have better things to do than to spy on Jeremiah Dalton? Next thing, she'd be peeking though the keyhole.

Shaking thoughts of the impossible man from her mind, she stalked across the room, and sat on the bed where she tugged at her boots. When she noticed the three lemon drops on her pillow, she smiled. Clarissa was such a thoughtful child. The very idea warmed Abigail, made her feel as though she'd done right by her daughter. Abigail's heart swelled with pride.

As Abigail reached for a piece of the yellow candy, she hesitated only a fraction of a second before popping it in her mouth where she slid it back and forth against her tongue, savoring the lemony flavor.

She closed her eyes and sucked on the candy a moment, the words to *Oh Susannah* going through her head. She'd never cared much for the song, but she couldn't shake it from her mind.

The more Abigail tried to rid herself of the song, the more it wedged in her brain until she found herself unknowingly humming the ridiculous tune.

"Hell and damnation," she said, not realizing that she'd spoken aloud until she heard the soft rap on the adjoining door.

"Everything all right in there?"

"Of course it is."

"Can I come in a minute?"

She heaved a deep sigh as Jeremiah wedged the door open.

"Since I'm right next door," he said with a taunting grin, his upper lip disappearing beneath a trim mustache. "I figured it wouldn't be neighborly if I didn't at least say goodnight."

My, he was a dashing man, bold and arrogant with enough magnetism to draw women from miles away. And he knew it. Confidence almost oozed from his pores. Charm, too. But Abigail had been charmed once before. It wasn't likely to ever happen again.

That didn't stop her from appreciating his rakish good looks or the way his hair fell over his forehead, all except for one lock that stuck up from his head like a small horn. She studied his dark hair, the color of rich molasses, and wanted to run her fingers over the cowlick and try to tame that strand of hair. No doubt, it would be no easier to control that lock than it would the man looking at her with fire in his eyes.

She took a quick breath, adjusted her gaze to his, pretended that she did not feel the heat building in her stomach.

"I can't have you dropping in here every two minutes."

"Good night, Abby," he said before closing the door.

Jeremiah had succeeded in driving that confounded song from her mind. Unfortunately, Abigail preferred the lyrics of *Oh Susannah* to the thoughts now running amok.

CHAPTER 11

Jeremiah slid between crisp sheets and looked forward to a good night's sleep. He extended his right foot toward one corner of the spacious bed, his left foot toward another and reached way out to the sides. Laying spread eagle, he enjoyed the luxury of finally being able to stretch.

He sighed in content. In another five months, he'd be back in Boston with Evelyn. When he'd first arrived in Texas, he'd missed Evelyn terribly, but now that he was busy from dawn to dusk, he didn't think of her as often. Deep in his heart he knew she was the woman for him. Unlike his parents, he didn't take commitment lightly. When he asked for Evelyn's hand in marriage, Jeremiah vowed to love her until the day he died. And Jeremiah's word was worth more than all the gold coins in his future father-in-law's bank.

Jeremiah sprawled onto his stomach. A gentle breeze ruffled the curtains in the opened bedroom windows. The sweet smell of wildflowers filled the air, stirring thoughts of the woman in the next room.

Never in his wildest dreams would he have imagined such a feminine undergarment beneath Abigail's manly shirts. And now that he'd seen it, the image was imprinted in his mind. He couldn't forget how the soft material hugged her gentle curves or the way her coppery curls had cascaded down her back. He'd wanted to run his fingers though the burnished locks. He'd wanted to feel their silken texture in his hand. He'd wanted to lose himself in that hair. When he'd said goodnight, she tilted her head slightly to one side before he'd shut the door. The simple gesture struck him as endearing and unbelievably feminine, a contradiction to the woman he worked with each day.

When soft footsteps approached the door that adjoined their rooms, he leaned up on one elbow to listen. Was his mind playing tricks? The doorknob jiggled. He toyed with the idea of Abigail entering his bedroom, wearing a wispy gown that revealed the dark peaks of her breasts and the golden triangle of fiery curls.

"Jeremiah," she'd say, her voice dewy with need. Since Abigail knew her way around the bedroom, would she be bold, take the lead? Would she dare him to love her? He tried to wipe the questions from his mind but found that he couldn't. Abigail did everything with confidence. And she approached life like a man. Jeremiah decided she'd be a wild cat in bed—untamed and unbridled.

His mouth dried as if he were standing bare-chested in the Texas sun.

When he tried to squelch such thoughts, neither his mind nor his body cooperated. Of course, if Abigail came to him, he'd have to turn her down—very gently, because he wouldn't want to hurt her feelings. He would never take Abigail into his bed while he was promised to another. He'd given his word, and that was the end of the matter. But Jeremiah could no longer ignore the facts. He clearly wanted Abigail, evident by his lustful thoughts and his throbbing groin.

What was Abigail up to? He held his breath, but when the door didn't budge, he figured he'd imagined the sound.

The doorknob jiggled again.

He climbed out of bed and went to investigate.

"Abigail, is that you?" he called out, crossing the room.

"Who else would it be?"

"What are you up to, sweetheart?"

"You needn't sweetheart me. I've just wedged a heavy chair under the doorknob."

After a night of tossing and turning, Abigail rose from her bed, meaner than a filly with a burr under its saddle. She threw on her clothing, damning the man who'd turned her life upside down. What was there about Jeremiah that drew her to him? He represented everything she despised. *And feared.*

He was a greenhorn.

An Easterner.

And handsome enough to turn her knees to jelly. No wonder she was drawn to him like a June bug to a flickering flame. Had someone been within hearing distance, Abigail might have sworn. There was no sense wasting the effort. Besides, she'd promised Clarissa that she'd stop cussing.

Abigail plopped her hair on top of her head and pushed back the wild curls that drooped over her brow. Sleep had eluded her last night, leaving dark blotches beneath her eyes. Abigail wished she'd inherited her mother's dark chocolate-colored hair. She took a closer look in the mirror and slid an index finger over the freckles dotting her nose. Until lately, she'd barely noticed the dang-blasted rust spots. They were there and that was that. But now she obsessed about the orange dots. Was a time she didn't care diddly about such things. There was no reason to care now. But the pewter eyes and trim mustache that flashed in the back of her mind told her otherwise.

When Abigail considered wearing a ribbon in her hair, she knew she'd lost her senses. Dang-blasted Jeremiah Dalton had better skedaddle before she outright made a fool of herself.

Again.

When she marched into the kitchen several minutes later, she spotted the empty seat beside Jeremiah along with the look in his eyes daring her to sit. She needed to prove a point. It would take more than the likes of him to frighten Abigail Wilcox. Besides, she was tired of sitting next to Mort, who belched between bites and scratched himself in plain sight. Abigail smiled in satisfaction when she plunked down next to Jeremiah and gave him that could-care-less look she'd perfected over the years.

"Good morning, Abby. Did you sleep well?" he asked, an infuriating grin lighting his face and making her stomach roll.

While stifling a yawn, she brushed the confounded lint from her pant legs, adjusted the fork by her plate and fidgeted with her empty cup before daring another glance at Jeremiah's handsome face. "Course I did." Over the years she'd also honed a cool tone capable of sobering most men, but the glint in Jeremiah's eyes said she'd failed.

Another yawn threatened. To cover her nervousness, she barked out orders. "Whip, you better check the beeves in the east pasture today. Bluc, you give him a hand."

Whip gave an easygoing shrug. "I told you yesterday that I'd already checked the steers. Today I aim to check those in the lower pasture."

"Oh, I guess it slipped my mind." Ignoring the quizzical looks directed at her, she turned to Pedro, who was jawing with Mort. "Didn't I make myself clear about breakfast? Six o'clock sharp," she said, pointing to the wall clock and noticing it was barely after six.

As Pedro scurried into the kitchen, he shook his head and mumbled, "Loco, estupido."

When Jeremiah stretched his long legs and brushed up against hers, Abigail suspected he was deliberately trying to fluster her, but she wasn't having any of it. She raised eyes capable of turning water to ice and was met with that grin she detested, that grin reminding her that she was indeed a woman.

"What are you gawking at?"

His mustache twitched. "I was waiting for my orders, Abby."

Abby. From his silken tongue, the word sounded indecent. She wished he wouldn't call her that and yet was thrilled that he did. Goosebumps sprouted on her arms. "A while back I promised to help you with your chores. I aim to do that today."

Looking confused, he leaned close and rested his chin on his upturned palm, bringing his face only inches from hers. "I don't remember you making that promise."

Abigail held her ground. Her gaze meandered to his trim mustache and the tempting lower lip. Lifting her eyes to his, she said in a wobbly voice, "We'd agreed that if you could outshoot me, I'd help with your chores."

"If my memory serves me right, I never hit a bottle."

Damn him for flashing that grin again. "You know darn right well you coulda beat me blindfolded."

His grin widened. "I'll admit I'm damn good, but blindfolded might be a stretch."

"I figured I'd help you clean out the loft. We need to get ready for the new hay."

Jeremiah straightened and gave her some much-needed breathing space.

Abigail sighed with relief.

Jeremiah drummed his fingers along the checked tablecloth, the rapid beat slower than Abigail's pounding heart. "Why do we put hay in the barn when it's easier to have the animals eat it right out of the field? In New England we have ice and snow in the wintertime, but in Texas it's warm all year." He ran his finger inside the collar of his shirt. "Hot as hell is more like it."

Those around the table muttered beneath their breaths. Someone chuckled.

Abigail knew the men considered Jeremiah an oddity. But she

saw no harm in asking questions. His reasoning was solid. Couldn't fault a man for wanting to learn.

"In the past, we've had long stretches without rain. Some winters are mild, but we've had some cold spells with enough frost to kill the grass. It's wise to have a decent reserve of hay."

Pedro and Blue arrived with trays laden with food. As Blue filled the mugs with coffee, Pedro laid the platters on the table.

Jeremiah took a swig of coffee and directed his gaze at Abigail. "If you have other things that need doing, I can handle the hay loft by myself."

She was disappointed with his comment. Didn't he want to spend time with her? Why did she care? She blew out a slow breath. "I said I was going to help, and I will."

He shrugged. "Suit yourself."

She couldn't decide which she wanted to do more—slap that wise look from his face or kiss him senseless.

On her way to the barn, Abigail spotted a rider approaching the ranch house. Dressed in a black riding skirt, a black blouse, and a wide black sombrero that hung over her back, Adele Diaz, Whip's mother, had come to call. Until Noah's death, she'd been a permanent fixture on the ranch.

Adele slid from her mount, tied the reins around the railing, and stepped onto the porch. "Morning, Abigail."

"Good morning. I haven't seen you in a while."

"Since the funeral." Sadness had aged Adele's face. She paused to gaze at the house and then the barn before continuing, "I miss Noah, and I thought being here might lessen the ache."

Abigail took hold of Adele's elbow. "Let's go inside and have a cup of coffee."

"I'm surprised you have time for coffee."

Abigail would let Jeremiah work by himself for a while. He'd made it clear he didn't need her help anyway. "There's no reason to rush."

They went into the kitchen where Abigail lifted the kettle from the cast-iron stove and filled two cups with the dark brew. She nodded for Adele to sit. "Get a load off."

As the light from the window tinted the white walls a golden hue, Abigail set the cups on the table along with the molasses and milk. She couldn't help noticing how Adele's raven hair shone like wet ink in the sunlight. Deep blue highlights accented the glorious mane. Abigail decided to sit on the shady side of the table; otherwise, her hideous hair would turn a ghastly orange.

Adele lifted her perfect face, not one spot marring her complexion. "What's wrong, Abigail?"

Abigail waved away the question. "Nothing. I'm just tired."

"It's no wonder. I've never seen a woman work the way you do."

"I don't have a choice."

"If you had yourself a man, you wouldn't need to work so hard."

Abigail yanked a chair away from the table, turned it around, and straddled it the way the men sometimes did. "I had myself a man once. All it brung me was heartache and shame. I'd have to be a jackass to want to go through that again."

"All men aren't alike."

"Maybe not, but I'm not taking any chances." She scraped her boot heel across the floor and studied the rip in her pant leg. It wasn't likely any man would want her, anyway. And she didn't want just any man.

She wanted Jeremiah.

The realization threw her, and she damn near tipped the chair over backwards. As Abigail scrambled to regain her balance, she saw the disbelief on Adele's face.

"Are you sure you're all right? I've never seen you looking this way."

"What way?" Abigail asked, turning the chair around and plunking herself down with a bang.

Adele waved a delicate hand with long tapered nails. "You seem flustered. Oh, it's probably just my imagination. Since Noah's funeral, I've had trouble thinking straight."

Glad that the subject had veered away from her, Abigail tapped Adele's hand. "It'll get easier. In time you'll be able to enjoy the wonderful memories you have of Noah."

Adele's forehead creased, and for the briefest instant, something flashed across her face that Abigail didn't recognize. "I loved him, you know."

Abigail nodded. "I could tell just by watching you with him."

"Did Noah ever talk to you about me?"

"Yes, many times."

Tears rimmed Adele's eyes. "He never told me he loved me. All these years I've waited to hear the words, and he never said them."

Abigail wasn't surprised. Once after several drinks of Tequila, Noah had confided that in his lifetime he'd loved only one woman—Jeremiah's mother. Abigail poured molasses into her coffee, took a sip, then added a little more of the sweetener.

When she glanced up, she saw the raw need in Adele's eyes.

Abigail decided a small lie would hurt no one. "Sometimes a man doesn't say what's in his heart. Noah loved you. He told me he did."

Adele blew out a small breath, a serene expression claiming her face. "You'll never know how happy that makes me."

Abigail chewed her lower lip and studied the woman's clear complexion. Not one single freckle. Not one! Figuring that Adele might know of a secret remedy to erase freckles, Abigail pondered the question embedded in her mind. She couldn't

117

just blurt the words without giving some explanation. Abigail was tired of seeing the ghastly specks. *When had vanity reared its ugly head?* She told herself it had nothing whatsoever to do with Jeremiah, but she knew differently. She wanted desperately to see the appreciation in his eyes when he saw her freckle-free face.

Abigail wiped her hands over her denim-clad legs. She stood and walked to the stove on the pretense of refilling her cup. With her back to Adele, she took a deep breath for courage and said in a rush, "Adele, you have very pretty skin."

"That's nice of you to say. I know you're trying to cheer me up."

Abigail turned, aware of the flush creeping up her neck. "I've been admiring the way you look and thought you might be able to share your secret with me."

Adele took a swallow of coffee, then set the cup down with a soft clunk. "What do you mean?"

Pussyfooting around the subject wasn't going to work. "You don't have a single freckle. How'd you manage to keep those confounded things away?" Abigail felt so silly, but the words were out. She couldn't take them back, and she didn't want to anyway.

Adele ran her fingers against her creamy complexion. "I don't do anything. I suspect my Mexican heritage is responsible. If there's a secret formula, I bet Emma Johnson would know. You should check with her."

Abigail couldn't very well stroll up to snooty blonde-haired, blue-eyed Emma Johnson, elbow her in the ribs, and settle down for a little woman-to-woman chat. The shock alone would have Emma sniffing smelling salts and waving her white-gloved hand in front of her face.

"Thanks," Abigail replied, chewing her lower lip.

Adele stood and ran a delicate finger against her throat.

"Would you mind if I have a look around?"

"Sure, look all you want. And come back any time you wish."

As Adele left the room, Abigail wondered if Emma Johnson knew anything about freckles. Abigail had never seen freckles on Emma's face, but then Abigail hadn't actually looked either. Emma had the irritating habit of carrying a bright floral parasol everywhere she went, which she twirled constantly. It was hard to look Emma in the face with that foolish umbrella whipping around. It was a wonder that Emma hadn't poked someone's eye out. Abigail couldn't fathom asking Emma for her beauty secrets, but she'd reached a point of desperation that made her consider doing just that.

On her way outside Abigail lifted her hat from the peg and saw the fresh buttercups in her hatband. Against her will, her heart skipped a beat, chipping another chunk from her already weakening resolve.

CHAPTER 12

When Jeremiah saw he was alone in the barn, he took several minutes to visit Moonbeam. The white stallion accepted the piece of buttered toast Jeremiah had tucked in his handkerchief. For the first time, the animal allowed Jeremiah to run his hand along its velvety muzzle. Jeremiah's heart quickened with joy and pride. He was convinced in time, Moonbeam would be his horse—at least until he returned to Boston. A fleeting moment of regret tugged at his heart, which he instantly dismissed.

"Moonbeam," he whispered. "You'd better get used to the feel of my hand and the sound of my voice, because I aim to make you mine."

As Jeremiah reached out to rub the horse's mane, the animal threw back its head and nickered loudly, emphasizing that their budding friendship had a long way to go.

Jeremiah had taken a few steps when Hamlet rounded the corner with an eager look, the pig's mouth opening in expectation. As the animal nudged Jeremiah's leg, Jeremiah reached into his pocket for a piece of biscuit he'd saved for his companion. The porker had gotten into the habit of following him around like a puppy, and though Jeremiah figured the two of them made a comical pair, he didn't care what anyone thought. He patted the hog's head before climbing up the ladder leading to the loft. Jeremiah only wished he could earn Moonbeam's trust as easily.

Some time later when Jeremiah looked out of the opened loft

door, he spied Abigail talking to a dark-haired woman dressed in black. It took a moment for him to remember who the woman was. Standing in the sunlight, the two women contrasted each other. Though Adele's jet-black hair might appeal to some men, it paled when compared to the flame-red curls that drew his attention and set his heart beating at an unsteady rate.

Guilt revisited him, reminded him that he was promised to another woman who trusted him and planned to be his wife. But guilt evaporated like a drop of water in the Texas sun when he remembered the camisole that had hugged Abigail's shapely curves. He leaned against the wooden handle of the pitchfork and admitted what had become evident. Sure as the sweltering heat, he wanted Abigail Wilcox more than he'd ever wanted another woman. Since he had no intention of validating that fantasy, he assumed there'd be no harm in allowing his mind to wander.

Jeremiah popped a lemon drop in his mouth, dropped down on the fragrant hay, and gave his mind free rein. What was Abigail wearing beneath her plain, cotton plaid shirt? Lace? Silk? Both? Would she object to a kiss? One small, innocent kiss? One taste to satisfy his growing curiosity. Did Abigail taste as good as she smelled? Would her mouth open under his? Would one kiss be enough? Instinctively, Jeremiah knew he could never settle for only one kiss. For that reason alone, he had to make sure he never gave in to temptation. When he remembered how she'd jammed a chair beneath her bedroom door, he realized he had nothing to worry about.

He was still sitting there, eyes closed, head propped against his bent knees when he heard Abigail's voice.

"Why in tarnation are you taking a nap this time of day?"

Startled, he leaped to his feet, glad that she didn't know what he'd been thinking about. "I sat down for a minute."

"Your eyes were closed."

"I do some of my best thinking that way." He sent her an innocent grin.

"Well, if you're through thinking, maybe we can get something done around here."

As they worked side by side, Jeremiah was amazed at Abigail's strength and endurance. By the time they'd pushed the hay into the lower level of the barn, sweat beaded her forehead and drenched the material of her shirt, pasting the fabric to her chest where he could make out the outline of two perfect breasts. Whenever she took a breath, he noticed the rise and fall of her chest and his heartbeat quickening.

When she caught him staring, Jeremiah discarded his shirt and dabbed at his face with the sleeve. "Is it always this hot in Texas?"

"Sometimes it's hotter," she said, never losing her momentum.

He threw his shirt into the corner. "You're really something, Abby."

Her brow furrowed when she faced him. "What's that supposed to mean?"

"It means that I'm impressed with all that you do."

She set the pitchfork aside and blotted her forehead with her arm. "I merely do what has to be done."

"Why don't you have someone take over for you?"

"I learned long ago not to depend on anyone." A haunted look claimed her eyes. Jeremiah saw the raw pain in her features, and he wanted to take her in his arms and have her lean on him.

She took a jagged breath. Through a forced smile, she continued. "When Noah gave me a place to stay, I promised him that I'd help around the ranch."

Abigail was the bravest woman he'd ever met. "It looks to me as though you've kept that promise and then some. I admire you, Abby."

She blushed, but the smile that lit her face warmed his heart. "That's the nicest thing anyone's ever said to me, Jeremiah."

The way she'd spoken his name was his undoing. In that instant her stained shirt disappeared, as did her soiled jeans and dirt-smudged face. All Jeremiah saw was a beautiful woman with fiery hair and emerald eyes. If Pedro hadn't banged a spoon against a metal fry pan, signaling dinner was ready, Jeremiah would have closed the distance between them. He'd have taken her in his arms and stolen a kiss from lips he had no business sampling.

Before he had a chance to make a big mistake, Abigail climbed onto the railing, let out a war cry, and leaped into the mounded hay below. Jeremiah was still laughing when he climbed down the ladder where she and Hamlet were waiting.

"You're lucky you didn't break anything," he said between spurts of laughter.

Her eyes lit with mischief. "You need to loosen up a little. You haven't lived until you've jumped into a haystack."

"If I jump and break a leg, what then?"

"It's not dangerous. The hay will cushion your fall."

Her laughter made him feel remarkably carefree. "Tell you what, I'll jump later this afternoon."

"Bet you're going to chicken out."

Jeremiah knew he was playing with fire when he rested his hand on her shoulder and gave a friendly squeeze. The thoughts sprouting in his fertile mind were anything but friendly. They were lucid and steamy. "That'll be the day when I let a bossy Texan like you get the better of me."

"Are you saying that I'm bossy?"

He loved her southern drawl. "I like your accent," he said, stretching his luck and brushing aside a curl that had tumbled free.

"I can tell when a man's trying to change the subject, and I'll let you get away with it this once. And just so you'll know, I'm not the one around here with an accent. You are."

When she looped her arm inside his elbow as they marched across the yard, Jeremiah knew they'd become friends.

He told himself that would be enough.

After washing up and donning a clean shirt, Jeremiah entered the kitchen and was pleased to see Abigail already seated in the chair next to his.

The mischief in her eyes was unmistakable. "Have you men heard? After we're through eating, Jeremiah is planning to jump from the loft into the hay below."

Whip took a swallow from his mug. "Planning it and doing it are two different things."

Blue, Mort, and Pedro snickered.

Jeremiah sat and patted Abigail's hand. He liked the way her pupils widened when he touched her. "The last time you people laughed at me, I turned out to be crack shot."

Mort squinted at him with his good eye. "Bet you jumped from plenty of hay lofts in that there bank back East where you worked." The comment brought rip-roaring laughter around the table.

Jeremiah scooped potatoes onto his plate.

"Hope he don't land on his head," someone said.

More laughter.

"Ain't likely to do much damage anyway. Near as I can tell, greenhorns only got hot air between their ears."

Knee-slapping, gut-wrenching hysteria ensued.

Jeremiah leaned back in his chair and gave the spectators a nonchalant shrug. "I don't know what the big deal is. I saw Abby make that jump, and it didn't seem that high to me." He'd been certain Abby would break her neck, but they didn't know that. He equated the height of the loft to a two-story building.

Blue speared a chunk of steak with his knife. "When I was a young whippersnapper, I used to love jumping into hay stacks." He cut a piece of meat and chewed. "Dang-blasted old age ain't 'bout to rob this old man of a little fun. I aim to fly into that hay just like when I was a young 'un."

The men thumped their hands against the old man's back. "We'll all be there to cheer you on."

Jeremiah saw the pride and anticipation on Blue's face. He figured if an old coot like Blue wasn't afraid of jumping from the loft, he wasn't either. Then why was his stomach tied in knots?

Lunch was over much too quickly. As everyone made their way toward the barn, Jeremiah decided he'd jump first and get it over with.

Blue kicked his feet up and flapped his hat around. "My old ticker's damn near busting with excitement. I almost feel like a kid again."

"Way to go old man," Whip said, his gray eyes sparkling.

Wearing a nonplussed expression, Jeremiah thought of this as sort of an initiation. If the jump didn't kill him, he'd be fast on his way to becoming a real cowboy. He'd be fast on his way to being like his father, and though the thought surprised him, it no longer repelled him.

Jeremiah knew if he didn't hurry, he'd be the last one to jump. The sooner he got it over with, the better he'd feel. He might even jump twice to prove to Abigail he could. The fact that he wanted to impress her worried him.

When they entered the barn, Abigail squeezed his arm. He looked down into her shining eyes and felt a closeness that didn't seem fitting. He told himself the feeling warming his chest was that of a brother to his sister. Out of the corner of his eye, he saw Blue hurrying toward the loft. Jeremiah smiled at Abigail one more time before turning away. Blue beat him to the ladder, but Jeremiah wasn't far behind.

"Blue," someone shouted, "maybe you should let the greenhorn go first. That way he can be down here watching to see how an expert does it."

Blue climbed over the top rung of the ladder. "Son of a gun, I think you fellows might have a point."

With a purposeful stride, Jeremiah took the few steps to the rail and eyed the distance to the mounded hay.

From behind him came Blue's words of wisdom. "Jump feet first. You don't want to break your neck."

Jeremiah nodded. "I've no intentions of doing anything fancy." That said, he climbed over the low railing, stood on the ledge a moment, and leaped. The fall was both frightening and exhilarating. The hay cushioned his landing. As Jeremiah scrambled from the haystack, he noticed the approval on Abigail's face and decided his adventure had been worth it.

She looped her arm into his, an unexpected bonus. "Ya done good, for a greenhorn, that is."

There was a time the word *greenhorn* would have dripped with sarcasm, but Jeremiah took no offense because he could tell she was teasing. "Nothing to it. I wouldn't mind having another go at it."

Whip hollered out, "Come on, hotshot, git outta the way so Blue can have his turn."

With Abigail by his side Jeremiah took a few steps and trained his gaze at the old man ready to jump. Wide grin, arms and legs flapping, Blue looked like a kid as he took flight, hooting and hollering like a drunk or someone who'd taken leave of his senses. Jeremiah threw back his head and laughed along with the others.

A blood-curdling scream tore from Blue's throat as his face

twisted in agony.

Figuring Blue had broken a bone, Jeremiah scrambled over the mound of hay. Blue's face had paled. His breathing was shallow.

Jeremiah ran his hand over the man's arms. "Where do you hurt?"

Blue gritted his teeth. "My leg."

Abigail and the others scooped handfuls of hay away from the injured man. Jeremiah supported Blue's shoulders. "Don't you go passing out on me, old man. You're made of tougher stuff than that." Jeremiah feared if Blue lost consciousness, he might never wake up again.

When Abigail gasped, Jeremiah followed the direction of her gaze. Blood everywhere! Lots of blood seeping from multiple wounds on Blue's right thigh, impaled with the tines of a rusted pitchfork.

Earlier that morning there'd been nothing under the hay. Jeremiah was certain someone had planted that pitchfork. Considering its location, it was a wonder Jeremiah had missed the sharp implement. Jeremiah was sure Blue was not the intended victim. Whoever planted the pitchfork was out to kill him.

If I didn't write in this journal, I'd lose my mind. For years I've waited, certain my patience would pay off. I'm done wringing my hands and waiting. I've given the Easterner a warning. He don't belong here. He never will. If he thinks he can just waltz in here and run off with everything, he's sadly mistaken. He'd better not try. Or I'll kill him.

CHAPTER 13

Jeremiah ambled onto the porch where Whip and the men were huddled together talking in low voices. "How's Blue doing?"

"Ain't too good," Mort said. "If infection sets in, Doc's gonna have to cut off his leg. Damn shame's what it is. An accident like that happenin' to old Blue."

Jeremiah studied each face, trying to decide who wanted to harm him most.

Whip hated Jeremiah's guts.

Mort was none too fond of him.

Pedro mumbled insults in Spanish whenever Jeremiah walked by. Every one of these men would celebrate if Jeremiah were to drop dead. Jeremiah gave each man a long searching look. "It wasn't an accident, and someone here knows that. When I started pitching the hay from the loft this morning, the barn floor was empty. Even if there had been a pitchfork lying around, it would have been flat on its side, not pointing toward the ceiling."

Whip never blinked. Mort's whiskered face always looked guilty so seeing guilt now meant nothing. Pedro mumbled insults under his breath, also as usual. If hatred were the motive, each man could have planted the pitchfork meant for Jeremiah.

Mort scratched his behind and leered. "Why'd someone want to hurt old Blue for?"

Jeremiah leaned against the porch railing. "I'm betting that pitchfork was meant for me."

No one looked surprised.

Whip lifted his head and spat across the yard. "Why would someone want to hurt you?"

"Hate or greed. If something happens to me, you men inherit half this ranch. And that half split three ways is a tidy sum."

Whip moved in closer. "Listen up, and listen good. If I had a mind to kill you, I'd have done it by now. I don't go sneaking around, planting hayforks, hoping you'll be fool enough to jump and I'll be lucky enough for you to land on it. That's not my style."

Mort gave a humorless laugh. "Now me, that's another matter. I always enjoy seeing the pain in someone eyes when he's about to kick the bucket. But I got nothing agin' Blue."

Jeremiah gave Mort a pointed look. "You'd probably love to get your hands on a sixth of Noah's estate."

A wicked grin stretched across Mort's face. "Can't argue 'bout that."

Pedro spouted in Spanish.

Jeremiah recognized the words gringo and loco. It was probably just as well he couldn't understand the rest of the message intended for him.

"Señor Dalton, if you think we are trying to kill you for a share of Noah's ranch, maybe you should question Miss Abigail. If something happens to you, she gets half of everything."

Jeremiah was unwilling to consider such a preposterous idea. Even if she were capable of planting the pitchfork, she could not have stood by with a smile on her face waiting for Blue to jump. Abby was not the culprit responsible for Blue's injuries. Jeremiah was willing to stake his life on that. "Abby doesn't have it in her to do such a thing."

Whip threw Jeremiah a mean look. "Don't underestimate Abigail Wilcox. I suspect she's capable of doing almost anything.

Meanwhile, if you're right about that pitchfork being meant for you, you might consider going back where you come from. You were lucky today. How long will your luck hold out?"

Later that night Jeremiah stretched out on his bed and pondered what each man had said. He was no closer to finding answers to his questions. Who had planted the pitchfork? Whip? Mort? Pedro? Could it be someone else?

Or maybe all of them?

If Jeremiah left town, all three men stood to gain. The will never stipulated Jeremiah had to be alive when he returned to Boston. He'd have to watch his back. He slid a chair under the knob of the door leading to the hallway. He was a heavy sleeper, and he was determined to wake up the next morning.

Abigail halted the wagon in front of Bufford's Mercantile and hopped down. She and Clarissa had come to town for supplies and something else—a present for Jeremiah.

Clarissa skipped alongside Abigail. "Maw, what do you think we should get Mr. Dalton?"

"I've been thinking of a silk vest. Green, like the one your goat ruined. Besides, Mr. Dalton looks good in green." But then, he looked good in anything. Especially with his shirt off, with sweat glistening along the contour of each well-defined muscle. Abby's throat grew parched like desert sand.

Clarissa nodded. "Mr. Dalton is funny, like his paw."

"You really think so?"

"Yup, he makes me laugh."

Jeremiah made Abigail feel like a woman, and that scared her, but she wasn't the sort to run from things that frightened her. Abigail had decided to take a stand and face facts. She longed for Jeremiah, and she'd seen in his eyes that he felt the same way. She wasn't prepared to do anything about it, but just admitting that she had feelings was a giant step.

"Maw, what if the mercantile doesn't have a silk vest?"

"It wouldn't surprise me none if they didn't. I can't picture too many men around here needing such a thing. But we'll do our best."

Clarissa lifted her hand. "I'm keeping my fingers crossed."

Abigail smiled at the childish gesture. She'd stopped making wishes a long time ago. Only lately had she allowed hope to creep into her heart.

As they entered Bufford's, Abigail spotted a spinning parasol. Figuring she'd try to catch a glimpse of Emma Johnson's face, Abigail left Clarissa in the millinery aisle, scooted around the corner and choked on the cloud of perfume surrounding Emma. It wasn't a dainty little cough, but a gut-wrenching, throat-clearing cough accompanied by fits of sneezing and wheezing. Emma gave Abigail a quick look of disdain before hiding behind her parasol, twisting the stem and blurring its painted silk flowers until Abigail grew dizzy.

When Abigail glanced away, Emma disappeared into the next aisle. Abigail filled her lungs with air before trying again. As she rounded the corner, she noticed that Emma's pink floral dress matched her parasol. Tiny white gloves covered her dainty hands. Such gloves were useless. How long would they stay white doing ranch work? But Emma didn't do farm work, and it showed.

Most likely, Emma had never milked a cow or stepped in manure. But that didn't matter to Abigail. What mattered was finding out if Emma had freckles, and if she didn't, Abigail wanted to know how she'd accomplished such a thing.

Abigail reviewed her options. She could either follow Emma around, hoping to see the woman's face, or she could find a reason to speak to her. Deciding on the latter, Abigail took one more deep breath, ignored the tickle in her throat, and charged toward her intended target.

Abigail cleared her throat. "Emma, I've been wondering where to get a parasol like yours."

As she turned, shock registered on Emma's face. "You want a parasol?" The small gloved hand dabbed at perfect pink cheeks that didn't have one freckle on them. "What, pray tell, do you need a parasol for?"

Abigail had no need for such a worthless thing, but she was biding her time until she could turn the conversation toward more important matters. "It gets mighty hot on the range."

Emma's perfect nose wrinkled as if she'd detected a foul odor. Had Abigail not been in desperate need of Emma's freckle secret, she might have spat at Emma's feet and enjoyed seeing the horror spring into her features.

Instead, Abigail fluttered her eyelashes. "While you and I are having this little friendly chat, maybe you can tell me how you keep your face free of freckles."

Emma fanned herself with her gloved hand. "A woman doesn't divulge her beauty secrets."

Abigail gritted her teeth, the last of her patience slipping away. "Emma Johnson, I've been about as patient as I can be. If you don't tell me your secret, the next time we have rain, and I see you crossing the street, I'll run my wagon right through a puddle, spraying mud from here to kingdom come. Won't that fancy dress and parasol look good, splattered with red clay?"

Disbelief stained Emma's face a deep crimson. "Well, I declare!" She whirled around, marched to the counter, ripped a piece of brown wrapping paper, and jotted down several words, most of which Abigail couldn't read. Regardless, Abigail felt pleased as she tucked the scrap of paper in her pocket. "What do I do with this stuff?"

Emma gave her a mean look. "Mix everything together. Afterwards, put slices of fresh lemon on your face."

Abigail reciprocated with a satisfied smile.

"Even if you succeed in getting rid of every freckle on your face, you won't be a lady. Lord knows you proved that today." Emma sashayed out of the store.

"Maw, what's taking you so long? I thought you were going to help me pick out a present for Mr. Dalton."

Abigail took her daughter's hand. "I had to attend to another matter first. But I'm all set now."

As they made their way to the men's clothing, Abigail could barely contain her excitement. She only wished she could yank out the paper and try to read the list of ingredients now. But that would draw attention to what she aimed to do, so she dug her hand in her pocket and fingered the paper, but left it there.

"Maw what about this?" Clarissa asked, lifting a bile-green handkerchief.

"That's awfully bright."

"You said Mr. Dalton looked good in green. I bet he'd love these, and I can buy three green handkerchiefs for only a dime."

Abigail figured color didn't matter much when the object was used for blowing noses and mopping sweat. "It's your gift. You decide."

With a nod and a grin, Clarissa said, "I'm getting these. The color reminds me of green grass."

Abigail smiled at her daughter. "Reminds me of sun-lit grass."

Looking pleased, Clarissa counted out three handkerchiefs. Abigail hoped that Jeremiah had the good grace not to say anything about the color.

As Abigail spied the display of vests hanging from the rafters, Lillian Bufford made her way toward them. "Anything I can do for you ladies?"

Over the years Lillian Bufford had honed her wagging tongue to a sharp edge. Abigail did not intend to be its next victim. "I'm looking for a vest."

Lillian pulled down a few vests and gave Abigail the once-over. "Even the smallest I got will be too big for you."

"I need extra large."

Lillian's eyes widened. "Oh?"

Abigail smiled innocently. "Yes, extra large."

Abigail sent Clarissa a warning look to keep her mouth shut. Clarissa shrugged and went back to folding the green handkerchiefs.

Lillian laid three vests over the display of towels. "These just came in. They're good quality, but . . ." she lowered her voice, "they're seconds."

Abigail didn't even know what that meant. Fortunately, Lillian continued. "On most of them you can't even find the flaw."

"You mean there's something wrong with these vests?"

Lillian raised her finger to her mouth. "It's not as though they have three arms or buttons that don't button. Each defect is minor."

"Would you happen to have a silk vest?"

Disbelief registered. "Silk? For you?"

"It's not for Maw . . ."

Abigail rested a heavy hand on her daughter's shoulder. Her fingers tightened. Abigail hoped Clarissa got the message.

Clarissa beamed a smile. "It's for Jeremiah Dalton, Noah's son from Boston."

Abigail's hand dropped to her side.

"I'm buying these handkerchiefs for him, too. Aren't they pretty?"

Sure as shooting, Abigail would be the brunt of local gossip for weeks.

Lillian's smile widened. "I think I saw him in here a time or two. Strapping, good-looking man, if my memory serves me right." She directed her gaze at Abigail. "Is it his birthday?"

"I wouldn't know."

"Special occasion?"

Abigail shoved her hands into her pockets. "No."

"Oh, I see."

Abigail saw red. She almost cussed, but remembered her promise to Clarissa.

Clarissa piped up. "We just wanted to cheer him up on account of we started out hating him and now we don't."

Pupils widening, Lillian inched closer to Abigail. "Good-looking son of a gun. Can't blame you for setting your sights on a man like that."

Abigail cussed silently to herself. "I'm not setting my sights, just trying to buy a vest, now show me the finest ones you have."

Lillian gave Abigail's shoulder a consoling pat. "I don't blame you. To impress a man like that, only the best will do."

Abigail gritted her teeth. "I'm not trying to do any such thing. Our goat ate his vest . . ."

Lillian dismissed Abigail with a wave of her hand. "You needn't worry about me. I won't tell a soul that you've a hankering for Mr. Dalton."

The breath left Abigail's lungs in a whoosh.

"Maw, what does hankering mean?"

"Means that a woman's lost her mind."

I never meant to harm Blue, but his getting hurt did some good. Jeremiah, smart-ass son of a bitch, figured out the pitchfork was meant for him. I'd imagined the rusted tines piercing his chest, driving through his heart, bleeding him dry like a gutted buck hanging from a limb.

Watch your step, Jeremiah Dalton, 'cause I'm watching. If you don't leave, I'm coming after you.

CHAPTER 14

Clarissa held a package wrapped in brown paper. "I got a surprise for ya, Mr. Dalton. Bet you can't guess what it is."

He sauntered onto the porch and sat on the wooden swing suspended by thick chains. Pushing with his foot, he rocked back and forth and studied the wide grin on the child's face. "I don't have a clue."

The door opened and Abigail came out. When she sat next to him, he feared his heart would explode. The creak of the swing helped to drown out its pounding beat.

Clarissa shoved the package at him. "I picked this out all by myself. Used my own money, too."

He untied the string. "Why are you buying me a present? Or does Christmas come early in Texas?"

Clarissa giggled. "Mr. Dalton, you're even funnier than your paw."

Jeremiah was aware of Abigail next to him. The smell of roses made him almost tremble with desire. He filled his lungs with her sweet scent and noticed the forest green ribbon fastening her wild curls to the top of her head. He loved the fiery color of her hair and couldn't fathom ever disliking its vivid shade, yet he knew that he had. He never pictured Abigail as the sort who'd wear ribbons. His fingers itched to tug the ribbon and free the flaming locks.

"Mr. Dalton, when you gonna open your present?"

He came to. "Oh, I was just thinking how considerate you are to buy me something." He unfolded the brown paper and was blinded by a bright shade of green.

"They're handkerchiefs. Maw said you look good in green. When I saw these, I knew they'd be perfect. You like 'em?"

He hadn't been around children much, but he knew this one was special. Though he hadn't always felt this way, he now believed Abigail had done a fine job with her. "Like them? I love them! These are the finest handkerchiefs I've ever owned." He folded one and tucked it into the pocket of his shirt.

Beside him, Abigail chuckled. "I suspect no one else in Boston has seen the likes of those handkerchiefs."

"No, but they will when I go back." His throat clogged. He forced a ragged breath and told himself he'd mistaken the regret that had seized him. "I'll bet everyone back East will be green with envy."

Abigail gave a deep laugh. "That's a fitting comment if ever I've heard one."

The laugh suited Abby. Unlike the polite titter he'd grown to expect from women, Abby laughed like she meant it. He joined in, feeling better than he had a right to.

She rested her hand on his arm and gave a squeeze that was both gentle and strong. "Clarissa wanted to get you something very special. It means a lot to both of us that you like it so much."

He suspected this was Abigail's way of saying she appreciated his tact. "Green's my favorite color."

"That's what I figured," Clarissa said, scooting in between Jeremiah and her mother. "Maw, when you gonna give it to him?" she whispered.

Jeremiah overheard the question.

Abby blushed and fidgeted, twisting her fingers, then lacing them together before rubbing her palms along her jeans. After several seconds she grimaced, stood, gave Jeremiah a sidelong glance, and grabbed another package from behind a chair. "This is for you." She heaved the gift at him as if embarrassed to be caught holding it. Her gaze became preoccupied with anything but looking at him.

"This is for me?"

Her rose-petal cheeks turned scarlet. "Course it's for you. I said it was, didn't I?"

Jeremiah got a kick out of Abby's obvious discomfort.

Clarissa nudged him. "What are ya waiting for? Aren't ya gonna open it?"

He yanked the string off, tore the paper from the package, and spotted a tan leather vest much like the one in his father's closet. The fresh smell of leather filled his nostrils as he stood, stuck his arms in the armholes, and glanced at his new vest with pride. Grinning, he said, "I'll treasure this always."

Abby took a step closer, her wide emerald eyes casting their spell on him. "I'd wanted to get you a silk vest, but Bufford's didn't have any. I had to settle for this one."

"Are you kidding me? I've had lots of silk vests, but none compare to this one." Clarissa eyed him, so he reached in his pocket and dabbed at his forehead with his new handkerchief. "You two gals are really something."

Before heading outside, Abigail dug in the bottom of her valise and pulled out a strip of lace that she'd saved off an old dress. As she closed her hand over the tattered remnant, she shut her eyes and imagined herself wearing a gown of dark green silk edged with the finest lace. Abigail was being silly. It would take more than a pretty dress to make a lady out of her, but as she pressed the lace to her throat, she felt the part of her she'd buried years ago come alive.

Jeremiah was mucking out the horse stalls when Abby marched into the barn with a gangly youth by her side.

"Jeremiah, this is Calvin, Hank Bufford's boy. I've hired him to take over in here."

Calvin nodded and grabbed the shovel from Jeremiah's hand. Jeremiah barely gave the boy a glance because his gaze was riveted on Abigail. Pinned to her shirt was a lacy bow that drew his eyes to that part of her anatomy a betrothed man had no business noticing. The tiny scrap of lace threw him, emphasizing that Abigail was indeed a woman, a very beautiful woman. But Jeremiah didn't need a reminder. He'd become overly aware of that fact some time ago.

Once more, his conscience gave him a hard time. Beautiful, perfectly groomed Evelyn was waiting for him back East. He did his damnedest to remember the fact that always escaped him whenever he was with Abigail. He tried to picture escorting Abigail to the *Fine Christian Woman's Charity Ball* he attended each July and found the thought ludicrous. Abigail would look as out of place as a buttercup surrounded by long-stem roses.

Abigail noted the disbelief in Jeremiah's eyes when he spotted the lace pinned to her shirt. *Dang-blasted fool,* she called herself. What did she expect? A man like Jeremiah wasn't likely to go all soft in the head for a woman dressed in smelly Levi's, a shirt not fit for a Sunday outing, hair a mess, and face covered with rust spots. His penetrating gaze flustered her no end. Turning away, she nodded for him to follow. Dang-blasted son of a gun had gotten under her skin. She tried to get rid of the quivery feeling that seized her whenever he was near. Abigail had lost control, and it terrified her.

"Follow me, nothing'll get done with us standing here gawking at each other." The stern tone of her voice gave her confidence until she glanced over her shoulder and saw that infuriating grin stretched across his face. Her insides quaked like a wind-tossed limb. Though Abigail no longer swore aloud, silently she cussed good and long. "It's about time you learn something about rounding up the steers along with roping and branding."

"I'd like that."

His penetrating gaze made Abigail's head spin. Jeremiah walked next to her. She was aware of the smell of leather, bay rum, and something else. She sniffed, but couldn't place the other odor. She could feel the heat radiating from his muscled frame. When he finally turned away, it pleased her to see the vest she'd bought him stretched tight across his broad shoulders, but it was the warm look in his pewter eyes when he faced her again that pleased Abigail most.

She recognized desire when she saw it. Although she knew about Evelyn, she shoved the unwelcome thought aside. The woman was back East and didn't pose a real threat from that distance. Maybe Jeremiah would forget about Evelyn. Abigail wasn't being rational. Jeremiah was a city man. He wouldn't likely settle for life in Texas. But she couldn't shake the thought that he might. Abigail called herself an imbecile, while she tried to figure out ways to persuade Jeremiah to stay.

As they approached Lancelot's stall, Abby placed her hand on Jeremiah's arm. "It's time you got yourself a real horse."

"Thanks."

One side of his mouth rose. His mustache twitched, drawing her eyes to his lips. She'd never kissed a man with a mustache. Would it tickle? Was it soft or bristly like a new broom? She fought the impulse to run one fingertip against the hair on his upper lip. She clasped her hands together so tight her knuckles turned white and reminded herself that kissing wasn't much fun anyway—a meeting of wet mouths that reminded her of a drooling hound dog. But providing the man was Jeremiah, Abigail was willing to give kissing one more try.

His smile reached his eyes, and he winked.

Abigail wanted to tell him to quit looking at her that way, but she didn't trust herself to speak. Gooseflesh the size of fresh berries pebbled her arms. She sucked on the lemon drop she'd tucked in her cheek earlier. She still hadn't gotten around to thanking Clarissa for the candy the child left on her pillow every evening. She also meant to question her daughter about her seemingly endless supply of lemon drops. "I noticed that your riding's improved."

"I've been practicing." He ambled toward the stalls that lined the inside of the barn. "Let me guess which fine animal you've chosen for me." He glanced over his shoulder, his smile warming her heart. "I'm hoping it's not another jackass."

"That didn't work the first time, so there's no sense my trying that again."

As he passed Moonbeam's stall, the white stallion didn't rear up and buck as Abigail expected. Instead, the animal's blue eyes followed Jeremiah's every move.

"Morning, Moonbeam," he said before glancing at Abigail again. "Before I return to Boston, I'm going to ride this horse."

Return to Boston. His words wounded, crushed any hope of his staying. "You'll break your neck."

"Do I detect caring in your tone?"

"More than likely what you hear is disbelief."

He threw back his head and gave a deep laugh. Abigail joined in, though inside her heart ached for what she feared would never be.

CHAPTER 15

As they walked toward the corral beside the barn, Jeremiah studied the frayed, discolored lace dangling over Abigail's right breast. What had possessed her to pin the bow to her shirt? Trying not to stare, he shifted his gaze and noticed a small rip on the back of Abigail's shirt revealing a speck of silky chemise. All he saw was a flash of white, enough to resurrect the images that had tormented him since . . .

Jeremiah put such thoughts out of his mind, slammed the door on his lustful imaginings, and threw away the key. Instantly feeling better, he reminded himself that unlike his father and mother, he valued commitment. When he returned to Boston, he'd make Evelyn his bride.

Evelyn was a wonderful woman. In time, she'd be his wife, the mother of his children. Unfortunately, as he gazed into vivid green eyes, he knew that Abby would always haunt his dreams.

Jeremiah was a practical man. He'd learned from his parents' mistake. They'd had little in common, which resulted in the inability to live together. As a child, Jeremiah longed for a real family with a mother and a father. He would never chance doing that to his children.

When picking out a lifetime companion, a man needed to use a healthy dose of common sense and not allow his heart—or other parts of his body—to overrule good judgment. Though sparks flew when he gazed into Abby's emerald eyes, he needn't act on the strong impulses telling him to kiss her senseless. He knew right from wrong. He had strength of character. No matter what, he'd remain true to Evelyn.

But he made the mistake of glancing down. His gaze met Abigail's. Warmed by her sweet smile, he ached to connect each burnished freckle with a gentle kiss. To save himself, he tried like the devil to conjure an image of Evelyn.

He failed.

His senses reeled from the scent of roses. Flames licked at the pit of his stomach. Though his heart ached for Abby, he ignored the overwhelming desire to run one finger over her forehead, to touch her hair, to taste lips he knew would be his undoing.

With every ounce of strength he possessed, he turned away. "How's Blue?"

A moment's silence.

Even with his back turned, he felt her presence. The tiny hairs at the base of Jeremiah's neck stirred.

Abby cleared her throat. "Blue's holding his own."

He recognized the sexual undertone in her voice. His imagination? Or was Abby thinking similar thoughts? Did she yearn for him as he did her? Would she settle for a roll in the hay if he suggested it? Guilt visited briefly, but he paid no mind.

Jeremiah wanted, no, he needed to wrap his arms around Abby. "I hear that Adele's moving in to care for Blue." His voice wavered, and he felt himself growing hard. To hide his sorry state, he lifted one booted foot onto the lower wrung of the fence and studied the horses in the corral.

She stepped closer. "Blue's lucky to have Adele. She knows a lot about herbs. She's making a poultice to draw out the infection."

"I hope the old man survives. I'd hate to have to live knowing he died because of me."

"You aren't to blame." Abby touched his shoulder.

The heat from her fingers sent sparks of awareness skittering down his spine. His breath lodged in his throat. If he turned and looked at Abby, he'd pull her against him. Jeremiah tightened his hands around the smooth rung of the fence. "Maybe not, but that pitchfork was meant for me. Someone is disappointed those rusted tines didn't go through my heart."

When she blew out a sharp breath, he caught the smell of lemon drops and wanted to sample her candied lips.

Her fingers wrapped over his shoulder. "Promise me, you'll be careful."

He dared a quick glance at her. "That's one promise I've every intention of keeping." Jeremiah noticed how pretty she looked with her face shadowed by the brim of her wide hat. The rays of the sun caught her lips just so, petal pink lips that almost drove him crazy. Without taking his gaze off her mouth, he asked, "Which horse will be mine?"

She stared up at him. "Huh?"

He grinned and pointed behind them. "Which horse will replace Lancelot?"

Her face flushed, adding to her natural beauty. "I thought Old Red would be perfect."

He rolled his eyes. "Let me guess, Old Red is about fifty years old, and he's missing a leg?"

He loved her hearty laugh and the lines around her mouth when she smiled.

"Nope, he has all four legs, and he's only four years old."

"Then why call him old?"

"He has a twin. Old Red got his nickname by being the first born." She climbed onto the fence and stood so close Jeremiah swore he could feel her heartbeat when her elbow touched his arm. "That's him over there," she said, pointing toward the reddish-brown horse with a thick black mane and tail.

Wanting to impress her, Jeremiah nodded, repeating the

information he'd garnered from Buck. "That's a fine-looking bay."

"I'm surprised you know that."

"Since arriving, I've learned a lot about horses."

"Really?"

"Try me."

"What kind of horse is that?" She pointed to the black and white animal hitched in front of the farmhouse.

"That's a piebald." Jeremiah nodded toward the farther end of the corral. "The chestnut-colored one is referred to as a sorrel."

"What do you call the long white streak running down the center of its face?"

"That's the blaze. Do I pass, Miss Wilcox?"

Pride swelled in his heart when he saw the approval in her eyes.

"Jeremiah, there's hope for you yet. You're sounding more like a Texan all the time."

He could stand beside Abby all day and never grow bored. "I'm glad you think so. I want to learn everything there is to know about this ranch. Maybe then, I'll feel closer to my old man."

"Noah loved this place," she said, scanning the surroundings. "This ranch was his life, and according to him, the only thing missing was you and your mother."

"There was a time when I wouldn't have let you get away with saying that."

"But now you will?"

"Yes." He was certain his father had cared for him. The chip on his shoulder that had weighted him down when he'd first arrived in Texas no longer existed.

"I don't see bitterness on your face when I mention your father."

He allowed himself to touch her hand, tracing patterns on her palm. "What do you see on my face now?"

Abby blushed and bit her lower lip. He could feel her discomfort, saw her tinted cheeks darken.

The fear that streaked across her features was replaced with a stubborn grin. "I see an Easterner who's trying to kill time. Let's get a move on, or nothing'll get done."

When Jeremiah swung onto Old Red, he felt the horse's powerful muscles beneath him. He tightened his hands around the saddle horn and gripped the animal with rigid knees, forgetting whatever Buck had taught him. Jeremiah reminded himself to relax. He closed his eyes for a moment and pretended he was still sitting on Lancelot. *Trust myself, trust Old Red,* he repeated silently.

He imagined Buck saying, "Relax, pretend you're with a woman. Use a gentle hand." Jeremiah had learned a lot from Buck, and the old geezer was the first to admit that Jeremiah had come a long ways in a short time. Unfortunately, Jeremiah was running out of clothes. His private lessons had cost him his derby, two silk vests, and a pair of linen trousers. At this rate, Jeremiah would have only the clothes on his back.

As Jeremiah's uneven breath steadied, he heard Abby's low chuckle. "You taking a nap?"

"No. I'm wide awake."

More laughter. "You sure about that?"

Had he been asleep, Abby would have been beneath him, and he'd be enjoying their erotic escapades. He grinned, a devil-may-care smile that mirrored his lustful thoughts. "I'm sure."

He leaned forward and patted Old Red's neck. "Red, you and I are going to be friends." He hoped the horse understood.

"You going to dally all day?"

"I'm ready," he said, nudging the animal with his heels,

almost tumbling off, saving himself just in time.

"You all right?" Her maple sugar drawl flowed over him like warm bath water.

"Why do you ask?"

"Just checking."

Jeremiah clamped his hand over the saddle horn, or he'd have lost his balance. Red's girth was far wider than Lancelot's, stretching Jeremiah's thigh muscles to their limit. He'd need a double dose of liniment come nightfall.

Every few minutes Jeremiah reminded himself to relax until, much to his surprise, he stopped worrying and found that he rode the horse with ease. "Where are we going?"

"I figured I'd give you a chance to ride Old Red. I can see you've everything under control, which is good because next week, you'll be taking part in the branding and roping of the steers." She looked at him for a long time. "I don't think you'll have any trouble."

Her faith in him filled Jeremiah with a deep sense of pride.

As they rode in companionable silence, Jeremiah steered his mount close to Abby, brushing her leg with his whenever he got lucky. She pretended not to notice. He noticed too much.

Evelyn never entered his mind. For now, only one woman existed—the one flicking nervous glances at him. The next time their knees connected, Jeremiah leaned over and took the liberty of reaching for Abby's hand. The fool-hearted maneuver almost knocked him off his horse, and he looked none too graceful with his arms flapping by his side until he'd regained his balance. But he didn't fall. And he was glad that Abby pretended not to notice.

Once he'd regain his composure, she cast a look that verified what he already suspected but refused to accept. The sparks between them would eventually dissipate the last of his willpower. He wanted to make love to Abby.

It was wrong.

It was out of character.

Jeremiah began to question his lack of character and his dwindling willpower.

He cared deeply for Abby, more than he wanted to. If they had more in common, if she knew more about his world, if she . . .

This was crazy.

Jeremiah understood why his father had been blown away by his mother's beauty. Jeremiah understood the attraction of opposites. He felt connected to Abby as he suspected Noah had been with his mother. Noah won his mother's heart and persuaded the lovely city girl to live on his Texas ranch. In time, his mother grew restless. The marriage of opposites crumbled. Their love died. In the process they ripped a small boy from the family he deserved.

Jeremiah was not Noah. He would not repeat his father's mistakes. He and Abby came from two different worlds.

And they'd remain that way.

"Oh, no." Abby kicked her horse to a canter, hopping off an instant later and running toward the steer that bellowed in pain.

Jeremiah didn't know much about animals or about giving birth, but he recognized the swollen belly and the agony in the animal's eyes. He knew something was seriously wrong even before he spotted the thin leg sticking out below the animal's tail.

"Abby, be careful," he said, fearing for her safety.

She approached the steer. "Take it easy, girl. I'm here to help you."

Emitting a mournful bay, the animal's long sharp horns dipped downward and came dangerously close to Abby. Jeremiah wanted to rush to Abby's side, but he'd only make matters worse. Abby knew what she was doing. He didn't belong here any more than she belonged in Boston.

Without looking back, Abigail called to him. "Get the ropes out of my saddlebags and look around for a thick branch. Hurry!"

Galvanized into action, he tripped over his feet as he scrambled to Abby's horse. His fingers fumbled with the buckles on her saddlebags. He searched the ground and found a sturdy limb. Finally, he ran toward Abby but stopped about fifteen feet from the large animal. "Is it all right to approach?"

"Yes, but be sure she sees you. And don't make any loud noises."

Jeremiah wondered if his pounding heart counted as a loud noise. With great trepidation, he neared Abby. "What can I do to help?"

"We have to get this steer closer to that tree over yonder. I want to tie her so she can't move away. Then I have to turn her calf. Otherwise, they'll both die."

Sweat popped out over Jeremiah's face; one bead slipped off his chin and landed on his shirt. Jeremiah wanted to help. He wasn't certain he could.

How would Abby turn the calf?

Abby wrapped the rope around the steer's neck and pulled. The giant animal let out a groan that made Jeremiah jump. Fortunately, Abby didn't seem to notice. Jeremiah was way out of his league. This wasn't a bank ledger that needed tallying or a fight on the docks that needed to be broken up. He brushed at his face with the back of his hand. The smell of blood was everywhere, twisting Jeremiah's stomach like a wind-tossed dinghy on the Atlantic. Jeremiah tried to ignore the bile rising in his throat.

"What can I do?" He hated the desperation in his tone.

"Here, grab the rope and help me pull. Once her contraction is over, maybe she'll walk for us."

When Abby gave the command, Jeremiah yanked with all his strength. The steer took several steps. Abigail tied the ends of the rope around the tree trunk. "I need you to hold her still while I reach inside. Try to keep her from kicking."

His pulse was pounding in his ears when he positioned himself beside the steer and clamped his hands over the beast's hind legs. Fluids gushed onto his pant leg. Feces landed on his shoes. Spots flickered before his eyes. His head spun. His stomach turned end over end. He feared he'd puke out his guts. Abby needed him. He took a slow breath, tried to settle his stomach, tried not to breathe in the pungent odors.

When he finally dared to look down, he watched Abby's arm disappear into the animal. She seemed unaware of the rancid smell. Or his fear. If he did something wrong, Abby might be hurt. Killed.

Panic squeezed his heart, made his hands slippery with sweat. If Abby was frightened, it didn't show. She was the bravest woman he'd ever known. His respect for her grew. He'd known Abby was strong and courageous, but he'd never guessed how brave until now.

Still clamping his hands over the steer's hind legs, he felt the muscles beneath his palms tighten. He heard Abby's cry, saw her face contort in pain. Tears filled her eyes.

"What can I do?" He couldn't even brush the wayward tear from her cheek.

She bit her lower lip and sucked in a breath through clenched teeth. Still gripping the animal, Jeremiah leaned forward so that his forehead rested against Abigail's. He wanted her to feel a connection. He wanted her to know he was here for her. As he stood, hunched over, his forehead pressed to Abby's, in a small corner of his heart love began to grow. In that instant, he forgot about the odors and his dung-covered boots. "Tell me what to do. I'm stronger than you are."

"I need to turn the calf. My arm is smaller. Yours is way too large." The pain on her face ebbed. "I've almost got it."

The calf's leg slipped out of sight. Blood oozed onto the ground.

Jeremiah damn near lost his breakfast.

Again, pain wracked Abby's features. She squeezed her eyes shut. Her chest rose and fell.

Jeremiah stood by helplessly. "Abby, I can't stand seeing you hurt like this."

Her eyes opened and she gave him a pathetic smile. "It's not as bad as it looks. Soon as this contraction is over, I'll be pulling out the calf's front legs. Get ready to tie a rope around them. Then secure the other end to the branch you brought over."

Though Jeremiah tried to unclamp his hands from the steer's legs, it took a moment for the message to reach his brain. His fingers were stiff, useless. He didn't belong here. As if to emphasize his point, his stomach heaved. He grabbed the rope and dropped it. Cussing, he managed to pick up the rope, and stared with mouth gaping at the spindly calf legs that appeared. How he managed to loop the end of the rope over the calf's legs was a mystery. Feeling sick to his stomach, he tied the other end to the limb at his feet. "What now?" he asked, dabbing a smelly hand over his face, getting a strong whiff of animal excrement, trying not to gag.

Abby rubbed the steer's sides. "When the next contraction strikes, I want you to pull, but not too hard. You don't want to tear the calf apart. Exert just enough steady force."

How the hell was he supposed to know what just enough was? He had visions of animal body parts lying at his feet. And he'd be to blame. Jeremiah had always considered himself a brave man. A man's man. Confronted with this situation, he realized he wasn't brave at all. He'd like nothing better than to turn tail and run. Only he couldn't.

He didn't belong here.

Abby did.

"Now," Abigail said, her voice strong and sure, her arm covered with what looked like bruises, but Jeremiah couldn't be sure because of the blood coating her flesh.

Praying he wasn't pulling too hard, he tugged until Abby said to ease up. About twenty minutes later, though it seemed more like two hours, the calf's snout appeared, then the eyes. The only hint of life was the slight wiggling of damp nostrils. Jeremiah felt like whooping for joy. He clamped his mouth shut. He didn't need to ruin everything by startling the mother steer. Once the top of the calf's head and ears appeared, the rest of the animal whooshed out onto the ground. Jeremiah collapsed next to the animal from sheer relief. He untied the rope and watched as Abby undid the other rope that tethered the steer to the tree. As the steer nudged her baby, Abby dropped down next to him. He wrapped his grimy arm over her shoulder and held her hand, which was caked with dried blood and only God knew what else.

He'd witnessed a miracle.

He'd felt as if he'd gone to hell and back.

CHAPTER 16

Abigail leaned against Jeremiah's strong chest and heaved a sigh of relief. "It's a good thing for that calf we happened along when we did."

Jeremiah's muscles bunched beneath her head. "It's a good thing *you* happened along."

"You done good, Jeremiah."

"You're being kind."

She'd seen the green cast to his face. It wouldn't have surprised her none if he'd passed out. But he hadn't. He'd stuck with her until the end. "You expect too much of yourself. It'll get easier with time."

"This has proven what I've known all along. I'm city bred. I don't belong here."

Her heart nearly collapsed from the crushing weight of his words. She knew Jeremiah would leave. Most likely, he wouldn't stay in Texas one day longer than necessary. She glanced at him, sitting there with his face streaked with grime, hair falling over his forehead, and she knew she loved him, had loved him for some time. The emotion she'd felt for Clarissa's father had been infatuation. She recognized that now. Jeremiah was the first man she truly loved, and he would probably be the last because she was too stubborn to let go even when she knew she should.

She loved him with all her heart and soul.

Now that Abigail accepted the notion, she repeated the words silently to herself. *I love you. I love you, I love you.* How would Jeremiah react if she outright blurted her feelings? That hair of his that he tried to keep slicked back would probably stand on end. He'd be the one sliding a chair beneath the knob of their adjoining doors. The thought of her heaving the door open as the chair splintered made her chuckle.

"What's so funny?"

She could see him eyeing her, felt his breath along the side of her face, felt a powerful yearning building deep inside. He flustered her no end. She didn't understand the wanting of him because she knew what that entailed. Pain, embarrassment, and when it was over, the overwhelming feeling of being used.

"Well, what's the joke?"

She gave him that cocky smile she'd perfected over the years. "I was remembering you running like a drunken cowboy when you took off to fetch the ropes from my saddlebags."

A low laugh rumbled. "I was nervous. I guess it showed."

She could have kicked herself for being so stupid. She certainly didn't want to add to Jeremiah's conviction that he didn't belong in Texas. She faced him square, met those deep silver eyes that tormented her at night. "I was damn proud of you, Jeremiah."

She hadn't meant to cuss. It had slipped out from habit. Pride claimed his rugged features. She watched her fingers reach for his face and linger on his strong jaw. How had her hand gotten there? Inside, her muscles turned to mush. Her bones melted, yet her fingers continued on to his neck where the hair peeking over his collar tickled her fingertips. More than anything she wanted to undo his shirt, run her hands over his chest, shed her clothes, and feel that springy hair rubbing against her breasts.

Scorching heat rose up her neck and onto her pale, freckled cheeks. What had come over her? Those pewter eyes had her thinking like a loose woman.

As Abigail's bold fingers traced the indentation over his breastbone, she saw the want on Jeremiah's face, saw indecision play across his features, saw his head dipping downward. When his large hand rubbed her arm, she yelped in pain.

If Abby could have recalled that cry, she would have. If she hadn't hollered, Jeremiah would be kissing her right now instead of examining her arm with a horrified look on his face. "Abby, your forearm's a mess."

Blood covered her arms along with dirt and she suspected a fair amount of dried steer dung. Embarrassed, she tried to pull free, but he wouldn't allow it.

"I should wash," she said, realizing for the first time how terrible she must look. Jeremiah was used to women all gussied up without a speck on grime on their hands. Shame brought tears to her eyes, and she batted them away with a vengeance.

"I'm not talking about the dirt. Your arm is bruised. By tomorrow it'll be black and blue."

Instead of revulsion, she saw caring. She stopped trying to escape.

He rested his forehead against the top of her head. "I wish I could have done more."

A tear slipped down her cheek. Abigail wasn't the sentimental sort. Why did she feel like crying like a baby? Her feelings were so close to the surface that if she didn't skedaddle, she'd tell Jeremiah what was in her heart. Sniffing and blinking away tears, she leaped to her feet and hurried toward her horse.

He caught up to her. "Abby," he said, halting her steps, his hands settling over her shoulders, then massaging her neck until shivers raced down her spine. "At least let me care for you."

She didn't know what he meant, but she turned and allowed him to lead her to the small stream about fifty feet away.

"Sit down, Abby." His gentle voice almost brought fresh tears to her eyes, but she held them back.

As if she were made of fine china, he helped her sit on the grass by the rippling brook. He withdrew one of the green handkerchiefs Clarissa had bought for him and dipped it in the cold water. When he turned, his heated gaze set her insides ablaze. With infinite gentleness, he dabbed away the dirt from her arm, rinsed out his handkerchief, and continued with his ministering. Abigail squeezed her eyes shut and pictured herself sitting naked in a tub of warm water as Jeremiah ran a wet cloth over her quivering body. When Abby looked at him again, desire washed across his face, mirroring the emotions running rampant inside her. She wasn't sure how it happened, but the next thing she knew she was lying on the grass, Jeremiah's face mere inches away.

"I want to kiss you, Abby . . . though I have no right."

He was giving her a choice. She knew he belonged to another woman. She knew he'd go back to her. So why did she reach up and pull his head downward?

The joining of their mouths was everything she'd imagined— and more. His mustache brushed her upper lip, and she was tempted to feel its texture with the tip of her tongue. For fear he'd think poorly of her, she clamped her lips tight and enjoyed the way his mouth moved over hers. Jeremiah Dalton was an experienced kisser. She wondered if he thought her experienced, too. After all, she'd borne a child. She knew the ways of men.

Did he consider her an easy mark?

When his tongue flicked across her mouth, she near died from the sensation. Gooseflesh covered her arms, legs, and everything in between. She'd never heard of such a thing. The embers that had glowed in the pit of her stomach flamed to life, soon raging out of control.

She wasn't sure if it was proper for his tongue to be doing what it was doing, but parted her lips and allowed his tongue to squeeze through. She kept her teeth clamped. A good case of jitters overtook her. She didn't want him to think her stupid, and she didn't want to do anything wrong. When she peeked through her lowered lashes, she was pleased to see his eyes were closed. And he seemed to be enjoying the moment. She took a relaxing breath and let her guard down for a fraction of a second. The next thing she knew, he'd wiggled his tongue into her mouth. After that, she lost track of everything. After that, she wouldn't have called a halt even if flaming bolts of lightning fell to the ground around them.

The steady pressure of his chest against her shirt pebbled her nipples beneath her silk camisole.

He sighed against her mouth. "Kiss me back, Abby."

The fog lifted from her brain. She was already kissing him. What did he mean? But the next time his tongue darted into her mouth, she thought she understood. Did she dare? Tentatively, she flicked her tongue against his lips, brushed against his mustache before retreating in haste. The first foray took the most courage. The second was easier. By the third, she'd begun to get the knack, and she poked her tongue into his mouth where it tangled with his, the moan from deep in Jeremiah's throat empowering her.

He tasted sweet, like lemon drops. She'd never be able to eat the candy again without remembering this moment. As she lost herself in that kiss, she felt his fingers toying with the buttons on her shirt. When he parted the cotton fabric and kissed her breasts through the thin material of her camisole, she was the one who moaned. His knee wedged between her legs, and though she couldn't understand the yearning that ran through her veins, she wanted Jeremiah to join with her.

"I love you, Jeremiah," she whispered, then instantly regretted the words as his hands stilled.

She opened her eyes and saw him staring down at her with

regret. She watched him jerk away and sit back on his ankles. He jabbed his fingers through his hair and glanced out at the horizon. "I'm sorry, Abby. I don't know what came over me." He turned and met her gaze as she yanked the sides of her shirt together and sat up.

He heaved a deep sigh. "I'm attracted to you, and I allowed that to get in the way of my better judgment." He shook his head. "This isn't right. It isn't fair to you."

"Let me be the one to decide what's fair to me."

"Abby, I'm going to leave. I won't lie to you about that. You deserve more than I can give you. You deserve a man who'll cherish you, a man who'll remain by your side until you both grow old together. I'm not that man."

"It could be you. There's no one forcing you to go back. I think you care."

"Of course I care for you. But . . . there's Evelyn. If you met Evelyn, you'd understand. We have so much in common. I admit I've had some misgivings since arriving in Texas, but I don't plan to give credence to my doubts. When the time is up, I'm selling the ranch and getting out of here as fast as I can. I can't stay. I won't."

She wanted to tell him she didn't care for him. She wanted to beg him to kiss her again. But then she'd look pathetic, and she still had some pride left. "You needn't concern yourself. It was no more than a few stolen kisses. If truth be told, I've kissed many a man." She wanted to wound, but she failed.

"Yeah, I could tell."

If she hadn't been so busy buttoning her shirt, she'd have slapped the arrogant smirk from his face.

Then his wise grin faded, and he grew serious. "Abby, you aren't experienced. You kiss like an innocent."

She couldn't follow his line of thinking. For years she'd stored the hurtful comments deep inside: whore, harlot, trollop. "Have you forgotten I have a daughter? I know what it means to be with a man."

"I suspect you've been with the wrong kind of man. There's much more you don't know. Only I'm not the man to teach you."

On the way back to the ranch, Jeremiah called himself every name he could think of. Abby deserved someone who would love her. A disturbing thought nudged the back of his mind, but he would have none of it.

Maybe, he did love her.

He cussed. Abby angled a sidelong glance as he nudged Old Red ahead. He needed to distance himself from Abigail Wilcox. He loved Evelyn, had loved Evelyn for some time. To consider another possibility would be preposterous, absurd, crazy, and proof that he had no more common sense than Noah had.

As Old Red plodded along, the horse's hooves thumping a steady beat on the hard-packed ground, thoughts of Abby's tentative kisses wreaked havoc with Jeremiah's mind. How could a woman who'd had a child know so little about kissing? He suspected her lover had been a selfish son of a bitch. Jeremiah had felt the fire in her touch, but he'd felt her nervousness, too. Pulling away from her had been the hardest thing he'd ever done. Had he not stopped himself when he had, there would have been no turning back. Quite honestly, he'd never wanted another woman the way that he wanted Abby. Since tasting her lips, his desire for her had multiplied.

They rode in silence. Jeremiah looked at the land that would one day be his. He admired the fertile fields, a great place to raise cattle, horses, and he suspected the perfect place to raise a family. He'd sell the property because he didn't belong here. He eyed the stream that zigzagged across the terrain and remembered Abby's passion-filled words. *I love you, Jeremiah.*

If only he could return that love.

This line of thinking was getting him nowhere, so he turned his thoughts to Boston and how much he'd changed since arriving in Texas. Working under the wide expanse of sky had given him answers to questions that had troubled him for some time. When he returned, he'd tell Evelyn that he was through working at the bank. She'd have to accept being married to a man with a little dirt under his fingernails. He wasn't meant to be a banker, to be cooped up in an office all day. He loved the outdoors. And he had loved working on the loading docks by the sea. He'd left his partner in charge of their warehouses and the shipping company that had provided a decent living. When Jeremiah returned, he'd let his partner manage the office, but Jeremiah would supervise the men on the docks, sometimes working elbow to elbow with the hired help, smelling the briny air and feeling the wind and the sun against his face.

The decision made him smile. Though he suspected Evelyn might not be delighted with the news, she'd accept the choice he'd made because she loved him, because she wanted him to be happy, and because there'd be no changing his mind. She'd shed a few tears, pout, cajole, and try her feminine wiles on him, but in the end, she'd accept his decision. Jeremiah was nothing like her father, who enjoyed working with figures. Though Jeremiah had a way with numbers, he found the work tedious. Why it took running off to Texas to open his eyes, he didn't know, but he was glad that it had.

Now that he'd made up his mind about what he'd do for work when he returned to Boston, he felt much better until he saw the tight smile on Abby's face. He'd hurt her. He regretted that. He wished he could turn back the time and undo the moment of weakness when he'd allowed himself to taste her lips and mold his fingers over her perfect breasts. If he had the opportunity, could he look temptation in the face and walk away?

Only one answer rang true—Jeremiah was a low-down creature like the snake winding its way along the tall grass.

The entire way back to the ranch, Abigail's insides tingled from the memories of Jeremiah's lips and the brush of his mustache. Maybe she'd been foolish to allow Jeremiah the liberties he'd taken, but she had no regrets. She had five months to change his mind about leaving. Though he was adamant about loving Evelyn, Abigail saw the doubt that flashed across his face. Evelyn's hold on Jeremiah had weakened. Time might completely dissolve their bond.

Abigail was willing to take that chance.

She cast a quick look at Jeremiah. Though his hat was tipped low on his forehead, she could still see the guilt in his darkened eyes. Her heart sang with happiness. The man had character. Otherwise, why did he look as if he'd just robbed a bank and shot up half the townspeople? He was a good man. He had morals. He had wit.

He had a *fiancée.*

Abigail's jaw clenched. She hoped to remedy that, or at least give it her best try.

When she glanced at Jeremiah, he managed a half-smile. You'd think he'd forced himself on her to see the grim lines around his mouth. A mouth that kissed like no other. Abigail wiggled in her saddle. She could daydream about that mouth from now until the cows came home. But she needed to act. She glanced down at the lace bow pinned to her shirt.

It was high time she dressed like a woman again.

They reached the ranch and Jeremiah finished up with his horse before she did. Instead of leaving her alone as she'd expected, he leaned against the wooden rail that divided the stalls. She felt his gaze on her. The tiny hairs beneath her collar stood on end.

"I didn't mean to hurt you."

"You didn't." She kept her eyes trained on the brush in her hand, did her damnedest to steady her fingers. She finished rubbing down her mount in record time, allowed herself to look at his hangdog expression. He caught her staring, and his hands fell to his sides.

"You kissed me. It was no big thing. So get over it." She saw the hurt and wanted to take her words back. A lady wouldn't speak in such a manner. A real lady would bat her lashes, cast her eyes downward in a coquettish fashion, and whisper in a timid voice that his kisses had mattered to her. Very much, in fact.

Feeling a bit silly, Abigail took a breath and flapped her eyelashes at him.

His right eyebrow rose. "Do you have something in your eye? Here, let me look."

Jeremiah stepped toward her, brought his fingers beneath her chin, and lifted her face. He angled his head over hers and stared into her eye. "I don't see anything."

She blinked again. "Are you sure?"

His breath pelted her face with unsteady beats, her own breath lodging in her throat. "Maybe I do see a speck. Here, let me." He reached in his pocket and withdrew his handkerchief, gently tapping the corner of her eye and the side of her nose, taking much longer than necessary. Where his handkerchief left off, his fingers took over. He traced the side of her face with callused fingertips, reached up, and undid the ribbon that harnessed her uncontrollable curls. She watched the wonder in his eyes as he crushed handfuls of her springy hair between his fingers.

"I've wondered about your hair. It's even softer than I'd expected," he whispered, his voice deep and rough.

Warmth skittered down her middle as if she'd gulped fine whiskey. His mouth edged closer, giving her a jolt of confidence.

Maybe it wouldn't take months to make him hers. As his mustache swept her upper lip, she wrapped her hands around his neck and welcomed his kiss.

"Well, I'll be damned." Whip's voice roared through the barn like thunder on a stormy night.

Abigail shoved Jeremiah away, expecting to see Whip's flint-gray eyes gawking at them, but was surprised that he was nowhere in sight. She hurried out of the stall and found him standing, back to them, staring at something in the yard.

Whip whistled long and slow. Fixated, he stared ahead and anchored one hand on his hip. Abigail reached Whip's side a fraction of a second after Jeremiah.

Abigail's jaw dropped. "What in tarnation . . . ?"

Slowly, Jeremiah stepped forward. "Evelyn! What are you doing here?"

CHAPTER 17

A feeling of defeat washed over Abigail as she looked with awe at the most perfect creature ever to set foot in Texas. Pride radiated from every inch of Evelyn—and rightfully so. She was beautiful and decked out in such frippery that even if Abigail dug out her best dress, she'd look plain and ridiculous in comparison.

Abigail could not compete with this woman.

Evelyn sat ramrod straight on the wooden wagon seat, her citified upbringing evident in the tilt of her head and the uppity look on her face. Though her creamy complexion was flushed from the heat, not one drop of sweat dared to dot Evelyn's brow. Abigail doubted Evelyn even knew how to sweat. Her earlier hopes of stealing Jeremiah from this woman vanished. Abigail had thought she stood a chance of winning his heart, but that was before seeing the competition. Now that she had, Abigail realized she'd lost.

Berry red lips rose in a welcoming smile as Jeremiah approached Hank Bufford's supply wagon piled high with boxes and four large storage chests. Hank, a lazy son of a gun by nature, wouldn't have come out in this heat unless pushed, emphasizing Evelyn's powers of persuasion. Or maybe Hank had taken one look at the raven-haired beauty and fallen under her spell like other men standing in the yard, acting as if they'd never seen a woman in their lifetime. Abigail took a closer look at Whip and wondered if he'd drawn a breath in the last few minutes. His pupils were dilated and his expression blank. One glance across the yard affirmed that Jeremiah was in a similar state. Abigail's heart clenched with disappointment.

Evelyn slanted her head to one side, her mouth disappearing behind the fluttering fan in her right hand, the gesture practiced and perfect. A ruffled parasol shaded alabaster skin the likes of which Abigail had never seen. Not even the layer of Texas dust clinging to her fine silk garments marred Evelyn's appearance.

The hat perched on her head and adorned with more feathers than a ruffled chicken caught Abigail's eye. Abigail had never seen anything as pretty. She yanked her Western-style hat off her head and slapped it against her thigh, raising a dust cloud that tickled her throat.

When Jeremiah reached the side of the wagon, Evelyn placed her parasol on the wooden bench and extended one white-gloved hand. Whip shot across the yard as if chased by a coyote and took Evelyn's elbow as she alighted onto the ground. The woman didn't walk but strode in a graceful manner, giving the illusion of an angel floating on a thin layer of air.

Feeling meaner than a cornered rattlesnake, Abigail stomped toward Evelyn and arrived in time to see the pride on Jeremiah's face as he introduced her to Whip.

"I'd like you to meet my fiancée, Evelyn DuBlois."

Nothing about Evelyn was plain, not even her name. It sounded classy and required a roll of the tongue to pronounce. Abigail decided she hated the woman but quickly changed her mind.

Hate was too mild a word.

Whip smiled like a jackass, flashing white teeth, his handlebar mustache twitching as if he had an itch he couldn't quite reach. He yanked his hat off his head, ran his fingers through his disheveled hair, and nodded. "Pleased to meet you, ma'am." His eyes glazed over with admiration.

Abigail felt like puking.

Since when had Whip turned into a gentleman?

Jeremiah took a possessive grip of Evelyn's hand and gave Whip a look that meant the lady was off limits.

"And I'd like you to meet Abigail Wilcox," Jeremiah said, his tone cool and impersonal when he spoke her name.

Abigail wished she could evaporate into thin air. What a fool she'd been to think she stood a chance with this man.

Evelyn gave Abigail's bloodstained shirt a quick assessment, her good manners coming to her rescue as she reluctantly took Abigail's hand in a gentle shake. When their palms connected, jealousy raged through Abigail, shredding her desire to act lady-like. She was tempted to spit at Evelyn's feet, tempted to see the well-shaped brows rise in disgust, but she controlled the impulse. She'd put that part of life behind her, and no one, not even Evelyn DuBlois, could change Abigail's mind once it was made up. Instead of puckering up, the urge strong in the back of her mind, Abigail mimicked Whip's shitty grin and tried to look real hospitable.

"Evelyn, what are you doing here?" Jeremiah asked, excitement ringing in his tone.

"I was bored. I thought if I came to Texas, maybe I could help, and we could get your will requirements done in half the time."

He chuckled. "Darling, that's not how it works. I have to be here for a full six months. To your way of thinking, if I hired a half-dozen men to help me, I could leave Texas in four weeks."

The blush that rose to Evelyn's cheeks added to her fragile beauty. "Silly me, I've never been able to keep such things straight. I guess that's why God made men to solve life's more complicated problems."

Jeremiah's chest puffed like a proud rooster. So did Whip's.

Whip piped up, "I don't fault your figuring. It was damn

clever if you ask me."

At the word *damn,* a startled expression seized Evelyn's face. "Oh my heavens, what foul language!"

Whip realized his error. "Forgive me. I know I shouldn't talk like that in the presence of such a fine lady."

Evelyn's long jet-black eyelashes lowered and rose, her warm chocolate-tinted eyes bestowing their approval on Whip.

If being a lady entailed acting helpless, Abigail would pass up the opportunity. She hadn't spent several years learning how to care for herself and Clarissa to stand around with a dumb look on her face, inflating men's egos.

Hank Bufford hopped down from the wagon. "If you'll tell me where to put your things, I'll get one of the boys to help me."

Abigail shook her head in disbelief. Was this the same man who ran for parts unknown when her supplies needed to be loaded in her wagon? "For now, put the boxes on the porch," she said. "We'll figure out what to do with them later."

A sweat-dampened shirt molded Hank's barrel-shaped chest. His belt buckle dug into his huge beer belly. Rivulets of perspiration trickled down the sides of his face as he strained to lift the largest box, setting it at his feet with a satisfied grin.

Concern furrowed Evelyn's perfect brow. "My, are all Texans as big and strong as you are?"

"Ain't nothin', ma'am."

Though Hamlet had never been one of Abigail's favorite animals, when the pig rounded the corner and plunked itself between Jeremiah and Evelyn, Abigail could have kissed the critter's snout. When an unsuspecting Evelyn glanced down and spotted the hog nudging Jeremiah's pant leg, to hear her high-pitched scream, you'd have thought a bear had taken a bite out of her.

Jeremiah laughed and tightened his hold on Evelyn's hand.

"You're safe. It's only a pig. We've become friends."

Evelyn's eyes misted. "A pig? Friends? But it's so . . . huge . . . and filthy. Surely, you jest."

Jeremiah's grin warmed Abigail's chest until she remembered it wasn't intended for her.

Whip leaped forward, ready to protect the damsel in distress. "Rest assured, we won't allow nothing to happen to you, ma'am."

"Thank the dear Lord for that, Mr. Whip."

Whip tipped his head a little. "Name's Alfonzo Diaz."

Jeremiah's frown shifted from Whip to Evelyn. "Trust me, it's a pig, but not just any pig. This is Hamlet. You've nothing to worry about. He's quite tame. If you'd like, I'll give you a piece of bread later, and you can try feeding him."

"I do believe I'll pass." Evelyn's forehead creased. "Jeremiah, what's happened to you?"

"What do you mean?"

"Your clothing . . ." She took a close look, her eyes rounding in disbelief. "What's that caked on your pants? And your shoes? And Lord, look at those fingers." Evelyn jerked her white gloved-hand from his grasp, stared down at the blackened palm, and gave Jeremiah a thorough going-over. She rested one finger below her nostrils. "Oh my, that foul odor is coming from you!"

Her face whitened. A small helpless cry fell from her lips. Her eyes rolled; her eyelids fluttered, and she swooned right into Whip's waiting arms.

Jeremiah recognized Evelyn's theatrical performance for what it was. He'd never met another woman who could pass out on command so he wasn't alarmed when she fainted dead away. He'd expected as much when he'd spotted the flapping eyelids and the cautious backward glance ensuring that someone was there to catch her.

As Evelyn collapsed, Whip bent down and swung her into his arms, cradling her head against his shoulder, his expression far gone, which was commonplace when men first set eyes on the dark-haired beauty.

Though he didn't approve of the lovesick look Whip was giving his fiancée, Jeremiah figured he'd better go wash up. If one whiff of him had made her faint, holding Evelyn in his arms would probably be the death of her.

Looking worried, Whip glanced at Jeremiah. "Should I get the doctor?"

"No, I wouldn't worry too much. I suspect she's exhausted after her trip. Take her inside, make her comfortable, and I'll be back as soon as I shed some of this dirt."

As Jeremiah ran into the house to get some clean clothes, he avoided the stricken look on Abigail's face. He'd taken advantage of her and now regretted his actions.

If only he'd kept his hands to himself. If only he hadn't kissed her.

Evelyn had not arrived in Texas one second too soon. Jeremiah had lost his head, and he'd almost lost his heart. Now that he'd seen Evelyn, his life was falling back into place. Clearly, she was the woman for him. How could he have doubted that? He'd only needed to glance at Whip's face to remember how very lucky he was.

Jeremiah entered his bedroom and poured water in the basin on the bureau. As he shed his clothing and left it in a pile at his feet, he wondered what he'd do to keep Evelyn amused. It was clear by the stack of boxes that she'd planned to stay awhile. Evelyn would die of boredom in Texas. And if she considered Whip's language inappropriate, she was in for a shock. Evelyn was delicate. She didn't have the stamina to live in Texas. She didn't fare well around loud, outspoken men, and she didn't have the wherewithal to keep her mouth shut when offended.

She would not stand for cussing in her presence, even if the person swearing up a storm had a six-shooter in his hands. For Evelyn's sake, Jeremiah had to persuade her to leave Texas as soon as possible.

Jeremiah hurried because he knew that Evelyn didn't like to be kept waiting. Even then it took a full twenty minutes to shave, wash his hair, and comb it back, using a liberal amount of pomade on the stubborn strands over his forehead. He'd stopped wearing the clothing he'd brought from Boston, but he wanted to look like his old self, so he dug in the bottom of the drawers. He yanked out linen trousers with a sharp crease but didn't take the time to iron out the wrinkles in the seat of his pants. Shrugging into a clean shirt and slipping on his leather vest, he plunked his Stetson on his head and glanced in the mirror. Jeremiah wished he still had the derby, not for his sake but for Evelyn's. He wanted her to feel a degree of normalcy. But the derby belonged to Buck, and Buck would no sooner part with that hat than he would his right arm, or so he said each time he saw Jeremiah.

Jeremiah threw his hat on the bed and followed the murmur of voices coming from the parlor.

Evelyn loved attention and it was clear by her expression when Jeremiah entered the room that she was having a wonderful time. Her feet were propped on a small stool, her slender fingers wrapped around a cup of tea, her smile lighting up the room when she spotted him. Evelyn had charm and charisma. She was amazing and given ten minutes could turn most men to mush, as was evident by Whip, who'd lost the hard edge to his face.

Evelyn's father liked to boast that his sweet Evelyn could twist most men around her little finger by simply fluttering her long lashes. Evelyn was a little spoiled, but that was all right with Jeremiah because he enjoyed indulging the beautiful creature. After all, women were weak and delicate; they needed men to help direct their lives.

The thought jolted him, made him cast a quick glance at Abby. His heart beat double time, and his mouth went dry. What had he done? Abby wasn't weak. She didn't need a man to tell her what to do. If a man tried, she'd set him straight in a hurry. But deep inside of her beat a heart with tender feelings, and he could see the pain beneath her strained smile. He felt rotten. At least he hadn't compounded the problem by taking Abby into his bed. He was thankful for that. Or was he? His jaw tightened at the selfish question. Of course, he was thankful . . .

He could tell Abby was doing her best to ignore his gaze as her green eyes focused on a spot across the room. Even in faded jeans and a shirt, she was pretty. He looked again. She wore a cotton top with gathered sleeves and a woven ribbon around her neck, tied in a bow that drooped over her small breasts. Jeremiah made himself turn away, relieved that Evelyn hadn't noticed his fascination with Abby's anatomy.

As he strode toward Evelyn, Jeremiah saw Abby leave the room. Relieved that she was gone, he rested his hand on Evelyn's shoulder, kissing her upturned cheek and basking in the approval in her eyes. Resting next to her on the sofa was her foolish-looking hat that resembled a dead duck. He moved the feathered monstrosity aside and sat down next to her. "I'm glad to see you're feeling better."

A healthy glow colored her delicate complexion. "Thanks to Mr. Diaz, who rescued me when I fell. Otherwise I'd probably be suffering from several broken bones."

"Call me Alfonso."

She glanced from Jeremiah to Whip. "I don't think I could be that familiar with a man I've just met."

Jeremiah'd about all he could take. "Darling, call the man by his first name so he can leave and go about his business. Things aren't as formal in Texas as they are in Boston."

Realization dawned in Whip's eyes. "Ma'am if you'll excuse me." He tipped his head and backed out of the room as if he couldn't bear to look away.

Once he'd shut the door and left them alone, Evelyn turned to Jeremiah. "I can't believe how rude that was of you."

"I don't know what you mean."

"I think you do. What's happened to your manners? You deliberately told that poor man to get out of here. And after all he's done."

Jeremiah decided to change the subject. "Did you come all this way to discuss my behavior?"

"Well, no."

"Then kiss me and make it worthwhile."

Jeremiah pulled her into his arms and settled his mouth over hers. She pulled away. "What if somebody sees us?"

"Then they'll think you're a loose woman."

She tittered, the sound irritating him for some reason. "You're impossible, Jeremiah."

"No, you are. It's impossible to kiss a woman while she's yakking."

As she leaned into him, the sweet smell of her perfume seemed a little too strong, too overpowering. He lingered a few seconds and then cut the kiss short. "I've missed you, Evelyn. I'm so glad you've come. I can't wait to show you around."

She looked confused. "Show me around, what difference does that make? You'll be selling this place anyway."

"Yes, I will, but I have something truly special I want to share with you. Come," he said, pulling her to her feet.

"Where are we going?"

"To the barn."

"Oh."

He laughed. "You needn't sound so distressed. It isn't like

you'll be cleaning out the stalls."

"I should hope not. And you shouldn't, either."

"You can be thankful I'm willing to dirty my hands, or I wouldn't inherit Noah's estate."

She waved her hand. "That dastardly man . . . he's a no good so-and-so."

"My father was a caring man."

"But you said . . ."

"I was wrong." He stopped in the hall. "Wait here, I'm getting a few biscuits."

When he returned, she planted her hands on her hips. "I hope you don't think I'm going to feed that swine I saw earlier."

"No, you needn't worry about that. I could tell my snouted friend didn't charm you."

"Don't call it that."

"Call it what?"

"Friend . . . it doesn't sound civilized. I know you aren't serious, but it still sounds . . . uncouth."

"I'll try to remember."

"What do you do for fun around here?" She sidestepped animal droppings as they crossed the yard.

"I've had no time for fun."

"You poor dear, it's a good thing I'm here to cheer you."

"I've been meaning to speak to you about that. Texas is hot as hell."

"Not you, too. You know I won't tolerate such talk in my presence."

"I've fallen into some bad habits since my arrival."

"I've noticed." She glanced at the back of his pants. "Have you stopped having your clothes washed and pressed at a laundry?"

"I haven't time for such things, and I wear Levis because they're more appropriate for the type of work I do. And I doubt the town has a laundry, anyway."

"No laundry? Where will I have my clothes laundered while I'm here?"

"You may need to do them yourself."

"Surely you jest."

Jeremiah didn't have the heart to tell her he was serious. "We'll figure something out."

It took some time to reach Moonbeam's stall because Evelyn stopped every few seconds to calculate her next step. She looked down in bewilderment. "I don't know how you can tromp through the animal excrement and act as if it's nothing. No wonder your boots are coated with . . . stuff."

"It's not stuff, it's shit."

"Honestly, Jeremiah, your gutter talk will be the death of me yet."

The righteous expression on her face made him laugh. "Darling, I was just teasing you. I've missed you so much."

"That doesn't give you the right to talk like a hooligan."

"No, but I missed seeing the shocked look that streaks across your face when you hear an impure word. It makes you look sexy as hell."

"Jeremiah, you're incorrigible."

"Yes, and deep inside you like me just the way I am. You love me because I'm one of the few men you can't control by batting those thick lashes."

"You may be right, Jeremiah. I do find you a tad wild, and I hate to admit . . . appealing."

"I could be a lot wilder. Just say the word."

Her cheeks turned crimson. "I'll not say any such thing." She brought her finger to her nose. "How can you stand the wretched odors in here?"

"You get used to the smell after a while."

"I never will."

"Take short breaths and it won't seem as bad. That's Moonbeam over there," Jeremiah said, resting his booted foot on the lower rung of the stall, pointing to the white stallion. "Isn't he a beauty?"

"Yes."

"Not a soul has been able to ride Moonbeam because he won't let anyone near. But he's beginning to trust me. Watch this." Jeremiah pulled the biscuit from his pocket and held it out. The horse meandered toward him and took the offering with a nicker. "I'm going to bring him back to Boston. I was thinking of giving him to you as a wedding present."

When Jeremiah looked into Evelyn's eyes, he saw disbelief. She didn't understand the significance of his offer. The horse represented time and effort, and something that he'd come to love very much. To give her Moonbeam was like giving a piece of himself. Instead of being delighted, she looked confused and hurt. "Of course, that was just a thought. I haven't made up my mind yet."

As they turned to leave, he noticed Evelyn walked with a limp. "Is something wrong with your leg?"

She seemed embarrassed. "No."

He watched her take another few stiff steps. "You aren't walking the way you usually do."

She heaved an exasperated sigh but remained silent.

"If you're hurt, tell me."

She stopped and looked around to make sure no one was listening. "It's of a delicate nature." A warm blush claimed her features. "That ride in that awful wagon on that hard wooden seat bruised the muscles on my backside," she finished in a whisper.

"Is that all?"

"Yes, but it doesn't seem right to speak of such things to a man."

"We're going to be married. You should feel free to tell me anything."

"We aren't married yet."

"I know that. If we were, I'd have you up in the hayloft right now . . ."

"Jeremiah, don't you dare!"

He smiled down at her startled expression. "Anyway, I have just the thing for your aches. But you have to swear not to tell a soul about it. Come with me," he said, leading her to the large wooden cabinet. He reached way in the back and pulled out the Sloan's Horse Liniment. "Sneak this into your bedroom and slosh plenty over your tired muscles. You'll be feeling good as new in no time."

Her eyes widened. "That's for horses."

"I know, but it gets the job done."

"You expect me to use that?"

"Why not? It works."

"There's a picture of a four-legged beast on the container, that's why."

To appease her, he glanced at the bottle.

She aimed her finger at his chest. "Surely, you don't think I would use horse liniment on myself."

"It'll make your muscles feel so much better."

"I'd shrivel up and die first."

CHAPTER 18

Earlier that afternoon, after Whip carried Evelyn into the house, Abigail had rushed to clean up and change her clothing. One glance at her freckled, dirt-smudged face in the mirror, and she'd cringed. The impulse to look feminine had been so strong that she dug into her trunk and yanked out a shirtwaist she hadn't worn in years. After rubbing some of the grime from her face and arms, she slipped into the garment and tied the ribbon at her neck. Abigail had felt pretty until she entered the parlor. When Whip glanced up, she expected him to comment, but his blank expression meant he didn't notice anything different about her. She hoped—no she prayed—that Jeremiah would say something nice, but after a cursory glance, he hurried toward his ladylove. Abigail had wanted to rip the stupid shirtwaist off her back and tear it to shreds. Jeremiah had not even noticed, and why should he? It would take more than ribbons and lace to transform Abigail Wilcox into a lady.

That night Abigail saw no need to shove a sturdy chair under the doorknob of their adjoining rooms. Jeremiah would never choose her over Evelyn.

Abigail sat down in front of the mirror and brushed her hair until it shone. Soft curls cascaded down her back and along the sides of her face. She hadn't even considered the possibility of marriage to Jeremiah. Her reputation had ruined any chance of that. Since Evelyn's arrival, Abigail's last chance for happiness had shattered.

Before slipping into bed, she noticed two lemon drops nesting in a small indentation on her pillow. She laid the candy on her nightstand and pulled back the quilt her mother had given her years ago. She missed her family, but as her father had pointed out, she'd brought this on herself. Grief filled her; she'd never see her mother again, but she quickly suppressed the depressing thoughts. There was no sense rehashing what couldn't be changed. She loved Clarissa with all her heart, and no matter how grave Abigail's sin, she did not regret giving birth to her daughter. And she would not subject Clarissa to her father's scorn.

When Abigail first discovered she was with child, she'd dreaded telling Frank Myers, but he'd seemed genuinely pleased with her distressing news. Relieved to hear him speak of their upcoming nuptials, she ran home to pack her clothing. Before dawn the next morning, she crept from her parents' house and waited for Frank outside of town. Frank never showed up. Later she learned that he'd run off in such haste he'd left behind half of his belongings in his hotel room. Something inside her died that day. She vowed never to believe the words that flowed from slick-tongued city men.

Shamed, she'd returned home and confessed her transgression to her parents. Abigail still remembered how dirty she felt, standing before her father as he quoted verses from the Bible.

The sound of muffled footsteps through the wall brought Abigail back to the present. She craned her head to the side and listened. Had Evelyn crept down the hall and stolen into Jeremiah's room? The hollow pain in Abigail's heart intensified. *Fool,* she called herself repeatedly, yet she still ached for the man in the next room.

She tossed and turned all night and before dawn climbed out of her bed and reached under her mattress for the scrap of paper with the recipe to remove her freckles.

English powdered mustard
Lemon juice
Oil of almonds
Make paste
(Rub freshly cut lemon on the spots)
She stared at the words in the wavering candlelight until her eyes grew tired, trying to sound out each letter and failing. Then a thought struck.

"Maw, isn't Evelyn the prettiest lady ya ever seen?"

Abigail glared at Clarissa, hoping she'd take the hint and change the subject. This was the last thing Abigail wanted to hear. "Yup."

"Did ya see how Whip gawks at Evelyn with big cow eyes?"

"Sure did."

"Why's he lookin' at her like that?"

"I think he's smitten."

"Is smitten the same as hankering?"

Abigail shoved her foot into one of her boots and tried to keep a calm tone. "I expect so."

"Oh." Clarissa's gaze landed on the lemon drops on Abigail's nightstand. "Can I have one, please?"

Abigail laughed. "Your stash run out already?"

"I ain't got no stash, Maw."

Abigail frowned.

"I mean I don't have no stash of candy."

"Not any more you don't." Abigail ruffled Clarissa's hair. "You're a sweet, generous child. I've been wanting to thank you."

Looking confused, Clarissa shrugged and brought up the same confounded subject. "Is Mr. Dalton smitten with Evelyn, too?"

Fool, fool, fool. Abigail had allowed Jeremiah to touch her breast, and her only regret was that it wouldn't likely happen again. She jammed her foot into her other boot and stood, taking care not to face Clarissa for fear her expression would give away her thoughts. "I expect he is. Seems the whole damn world is smitten with Miss Evelyn DuBlois." The last syllable rolled off Abigail's tongue, made her sick to her stomach.

"I bet Miss DuBlois would have a conniption fit if she heard what you just said."

"Huh?"

"You cussed. You promised you wasn't gonna cuss again."

"Well, I guess that about makes us even, don't it? You promised not to say ain't."

"I do my best, Maw, but sometimes it just slips out."

"Same here." Abigail glanced at her daughter. She could understand the child's curiosity about Evelyn. Clarissa had never seen a real lady until yesterday, except for Emma Johnson, who'd looked like a field mouse compared to Evelyn DuBlois. Unfortunately, Clarissa had never seen her own mother dressed like a woman. Abigail feared she'd failed her daughter.

"I'll be going into town for supplies. Care to come along?"

"Can I buy some peppermint candy?"

"I don't see why not." Abigail left her room with Clarissa at her side. They entered the kitchen where Pedro was kneading dough for loaves of bread. "Do you need anything?"

Pedro glanced up from his chore. "Si, we are running low on flour, and we could use some more coffee. Make sure it's Arbuckle or the men will squawk."

"Write down whatever you need."

He looked suspicious. "You never had me write down stuff before."

"I don't have all day to dally around the mercantile. I figured I'd drop off the list and mosey over to the sheriff's office."

Pedro wiped his hands and reached for a pencil and paper.

He jotted several words and handed the list to Abigail.

Satisfied that her plan would work, Abigail smiled and took the paper, shoving it into her pocket. "Thanks, Pedro."

A moment later Clarissa watched Abigail buckle her gun belt. "How come you're wearing your gun, Maw?"

"It makes me feel safe."

"Oh."

Ever since Blue's accident, Abigail had gotten into the habit of keeping her six-shooter by her side. She feared for Jeremiah's safety. Whoever had planted that pitchfork had to be mentally unbalanced and could be a danger to everyone. Abigail preferred to be cautious.

They entered the barn and Abigail started to hitch up the wagon as Clarissa hooked the harness to the horse. "Maw, when I grow up, I want to have pretty clothes like Miss DuBlois."

"Then you'd better mind me and learn your lessons. It takes more than looking like a lady to be one." The words knifed through Abigail.

"Aw, Maw, I shoulda known you'd say that."

As they led the horse out of the barn, Jeremiah strode toward them. "Good morning," he said, with a tip of his hat and a grin that rubbed raw wounds.

"Good morning, Mr. Dalton," Clarissa chirped, her voice ringing with excitement. "We're going into Lowdown and I'm gonna buy some peppermint sticks."

"Is that so." His gray eyes flashed toward Abigail before turning back to Clarissa. "Do you two gals have room for someone else?"

Abigail's heart leaped to her throat, thinking he meant himself. "We could make room," she said, figuring Clarissa could ride out back. Was this Jeremiah's way of spending some time with her?

His smile lit his entire face. She remembered the feel of his mustache against her mouth. The memory of his tongue slipping between her lips sent a shiver down her spine. She couldn't deny that she loved him. And always would.

He patted Clarissa's head. "If you gals will wait a minute, I'll go check and see if Evelyn would like to ride along. She'll get bored in no time if we don't keep her busy."

Abigail's heart slammed into her stomach.

Fool, fool, fool.

It took damn near thirty minutes for Miss High-and-Mighty to get ready. Meanwhile, Abigail near burst from the inconvenience. When Evelyn finally made her grand entrance, she had hold of Jeremiah's arm. Whip appeared out of nowhere, and both men helped her climb aboard. Abigail wondered how she'd managed to get down without the men's help. As far as Abigail was concerned, the woman would stay on the wagon and die of heat stroke in the Texas sun before she'd assist her.

If Clarissa hadn't been around, Abigail would have cussed the entire way into town, but she minded her manners and managed to keep her replies short and proper. The problem of Evelyn climbing down from the wagon was solved immediately upon their arrival because a small cluster of men gathered, adoration in their eyes, more than willing to help.

As Evelyn, Abigail, and Clarissa strolled toward the mercantile, Abigail felt like a caterpillar next to Miss Butterfly who drifted on a cushion of air. Abigail's loud boot heels clomped on the boardwalk, the hollow sound mimicking her heartbeat. She'd never felt lower until she remembered the recipe in her pocket. The thought of banishing the rust spots from her face gave her hope.

Abigail spotted Gordy coming toward them at a fast clip.

He waved. "Abigail, wait a sec. I want to place another bet."

Abigail felt like a critter with a leg stuck in a trap. "Not now, Gordy, I'm busy." She tucked her chin down and hoped he'd leave her alone.

Instead, he caught up to them and doffed his hat. "Ma'am," he said, directing his gaze at Evelyn before turning back to Abigail. "Joe Wall just heard about our bet. He wants in, too, and I'm placing another bet for myself."

Abigail instructed Evelyn and Clarissa to go on without her, but she noticed they were waiting about fifteen feet away. She yanked the coins and the piece of paper from Gordy. "This is it, the last ones. I've had it up to here," she said, running her finger along her throat. She yanked on the collar of Gordy's shirt, brought his ear down to mouth level, and whispered. "Jeremiah isn't going anywhere. He's not a quitter."

Gordy straightened and smiled. "You may be right, but since the lady's arrival, odds of him hightailing East have increased. I expect a lot of men would love to up their odds of winning. And you needn't stand there lookin' so uppity. I heard you placed a bet, too."

She ignored the last comment. "Tell them bets are closed, ya hear?"

"Will do." Gordy grinned and took off in the other direction.

Abigail wondered if Evelyn had heard but decided she'd probably hadn't due to Clarissa's incessant questions. For once, she was thankful her daughter was a curious child.

As they entered Bufford's, Evelyn said, "Back in Boston we have stores that are ten times larger than this one."

Abigail didn't give a hoot, but Clarissa did. "Wow, maybe when I grow up, I'll go to Boston and see for myself."

Evelyn smiled down at Clarissa. "When you do, you can stay with Jeremiah and me. I suspect we'll have a child by then, but my house will have lots of rooms so you'll be welcomed anytime. I'd like for you to come, too, Abigail."

Abigail swallowed twice before she found the strength to answer. She'd never go East to see what kind of life Jeremiah had built for himself. "That's right nice of you to offer." There'd been a sight sarcastic ring to her words, but Abigail smiled in hopes of hiding her true feelings.

Evelyn's long lashes fluttered down, shading cream-colored cheeks for an instant. As much as Abigail hated to admit it, the woman was beautiful.

"What's that sticking out in back of you?" Clarissa asked.

Evelyn glanced behind her and then smiled at the child. "That's a bustle. It's the newest style back east."

"That's the prettiest dress I ever did see." Clarissa ran her fingers along the silk material. "But that bustle would get in the way if you were riding a horse."

A melodious laugh fell from the perfect mouth. "You're such a delightful child. This outfit wasn't meant for horseback riding. When we return to the ranch, I could help fix up one of your dresses if you like."

"I don't have a dress," Clarissa said, sticking her hands into the pockets of her pants.

"Maybe I'll buy you a dress today, and I'll accent it with tiny flowers and leaves. I'm handy with an embroidery needle," Evelyn said with a gentle tilt of her head.

Clarissa glanced at Abigail. "Isn't Miss DuBlois the nicest lady ya ever met?"

It took great effort for Abigail to nod in agreement. If she'd wanted to be honest with herself, she might have found it in her heart to see the woman's generosity, but she closed her mind. She hated Evelyn DuBlois. Period. End of discussion.

Abigail had never embroidered a stitch in her life. If she knew how, she'd tell Miss Fancy-Know-It-All to keep her nose out of her business. "If you want a dress, I'll buy you one."

"Aw, Maw, you mean it?"

"Course I mean it. I said so, didn't I?"

Worry creased Clarissa's forehead. "I don't think Bufford's is gonna have a dress as pretty as this one," she said, running a hand over the shiny material of Evelyn's skirt.

"Maybe not, but I bet we can find a nice cotton calico that will bring out the color in your eyes."

Evelyn rested her palm on Clarissa's shoulder. "I bet my couturier would be happy to make you a fine dress. We could wire her your measurements. If I told her to hurry, we could have the garment in a couple of months."

Abigail put a halt to this nonsense. "That won't be necessary. Clarissa won't be needin' a highfalutin' fancy dress. I'm sure whatever I find at Bufford's will suit her just fine." Abigail didn't bother to tone down her irritation, but instead allowed every word to snap out with sharp intensity.

"Aw, Maw."

Abigail knew Clarissa was disappointed, but for once, she recognized Abigail's warning look and dropped the subject. It was bad enough Abigail had lost Jeremiah to Evelyn without losing her daughter, too. Abigail took a deep breath and admitted Jeremiah had never been hers to lose. From the start, he'd belonged to Evelyn. Like it or not, that was something Abigail had to learn to live with.

Abigail felt a moment's guilt for treating Evelyn rudely. She considered apologizing but couldn't find it in her heart to do so. Realization dawned with a fact that sounded preposterous. The feeling tightening her chest was jealousy.

Lillian Bufford greeted them, her curious gaze following their every move. "Good day, ladies. My, what a beautiful hat."

Abigail had found this hat even prettier than the one Evelyn had worn yesterday. Multicolored ribbons edged the tan felt along with long white plumes sticking out from each side like angel wings. A piece of white netting with tiny beads fell gracefully over Evelyn's forehead. Abigail was fixated by the hat, and by the look on Lillian's face, so was she.

Though Abigail hated to add to the gossip around town, she felt the need to make introductions. "Lillian, I'd like you to meet Miss Evelyn DuBlois."

Lillian hurried forward. "Pleased to make your acquaintance."

Evelyn extended her white-gloved hand and tipped her head with poise. "Likewise, I'm sure. My chapeau is from Paris."

Lillian reached up to touch the feathers. "Do you mind?"

Evelyn, always the lady, dipped her head to accommodate.

Lillian glanced at both women. "I've been thinking of carrying a line of fine women's clothing. Lowdown is an up and coming town. I believe in changing with the times."

Abigail figured Lillian's talk was a bunch of hot air, but she kept her mouth shut; she'd already filled her quota of rudeness for one day.

Evelyn pulled out two jeweled hatpins and took the hat off her head. "The address where these can be ordered is stitched inside. Feel free to copy it down while I have a look around."

Evelyn was nice, or so it seemed, but Abigail wasn't ready to admit it yet, though the damn thought kept creeping up on her when she least expected it.

Lillian took the hat and smiled. "Thank you, dear. What brings you to our humble community?"

"I've come to spend some time with my fiancé."

"She's gonna marry Mr. Dalton," Clarissa added.

Lillian gave Abigail a consoling pat on her shoulder, which Abigail pretended not to notice. She thrust the two pieces of paper at Lillian, hoping she'd attend to business and leave them alone. "I want you to fill out these two lists. When you're through, wrap each order separately."

"Whatever for, dear?"

"They're going to different places," Abigail replied without explanation.

Lillian took the pieces of paper from Abigail and swirled around, heading for the front counter.

Abigail steered Clarissa toward the display of girl's dresses. The blue cotton one with yellow buttercups on the skirt caught her eye, so she lifted the garment and held it in front of her daughter.

"Maw, I wanted a pretty dress, like Evelyn's."

"Honey, this one is pretty."

Clarissa didn't look convinced.

Evelyn sashayed toward them, inspecting the garment. Abigail was waiting for her to comment, to say anything against the dress she'd chosen for Clarissa. Abigail was prepared to give the woman a piece of her mind.

"That's such a darling dress," Evelyn said much to Abigail's surprise.

Clarissa chewed her lower lip. "Ya really think so? Don't you think it looks kinda plain?"

Evelyn fingered the simple collar. "It could be spiced up a little with a touch of ribbon here and there, that's if it's all right with your mother."

Jealousy struck again, surged though Abigail's bloodstream at the adoration in Clarissa's eyes directed toward the other woman. "Of course it's all right with me." But it wasn't. Abigail wanted Clarissa to look that way at her. Abigail knew her hurt feelings were unfounded, but she couldn't help herself. She handed Clarissa enough money to purchase a peppermint stick. "Honey, buy yourself a piece of candy. I'll let you and Evelyn decide what you need to spiff up this dress, and you can put it on our account. I've some other business to attend to." Without a glance toward Evelyn, Abigail hightailed it out of the store and hurried toward the jailhouse. As her feet pounded on the walkway, she wondered how long Evelyn would remain in Texas.

If she stayed much longer, Abigail would lose her mind.

I've taken a breather to decide what to do next. Since Blue's accident, everyone is edgier than a pregnant mare about to foal. I'm laying low for a while, giving that cussed Easterner two weeks to leave on his own. I've seen his lady friend. If anyone can persuade him to go home, she can.

Otherwise, I'll be doing a little persuading of my own!

CHAPTER 19

During supper Abigail could barely eat. Her mind was riveted on the magic cure that would dissolve her freckles. She pushed the food around her plate and took a few bites, tried not to act suspiciously. After tucking Clarissa in bed and telling her a story, Abigail vanished into her bedroom and waited until everyone had gone to sleep before creeping out to the barn to retrieve the package she'd tucked beneath the wagon seat earlier that afternoon.

The inky blackness of the interior made seeing impossible, yet she didn't dare light the lantern by the door, but chose instead to use the candle she'd brought with her. If someone showed up, she could blow out the flame and hide. Her heart drummed in her chest as she climbed onto the wagon and pulled out the package wrapped in brown paper and tied with a string. The urge to open it right away was strong, but she decided to wait until she'd reached the privacy of her bedroom.

She hopped down from the wagon and heard someone entering the barn. Blowing out the candle, she dropped to her knees and peeked between the spokes of the wooden wheels. She watched someone strike a match and light the lantern by the door. The swaying, wavering light got nearer, and though she strained to see, she couldn't make out who was inside the barn. Maybe this was the person who'd planted the pitchfork. Why hadn't she brought her gun with her? She'd had her mind full of nonsense, that's why. She bit her lower lip and glanced around the dark interior for a weapon in case she needed one.

The person neared, and she could tell by the shadowed broad shoulders that it was a man. As she studied the large form, she decided she was looking at either Jeremiah or Whip. Until now, she hadn't stopped to consider the similarities in their build. Even by Texas standards, both men were larger than average.

When he hung the lantern on a nail, she caught a glimpse of Jeremiah's face. Abigail wanted to jump up and strangle him for scaring her out of her wits, but she held her breath and watched. What was he up to?

He strolled toward Moonbeam. "I have something for you," he whispered, his deep voice doing strange things to Abigail's insides. She was surprised when the white horse allowed Jeremiah to rub its mane and nibbled food from Jeremiah's extended hand.

"That's a good boy. It's time you and I got better acquainted." Jeremiah swung open the gate to the stall, entered, and latched it behind him.

Abigail was ready to scrape Jeremiah off the sideboards any second. She held her breath and prayed he had the good sense to keep some distance from the stallion. Just the other day, Whip had tried to break in the wild beast. All he'd gotten for his trouble was a kick in the leg. It was a wonder he hadn't broken a limb. Whip declared the animal a lost cause.

Abigail wanted to shout out a warning, but she couldn't very well do that without explaining why she was here.

Jeremiah ran his hand along the horse's back. "I won't hurt you. You know that, don't you? I can see it in your eyes."

For a few seconds she squeezed her eyes shut and pretended his soothing voice had been directed at her, but reality returned when Moonbeam threw back his head and whinnied.

Abigail had never seen the likes of it. Jeremiah had a way with the horse. And even though Jeremiah wasn't hers, pride swelled inside. She'd known all along that he'd succeed. The man was really something.

Then, just like a greenhorn, he pushed too hard and too fast. She watched in horror as he climbed up the boards dividing the stalls and swung onto Moonbeam's back. The barn exploded with noise as four hooves pounded the wooden stall and the hard-packed earth. This was followed by a painful curse and a loud thud; Jeremiah jumped to safety and brushed the dirt from his behind.

Abigail couldn't stand seeing him hurt, but when he tried the fool-hearted stunt again, every cell in her body tensed. Again, he fell; again, he barely missed the hooves capable of doing deadly harm. When he climbed onto Moonbeam a third time, Abigail was certain her heart would not take the strain.

Moonbeam hesitated, glanced at the rider a moment before ridding himself of his burden.

Legs and arms flapped. Jeremiah's backside landed hard. He cussed and scrambled from the stall, a limp evident in his gait.

"Like it or not, I'm going to ride you. So get used to the idea."

And though Abigail didn't see how he'd ever manage to ride Moonbeam, she had faith he would somehow succeed.

She watched Jeremiah hobble several steps and set the lantern on a shelf. The golden flickering light emphasized the strong planes of his face, hiking her body temperature several degrees. My, he was a handsome devil. She could make out his mustache, or maybe she couldn't, but she didn't need to see it to remember how it had felt against her mouth.

He turned and glanced around before yanking the cabinet door open and reached way inside, pulling out a tin of something she couldn't see from beneath the wagon. She craned her neck to get a better look but still couldn't make out the label. Again, Jeremiah glanced behind him, reminding Abigail of a bandit about to rob a bank.

He removed the cap on the metal tin, turned around, and scanned the inside of the barn one more time. Her curiosity was at an all-time high. When he unbuckled his belt, Abigail grew dizzy. When he unbuttoned his fly, her breath lodged in her throat. When he dropped his pants in plain view of her, she felt like fainting, only she wasn't the fainting kind. Besides, she didn't want to miss anything. Ashamed at her outrageous behavior but too weak to turn away, she studied the bulge in his drawers. She was wicked to the core, a core that was fast becoming a ball of fire.

She was barely aware of his hands dabbing a liquid over his muscled thighs until a familiar smell radiated toward her nostrils.

Sloan's liniment.

Why, that low-down sneak. Nothing she'd have loved more than to jump up and let him know the jig was up. But she couldn't. She clamped her lips together and vowed never to say a word. Jeremiah would never be any the wiser.

Abigail thought she heard soft scratching nearby. Calm down, she told herself, closing her eyes and praying she could ignore the fear welling inside. No matter what, she mustn't move a hair. Her heart stilled. She listened intently. Abigail feared very little. She'd looked danger in the eye, had stood toe to toe with large men, shot coyotes and bears, but she could not tolerate mice. She'd rather arm-wrestle a grizzly than have one tiny mouse cross her path. When the little critter scurried over her extended legs, she reacted on impulse. Her scream was long and shrill. She leaped from her hiding place and hopped onto the wagon.

"What in the hell are you doing there?" Jeremiah shouted as he bent to yank his pants up, tipping over the odorous can of liniment, cussing and shaking his head in disbelief. "Sneaky female is what you are. Can't a man have a little time to himself without everyone knowing his business?"

She couldn't speak, and when she glanced down she saw her fingers were still wrapped around her package.

"You could have given me a heart attack. What's all the fuss about?"

"A mouse." She hated that her voice trembled. Even now, her hands shook so much she could hear the crinkle of the paper wrapping on her parcel.

"You telling me all that noise was for one small, harmless mouse?" A corner of his mouth rose. "Tough Abigail Wilcox, scared of a mouse? Well, I'll be damned." She didn't like the way he laughed, or the way he shook his head from side to side. She especially didn't like the way he stood there looking so dog-goned handsome with her thoughts still stuck on the image of his pants down around his ankles. She was thankful for the dim light that hid her crimson cheeks.

"You needn't stand there laughing at me. I saw the Sloan's you splashed all over your legs. You're a sneaky son of a gun."

He laughed deep and long. "I can't argue with you about that." He walked over to where she stood all tense and rigid, still on the alert for the mouse that had run over her. "Are you going to stay up there all night?"

"Of course not," she answered, taking one more look around.

"What's that?" He nodded toward her package.

"Oh, this?" Her voice came out an octave too high. "Supplies that I picked up at Bufford's today."

"What's wrong with your voice?"

"Absolutely nothing."

"You sound guilty as hell."

"Sounds about right coming from a man who just got caught with his pants down."

"You have a point." He hesitated a moment, his face turned toward hers. She couldn't see his eyes, but she could feel their intensity directed at her. She could smell the liniment on him, could feel his presence and the overwhelming magnetism drawing them together.

He cleared his throat, ran his fingers through his hair. "Well, are you coming down or not?" He extended his hand for her to grasp.

Like a ninny, Abigail stared at the dark outline of his fingers. She didn't trust herself to touch him but wanted to so much she ached. The decision was made for her when he grabbed her hand and gave an encouraging tug. "I have my guns with me so I'll protect you if the mouse comes back, though I suspect after the way you screamed, it's halfway to Boston by now." The humor in his tone vanished, replaced with a deep timbre that radiated desire.

When she hopped down, he didn't release her hand, but instead tightened his hold. Once he let go, he'd never touch her again, and for that reason, Abigail tried to memorize the texture of each finger. Staring into the darkness, her pulse drumming in her ears, she was tempted to stand on tiptoes and press her mouth to his. She wanted to part her lips and feel the flames in the pit of her stomach, but Jeremiah wasn't hers.

And he never would be.

But one kiss, would one kiss be so bad?

Abigail dropped his hand as if burnt by a cast iron pan on a hot stove. She'd reached an all-time low. Until now, she'd had morals. She wasn't the sort to cavort behind another woman's back and try to steal her man.

Hot tears fell, but she didn't bother to brush them away. "I have to go," she whispered and ran from the barn.

Once Abigail's hands stopped trembling, she pulled back the wrapping and glanced down at a tin of mustard powder and bottles of lemon juice and oil of almonds. One round lemon rolled across her quilt.

Though she'd never given her freckles much thought until recently, now that she'd made up her mind to erase them, she couldn't wait to begin.

Abigail cut the fresh lemon into thin slices. She didn't know how much of each ingredient to mix together but figured the stronger the solution, the more immediate the results. With that theory in mind, she emptied everything in a bowl, and after mixing, she applied a thin coat over her face. As excited as she was, she woke up several times during the night, on each occasion dabbing a generous amount of the magic formula over her cheeks and nose. Between applications, she laid slices of lemon on her face. She ignored the slight burning sensation, proof that the concoction was working.

When dawn arrived, Abigail was tired, but she could hardly wait to look at herself in the mirror. She was certain her freckles had disappeared. Her skin felt different. It was tight and burned like the dickens. She leaped from her bed and rushed to the mirror, where in the dim light she could barely see her reflection. With anxious hands, she struck a match and lit the lantern. After turning up the wick, she stared in disbelief at her image: face beet-red, swollen eyelids, and chapped lips. It hurt to move, she discovered when she angled her head closer to the looking-glass, certain she'd been mistaken, horrified that she wasn't.

To make matters worse, the solution had dripped down her neck. Her face was completely scarlet, which was an improvement over the crimson crooked lines zigzagging across the area between her chin and her collarbone.

Tears surfaced. When Abigail tried to brush them away, her gentle touch scorched her cheeks. Flames licked each pore. She fanned her face with her hand, getting no relief from the growing heat.

★ ★ ★ ★ ★

When Jeremiah sat opposite Evelyn at the breakfast table the next morning, he avoided looking at her, fearing she'd see the guilt in his eyes. All night he'd dreamed of Abigail. He'd kissed her mouth and had worked his way down to her knees and back up again. Several times. He couldn't be blamed for his dreams, but he'd enjoyed himself way too much.

"Are you feeling all right, Jeremiah?"

He was forced to face Evelyn, who didn't suspect how he felt about Abigail. How did he feel? He wasn't certain, and it didn't matter anyway. He'd leave and build a life with Evelyn. He wasn't like his parents, who'd allowed their strong attraction to overrule their good judgment. They had later paid the price and so had he. Jeremiah had made a commitment, and he would not go back on his promise.

"I'm feeling fine, why do you ask?"

"You seemed so far away."

He smiled and kissed her cheek. "Did you have a good time in town yesterday?"

Her eyes lit with excitement. "As a matter of fact, I did. And I saw a poster for an upcoming dance. I was hoping we could go."

"It sounds fine to me."

Whip scraped his chair back and turned toward Evelyn. "The hoedown will be at Buck Ridley's Livery. He has a big to-do several times a year. Everyone from miles around will be there."

Evelyn laced her fingers together. "It sounds like fun."

Jeremiah noticed Whip had cleaned up his act. His mangy mustache, which until now had hung from his face, reminding Jeremiah of a tired walrus, was trimmed to just above his upper lip. His hair was slicked back and parted down the middle. His gray eyes focused on Evelyn as if she were the main breakfast entree. Upon closer inspection, Jeremiah noticed Whip's shirt looked new and had enough starch in the collar to chafe the man's neck, which Jeremiah felt like wringing.

Jeremiah reached for Evelyn's hand and glared at Whip, making it clear he was to keep his distance.

The fool stretched and leaned his right leg against Evelyn's skirts. If Clarissa hadn't shown up just then, Jeremiah might have ripped the starched collar off Whip's new shirt. Deep inside Jeremiah realized he was playing a part. Whip's behavior didn't bother him as much as it should have.

"Maw says to eat without her. She's sicker than a dog that's been drug behind a wagon for a mile."

Jeremiah was concerned. "Maybe I should check on her."

"Maw says the first person to stick their nose in her room will have it shot off. She's in a right mean mood. I wouldn't go in there if I were you."

Even during good times, Abigail could be ornery. Jeremiah hated to imagine what she must be like now. Still, he couldn't just leave her in there with nothing to eat or drink.

He glanced at Evelyn. "Maybe it's woman problems. Why don't you go check up on her?"

Evelyn stared at him with an incredulous look.

Since she didn't say a word, he figured he'd elaborate. "Maybe it's the monthly curse."

You'd have thought by the expression that sprung onto Evelyn's face, he'd whispered dirty words in her ears, which was something he liked to do during lovemaking. He doubted Evelyn would ever stand for that.

"Jeremiah," came the righteous voice as she fanned herself with her napkin. "You know better than to talk thusly in mixed company." She paused and gave him an encouraging nod. "Maybe you should check on Abigail, see if she would like me to bring her in some tea. I don't think she wants me in there. If

Abigail tells you she needs my help, I'll gladly see what I can do."

Jeremiah slid his chair back and strolled down the hall. He knocked on Abigail's door and waited for a response. Not getting one, he slid the door open and stepped inside. "Abby."

The room was dark like a tomb, and the voice that answered from the vicinity of the bed sounded strong instead of deathly ill. "So help me, if you don't get the hell out of here, I swear I'll skin you alive and stretch your mangy hide on the barn door as warning for others to leave me alone."

He held in his laugh. "If you're strong enough to swear, you can't be that bad off."

He took several steps, giving his eyes time to adjust. She'd drawn the heavy shades and he could barely make out her small frame beneath the quilt. He was surprised when she wrenched her hat from her bedside table and plopped it over her head. "I got a bad case of the grippe. You better stay away."

"This came on suddenly. You looked fine last night."

"Is there something wrong with that?"

"Would you like me to bring you something to eat?"

"No."

"Drink?"

"No."

"Anything at all?"

"Confounded man, can't you tell I want to be alone?"

"You don't sound sick to me. Let me have a look at you to ease my mind."

"I've got fever and red blotches covering my person."

He tiptoed next to the bed, lowered his head, and caught a lemony scent. The slight part in the heavy shade allowed one narrow sliver of light to penetrate the gloomy interior. Her hat was inclined over her forehead, meeting the blankets pulled over her nose. Part of one cantankerous eye peeked up at him, looking none too pleased to see him.

"How long are you going to stay in here?"

"Till the fever goes down."

"Let me check your brow in case you're burning up." When he started to lift her hat, she slapped his hands away.

"I'll be fine."

"If there's something wrong, I want to know. I'm worried about you. You don't sound like a sick person. Your voice is much too strong."

"Did you get your medical degree at Bufford's the last time you fed your sweet tooth?"

He laughed. "See what I mean? Your mind's sharp. You aren't any sicker than I am. Unless . . ." He hated to pursue the subject but decided he didn't have a choice. "Is this dealing with . . ." The question lodged in the back of his throat. He took a breath and pushed ahead. "With your time of the month?"

The next thing he knew he was dodging a boot aimed at his head, which he took as a yes to his question. He escaped into the hall and shut the door, then heard a hollow thud on the other side of the wooden surface. He hated to send delicate, unsuspecting Evelyn into that bear's den, but he couldn't come up with a better solution. Abigail needed help, and he wasn't the one to give it.

CHAPTER 20

Abigail was so hungry she could have bitten off a steer's leg and eaten it raw. Well, not quite that famished, but close to it. She'd had little for supper last night because of her excitement over the freckle remedy, so her stomach growled in protest as she lay in bed, pretending to be sick, which was easy with her stomach churning and her head spinning each time she remembered her reddened face.

What if her skin stayed like this? For the rest of her life, she'd have to wear a neckerchief over her nose and go out only at night. There was no way she'd allow another living soul to get a glimpse of her.

And especially not Evelyn DuBlois!

Abigail had never considered herself vain, and she'd never cared diddly whether her hair was messy beneath her hat or whether her face was smudged with dirt. But vanity might be playing a strong role in her seclusion.

Mired deep in self-pity, she heard a light tap on the door, and before she could discourage the intruder from trespassing, the door opened and shut again.

"Abigail, I've brought in a cup of sweetened tea and a piece of buttered toast with a little jam. I've removed the crust from the bread and cut it into small triangles because that always comforts me when I'm feeling poorly."

At the sound of food, Abigail's mouth watered.

"I thought I'd stay and converse with you awhile."

Had Abigail's voice not lodged in her throat, she might have cussed the woman away, but not one sound rose. Panicked, she looked for an escape and decided to rely on fear—not hers, but Evelyn's.

"I've red bumps all over my person. You'd better run before you catch this. Just leave the tea and toast on the bureau and skedaddle before we're both quarantined." Not wanting to repeat the same mistake she'd made with Jeremiah, Abigail made sure her voice was feeble and scratchy.

There was a long pause. "You poor thing, I must admit I feel bloated sometimes, but I've never had red bumps. Let me take a look." Evelyn strolled toward the bed. Before Abigail could snatch her hat, Evelyn had tossed it across the room and set down the tray in its place.

Abigail ran shaky fingers through her hair, pulling thick strands over her forehead and eyes. "You'll be sorry if you come down with what I have."

"I wouldn't be able to live with myself if I abandoned you in your time of need."

"At a time like this, you should look out for yourself." Abigail breathed a sigh of relief at the sound of retreating footsteps, but instead of charging for the door as anticipated, Evelyn flung open the heavy drapes and flooded the room with light.

Abigail dove under the blankets.

"Sunshine is the best medicine there is. I'm sure of it."

"The light hurts my eyes," came Abigail's muffled reply from beneath the covers.

"You mustn't look at what you have as an illness. There's a new book I've read lately that says women need to stop considering that time of the month an illness and a curse."

Abigail didn't pay much attention to Evelyn's prattle. She had problems of her own. How would she persuade the wretched woman to leave?

"It's mind over matter. There's even a chapter about birthing. Do you realize that with the proper mindset, childbirth needn't hurt?"

Abigail did not say one word at that lunatic comment but instead clasped both hands tightly on the quilt over her head.

"I won't go until you give my theory a chance. It's been proven that sunlight will do wonders for swaying moods. Your mind is stuck in the doldrums. There are times each month when I could weep and hide out in my room as you're trying to do now. We women have to stick together. I'm certain I've found the answer to our female problems. Get out of that bed, sit in the sun for a half-hour, and you'll be amazed how much better you'll feel."

"You don't understand." This time Abigail didn't fake the wobble in her voice. Not knowing what to expect from the stubborn woman, she clenched the blankets tighter.

"I won't abandon you."

"All right, you win. I'll sit in the cussed sun, but not until you go. If you leave me alone, I promise to eat the toast, drink every drop of tea, and sit with my face turned toward the sky."

"I don't believe you. You've sunk too low to do this on your own."

And while Abigail clung to the blankets over her head for dear life, Evelyn undid the covers at the foot of the bed and flung them up and over Abigail, who was too startled to scream. Instead, she stared into Evelyn's pale, anxious face.

"Ohmygoodness!"

That one word confirmed to Abigail her complexion had not improved one iota.

Evelyn collapsed onto the nearby chair, eyed Abigail warily, and waving her lace handkerchief in front of her, proclaimed, "We're all going to die!"

Abigail leaped from the bed and stalked toward the woman

who'd not taken no for an answer. "What say we both gawk at the sun awhile. That should do a lot of good, don't you think?"

Evelyn shook her head and mumbled, "Ohmygoodness."

There was nothing Abigail would have liked better than to frighten the woman out of her shoes, but she figured she'd rather eat first. Turning, she took a few steps and grabbed a dainty triangle of toasted bread. "It's too bad you cut off the crust. I'm starving." She ate another piece and drank several swallows of tea before facing Evelyn again. "You needn't sit there acting like I have the plague. Don't worry, this isn't catchy."

"Are you certain?"

"I'm suffering from a severe case of stupidity."

"Do your cheeks hurt?"

"What do you think?"

"It reminds me of a bad sunburn. How did your face get that way?"

"I used a concoction to banish my freckles. I mixed it too strong, and I may have overdone the application a bit."

"Why'd you do that?"

"Right now, I can't think of one single reason." Abigail wiggled her nose. "Ouch." She fanned her face with the napkin on the tray.

"I've got just the thing for you." Evelyn hurried from the room and returned a few minutes later with a can of Camphor Cold Cream.

"Lie down, Abigail, and let me gently dab this salve over your face. You'll be looking good as new in no time."

"You really think so?"

"There's nothing better on the market. It's good for sunburn, pimples, and cracked and chafed skin."

"I only wish this was nothing more than a pimple."

Evelyn laughed, her light tone ringing throughout the room

like musical chimes. When Abigail joined in, she compared the sound she made to a braying donkey.

Abigail hated to bring up the subject, but if she didn't, she'd lose another night's sleep. "Are you going to tell anybody about this?"

Evelyn looked offended. "It hurts me that you need to ask. Your secret is safe with me. We women stick together."

Abigail could tell Evelyn was sincere, and it took a great weight off her chest to hear her reassuring words. As Evelyn applied the soothing salve to Abigail's face, Abigail closed her eyes. "That feels better already."

Through squinted lids she watched Evelyn take a close look at her nose and cheeks. "You know, I do believe you have fewer freckles."

"Really?"

"Definitely."

Abigail knew she was being kind. She finally admitted Evelyn was a nice lady. Try as she might, Abigail didn't hate her any more. Not even a little.

For two days Jeremiah kept his distance from the house, and except for sleeping in his bed at night, he did everything else as far from Abigail as he could. Unfortunately, he felt guilty as hell for ignoring Evelyn. He knew he wasn't being fair to his fiancée, but he felt better distancing himself from the red-haired beauty who lived and breathed in his dreams. *And daydreams.* Jeremiah feared he had fallen in love.

With the wrong woman!

This unexpected circumstance was a mystery, but it was not one he had any intention of solving. If he stayed away from Abby for a few days he'd be able to clear his mind, then focus all his attention on Evelyn. Whenever his thoughts strayed, he remembered the way Whip looked at Evelyn, or the way most men's eyes glazed over with jealousy when they'd spot Evelyn, her arm draped through his. Jeremiah was indeed a very lucky man.

For the evening meal, he ate at the Rattler Saloon in Lowdown where smoke hung heavy in the air, raucous laughter roared, and the beer and whiskey flowed like water from a swollen creek. If Jeremiah had been a drinking man, he'd have been in his element, but except for an occasional shot of whiskey at weddings and funerals, he pretty much stayed away from the stuff.

He'd just finished a plate of corned beef hash when Whip pushed through the swinging batwing doors and greeted the men at the bar. "Hey, Gus, Gordy, Tom, how's it going?"

Whip spotted Jeremiah and swaggered toward the table where he sat. "What are you doing here while that lit' gal is waiting at the ranch?"

"I had some things to pick up in town. It got late, so I decided to grab a bite here."

"If I were you, I'd be at Miss Evelyn's side every chance I got. You should have your head examined."

"And you should keep your opinions to yourself and your eyes off my woman." Jeremiah glared at Whip, hoping he'd take the hint and leave.

Instead, he yanked a chair back, turned it around, and straddled it, leaning forward on his elbows and directing his gaze toward Jeremiah. "You don't deserve the lady. You take her for granted."

"Lay off. This is no concern of yours."

"I'm making it mine."

"Look, why don't you let me buy you a beer and we'll let bygones be bygones."

"I have a better idea, why don't you meet me outside and allow me to rearrange your face."

"Back in Boston we don't settle our differences of opinion with our fists."

"You're in Texas now."

"What are we fighting about?"

"I hate your guts, that'll have to be enough."

"You hated me when I first arrived."

Whip's mustache twitched. His steely eyes narrowed. "You're wrong, I hated you long before you ever set foot on the ranch."

"Why would that be?"

"I have my reasons."

When they strolled outside, not a soul suspected they were anything but friends. When the first fist flew, no one heard the bone-jarring impact, but when the two men reentered the Rattle Snake twenty minutes later, every head in the joint turned to stare at their disheveled appearance: reddened eyes that would blacken by morning, bloodied lips, ripped clothing, and bruised knuckles. If someone had won the fight, it wasn't instantly apparent.

Whip threw back his head and laughed at the startled glances aimed toward them. As he clapped a hand over Jeremiah's shoulder, Jeremiah noticed the animosity between them had vanished.

"In case anyone's wondering, I was fixin' to teach this Bostonian a thing or two, but the fight was a draw. It wasn't until his fist connected with my jaw that I realized I'd forgotten one very important fact."

"What's that?" someone shouted from the bar.

"He was born in Texas. He's one of us."

Laughter erupted around Jeremiah as Whip steered him to the bar and bought him a double, which Jeremiah tossed back without a blink. It was damn fine whiskey, and he figured Whip was being a good sport. Jeremiah reciprocated by buying a round for everyone. After that, it wasn't clear who did the buying or how many times the glasses were filled, except to say the bartender had his work cut out for him.

Much later that night as another swallow of hard liquor trailed a heated path down Jeremiah's throat, he felt camaraderie with the men around him.

Even Whip seemed more friend than foe.

The next morning Jeremiah awoke, turned his head to one side, and instantly realized something was terribly wrong. It hurt to move. It hurt to blink. It even hurt to breathe. Hay cradled his head, and the stench of fresh manure rose to his nostrils. If he didn't know better, he'd swear he'd spent the night in the barn. It wasn't until he inched an eyelid open, light instantly spearing his brain, that he saw the fuzzy boards of a stall above his head. For the life of him, he couldn't figure what he was doing here or how his tongue had sprouted a thick layer of grass overnight. A freight train roared through his head, and the slightest movement jarred the metal wheels, the ensuing screech shredding his fragile eardrums.

As he lay there, he noticed subtle differences. His right eye didn't open as wide as it once did. His upper lip felt thick. Even the light breeze coming though the open barn door, stirring his hair, made every follicle throb. He was in sad shape.

In the recesses of his mind, he faintly remembered laughter, lots of laughter, and possibly tipping a glass a few times too many.

When he managed to sit up, the interior of the building spun; his stomach lurched. He had the good sense to clamp his eyelids shut. He took a breath. Though the oxygen helped to revive him, the sharp jab to his ribs cut the breath short.

He leaned forward and supported his head in hands propped on bent knees. As his face dug into his palms, images of the previous night flicked through his mind like a sharp blade, jabbing, jabbing, jabbing unmercifully.

He was aware of dried blood on his right cheek. The corner of his mouth was split, the flesh around his right eye tender and swollen. He wasn't the sort to brawl, yet he could almost remember accepting the challenge. In his wretched state, a foggy image materialized, he and Whip with arms entwined, leading the gang at the Rattle Snake in a rowdy chorus fit for male ears alone. Was this a nightmare? Would he wake up any second and laugh at the absurdity?

He sat there for a moment, hardly daring to move, torn between wishing he'd died instantly and pondering the merits of surviving the day when a harsh sound pierced his brain.

"Jeremiah, where have you been? I've looked all over the place for you. Last night when you didn't come home, I was certain you'd been eaten by some wild beast or killed by outlaws."

He couldn't find the strength to answer.

Between the slits of his narrowed eyelids, he made out a blurry image of Evelyn, her hands over her hips. "And there you sit resting while I'm worrying myself half to death. Well, what do you have to say for yourself?"

Jeremiah heaved a slow sigh, prayed the pounding in his head would ease, and with as much strength as he could muster, glanced up at Evelyn, whose image wavered before his eyes.

"Ohmygoodness, you barely escaped with your life." She was by his side in an instant. Her gentle touch did make him feel somewhat better until she ran her fingers along his ribcage and awakened a particularly sensitive spot.

Jeremiah winced.

She studied the hay by his side before kneeling next to him. "You poor dear, when I first arrived in Texas and saw the uncouth hooligans around here, I knew you didn't belong."

He offered a weak smile to let her know he appreciated her support.

"Someone should summon the sheriff. You poor dear, do you know who's responsible?"

The thought of blaming Whip struck him as hilarious, maybe a residual effect of the alcohol he'd consumed. "Whip," he mumbled through swollen lips.

"Alfonso, did this to you? Lordy, your right eye is black."

He nodded.

"When I get my hands on him, I'm going to let him know just what I think of his savage ways. Doesn't the man have one bit of civility in his body?"

"I doubt it." Though it hurt like the devil, Jeremiah smiled.

"The man's a barbarian. He belongs in jail."

Her outrage made Jeremiah feel better.

"It's a good thing Daddy can't see you now or he'd give you the speech we've both heard many times. 'A banker has an image to uphold. You can't expect people to trust you with their earnings if you run around looking like a beggar and a drunk.' I realize you aren't at fault, but Daddy has his standards. But I'll not whisper a word of this."

Jeremiah straightened and leaned against the boards behind him, stretching out his legs. He heaved a disgruntled sigh and wondered if he had the courage to broach the subject or whether he should wait until he was stronger.

"You look so dapper with your derby and suit. You're the handsomest gentleman in the bank." She eyed him seriously a moment. "Though I suspect you'll have to buy new clothing when you return because your shoulders have widened with all the menial tasks you perform."

"I enjoy working outdoors."

"Yes, but it'll be wonderful to be able to hug you again without pinching my nostrils shut." She looked at him suspiciously. "Do I detect alcoholic spirits on your breath?"

"I may have had a drink or two."

She gasped. "You smell no better than a saloon."

"You exaggerate."

"I'll admit I sometimes do, but not this time." She studied his attire. "You know how I feel about fighting. I cannot think of one single excuse for a man to use his fists. Not while he has a perfectly good brain to solve his problems."

Jeremiah gave a feeble nod. He'd heard all this before. Until yesterday, he'd lived by that code of ethics.

"What's come over you? You've changed. Look at the way you dress." She reached down and ran a tentative finger over his rawhide vest that was none too clean. A shudder racked her body. "What happened to the silk vest I bought you, the maroon-checked one with the tiny gold triangles you said was your favorite?"

It was also Buck Ridley's favorite. Jeremiah had traded it for six horseback riding lessons. "I've looked around, but it's not in my room," he said with an innocent grin.

"Have you also lost track of your Derby?"

"I'm afraid so."

"That's too bad, but we'll get you another as soon as we get back to Boston."

He took her hand. "I've been meaning to discuss something with you."

"If you're concerned about our forthcoming nuptials, Daddy's planning a grand affair. Everything should be ready when we return. All I need to do is wire our arrival date and he'll take care of the rest."

Jeremiah took a shaky breath. "This has nothing to do with that."

Her lower lip jutted out and wobbled. "Oh."

"No, it's about the job at the bank." Suddenly, he wished

he'd waited until he was in better shape to argue his point.

A small tremor shook her body. "What about the bank?"

He took a reinforcing breath. "When we go back to Boston, I've decided to work on the docks. I'm not going back to the bank."

Her hands flew to her mouth. "Has the Texas sun fried your brain?"

She leaped to her feet and turned, her skirts swirling around her ankles. When she stomped from the barn, he wondered how long she'd remain angry.

Then he heard her say, "Alfonso, you look as bad as Jeremiah does. It serves you right for picking a fight."

"Jeremiah and I settled our differences last night. But don't look at me like that, ma'am, I didn't throw the first punch."

"Are you telling me that Jeremiah struck the first blow?"

From inside the barn a satisfied grin stretched across Jeremiah's face as he remembered the shock that had registered on Whip's face when he'd knocked him on his ass.

"Yes, ma'am, but it was a good match, and we had ourselves a high old time afterwards. Did you know Jeremiah can balance a tumbler of beer on his head while singing a tune and clapping his hands? It's a sight I'll never forget."

Evelyn voice rose in disgust. "The very image causes my heart to palpitate."

Whip laughed. "You really should have seen him."

Evelyn huffed. "If I had been there, I'd have blackened that scallywag's other eye."

CHAPTER 21

Two days before the dance, Abigail still had nothing appropriate to wear. It didn't matter because she had no intention of going. Not only would she look like a frumpy old lady next to Evelyn, Abigail would die if she had to watch Jeremiah dance with the woman he intended to marry. Over the years, Abigail had shielded herself with a couldn't-care-less look that had fooled many. But she could not pull this off; no one would miss the love in her eyes if they caught her glancing at Jeremiah.

With all the feelings tearing her apart, she couldn't bring herself to dislike Evelyn. The woman was generous and kind. She'd helped Abigail in her time of need. The cream she provided did wonders for Abigail's complexion and quickly diminished the redness. Within two days not a trace of the irritation remained, though unfortunately, she couldn't say the same for her freckles.

It galled her; though Abigail had tried hard to find fault, she could not find one thing wrong with Evelyn. She was not only beautiful, but she had a heart of pure gold—a fact everyone around kept voicing whenever Abigail bothered to listen.

Pedro, who never allowed another soul in his kitchen, had made an exception and still praised Evelyn's braided bread. Blue had risen from his deathbed and crossed the room on crutches, all because Evelyn thought it would do him good to sit outside in the sun. Blue's recovery started that day, and he'd improved greatly since. She'd befriended Adele Diaz, who seemed better able to cope with Noah's death because of their alliance. Evelyn could be bossy, but in a nice way. She wouldn't take no for an answer, and those around had benefited from her stubbornness.

And then there was Whip, hair slicked back, spiffed up in another clean shirt each time Abigail turned around, looking like he was going to church instead of herding longhorns. He'd gotten into the habit of wearing a string tie even while he worked. Abigail would have choked some sense into him with that tie if she'd thought it would have done any good.

Whip was in worse shape than she. At least Abigail had accepted her fate. Darn fool didn't stand a chance with Evelyn. Whip didn't seem to know it. Or care.

Abigail popped a lemon drop in her mouth and closed her eyes, enjoying the taste and smooth texture against her tongue.

A light knock on the door broke into her reverie. "Maw, can I come in? I have a surprise to show you."

"Sure thing."

The child who entered was barely recognizable. Her hair piled on her head, adding four inches to her height, was swept up off her face and braided in a style emphasizing that Clarissa was indeed a very pretty young lady. Colorful ribbons were woven among the thick strands of her daughter's mahogany hair. The dress Abigail had chosen had been gussied up with delicate embroidery around the neck and sleeves. When Clarissa twirled around, Abigail noticed the jeweled comb along one side of her daughter's head. Abigail's thoughts turned melancholy; tears built behind her eyes when she realized Clarissa would leave her some day to go to school. Though it was the proper thing to do, a great ache tugged at Abigail's heartstrings.

"What do you think, Maw?"

"You're a sight for sore eyes, that's for sure. Where are you going all decked out like that?"

"To Buck Ridley's shindig."

"Land sakes, that's still two days away. Why are you dressed like that now?"

"I'm practicing walking. Evelyn says I should glide when I'm wearing a dress, not clomp around like I've got heavy boots on my feet."

"Are you gliding yet?"

"Watch, and you tell me." Clarissa took several delicate steps across the room before forgetting herself and running back at breakneck speed, skidding the last few feet.

"You may need to work on it a little more, but I think you're real close to being the best glider around." Abigail took a moment to admire her daughter. The child was gorgeous. "I haven't decided whether we're going to the dance."

"Aw, Maw, everyone's gonna be there. I hear there'll be games and all kinds of food. We are going, aren't we?"

Abigail saw the excitement in Clarissa's eyes and didn't have the heart to refuse. She deserved to be among children her own age. Although Abigail would dread going to Buck's get-together, she'd do it for Clarissa. Maybe Abigail could help with the children's games and ignore the goings-on at the dance. With her heart overflowing, Abigail nodded. "I guess we could go for a little while."

Clarissa sniffed. "What's that you're eating?"

Abigail smiled down at her generous daughter. "The lemon drop you left on my pillow last night."

Clarissa's eyebrows rose. "I don't know where you got that notion. I ain't . . . I mean I don't have any candy."

"You didn't put a lemon drop on my bed?"

Clarissa shook her head.

"Have you ever?"

Again, a definite shake of her head.

Abigail's heart fluttered like a trapped bird beneath her

breastbone. If Clarissa hadn't left the candy, then who had? Only one person came to mind. Jeremiah. He'd sashayed into her bedroom as if he had a right.

Torn between outrage and pure joy, Abigail considered the situation. He'd stood next to her bed, his fingers brushing her pillow as he laid the candy for her to find. The thought brought a flush to her cheeks. How dare he invade her room like a thief in the night? But instead of wringing his neck, Abigail wanted to wrap her arms around it and draw him close. Jeremiah might not love her, but he did care. She'd have to content herself with that.

"What are you gonna wear, Maw?"

Abigail glanced down at her loose-fitting britches. "I expect you're looking at it."

Disbelief streaked across Clarissa's face. "You joshing me?"

The time when Clarissa would be ashamed to be seen with her mother was fast approaching. Abigail glanced at her daughter's innocent face and forced a smile. Great trepidation took hold when she pictured herself standing beside Evelyn, Jeremiah and others making the comparison. "I could probably get myself a dress at Bufford's."

It would take more than a dress to transform Abigail Wilcox into a lady. Though she got along with most of the townsfolk, there were several busybodies who'd forever look down their noses because of what Abigail was—a loose unmarried woman with a bastard child. Abigail kissed her daughter's upturned cheek and prayed Clarissa would never have to pay for her mother's sins.

To see all the goings-on at the ranch for one of Buck Ridley's shindigs, you'd have thought everyone had taken leave of their senses. At least, Abigail thought so.

Adele was in a dither trying to select the right dress. Whip bought another shirt—God forbid Evelyn should see him in one he'd worn once before. All spruced up, Blue planned to sit and watch the activities from the sidelines. Mort even took a bath for the event.

After hours of gliding under Evelyn's watchful eye, Clarissa was rewarded with an approving nod. To Abigail's way of thinking, if God had meant people to glide, he'd have given them wings like the eagles that soared overhead. Feet were meant for walking, stomping, clomping, and pounding. Yet, at night when no one could see her, Abigail practiced taking dainty steps across her bedroom floor. As she slid one foot in front of the other with her shoulders back and chin up, she almost felt as if she were strolling real lady-like, which had to be darn close to gliding. What difference did it matter anyway? The one man she wanted to impress would be busy admiring another woman. At that thought, Abigail dropped onto her bed. A lemon drop rolled alongside of her, making her smile despite her low spirits.

Although the dance didn't matter diddly, Abigail still took a long bath, pampering herself with her favorite rose-scented soap. After toweling herself dry, she stood in a lace camisole in front of her bedroom mirror as she fastened her hair on top of her head with a velvet green ribbon that allowed her fiery curls to cascade mid-back. Abigail deliberately pulled tiny ringlets along the sides of her face and pinched some color into her cheeks. She slipped on a simple emerald green cotton dress that had puffy sleeves and a lace-edged collar. Around her neck hung the cameo her mother had given her the day she'd left home. Abigail ran her hand over the pendant and glanced in the mirror. She looked fair to middling.

When it came time for everyone to leave, there was a big hullabaloo and when Abigail finally entered the parlor, everyone was scurrying like rodents being pursued by a pitchfork. Voices rang. Footsteps echoed.

As she looked around her in disbelief, she found herself standing in front of Jeremiah, his eyes widening at the sight of her. Abigail grew lightheaded as anxiety dashed up her spine. How would she survive the night?

"You look beautiful," he said, and she stored the compliment inside her heart and looked into pewter eyes capable of igniting a woman's clothing.

Abigail swallowed and stared at him like a ninny. "You don't look bad yourself," she said, forcing the words over a thick throat, thinking he had to be the handsomest man alive.

He'd chosen black trousers, a white shirt, and a belt she'd never seen until now, its thick metal buckle engraved with a wild stallion. It pleased her to see him wearing the leather vest she'd bought. On his head cocked to one side was a black Stetson, which shaded his face and emphasized his kissable mouth and the trim mustache that would never again . . .

She had to get hold of herself.

Lost in his gaze, she looked up helplessly, so in love that she ached inside from the impossibility of it all. The air crackled between them, and Abigail knew if she didn't say something, she'd go up in smoke. "I like your belt buckle."

He didn't break eye contact. "Thanks, I bought it the last time I was at Bufford's. It reminds me of Moonbeam."

"Oh."

"Pretty dress." His gaze meandered down the length of her and back up again, settled on her small breasts where it lingered a fraction of a second before making eye contact.

Every touch and every kiss they'd shared haunted Abigail at that moment. He wanted her. She saw it on his face. The heat of him enveloped her like a warm blanket. With every fiber of her being, she wanted to reach up and run but one finger along his mouth. Just one finger, one touch, but she didn't dare. She clenched her fingers over handfuls of the cotton fabric by her sides for fear she'd be tempted to act on her impulses. And when she was certain she would die from the strain of seeing the desire in his eyes, her own need evident on her face, Evelyn arrived.

Jeremiah swung his gaze toward the woman of his dreams. Abigail couldn't see his expression, and she was glad not to witness the adoration in his eyes.

Evelyn was breathtakingly beautiful.

Jeremiah already belonged to someone, and if Abigail had forgotten that fact for a moment, she was reminded of it now. Evelyn's cobalt satin dress with a scalloped neckline and wide sleeves was the prettiest thing Abigail had ever seen. It was too fancy for one of Buck's shindigs, but the men wouldn't complain. Around her neck were strands of pearls. The hair woven around her head emphasized a long graceful neck and tiny shell ears adorned with pearl earrings. Perched atop her head was a matching satin hat with a long white plume, sticking out a good six inches from the back. A delicate veil covering her deep chocolate eyes added an air of mystery to the raving beauty.

Abigail wished she'd thought to look for a hat at Bufford's, but it was too late to ponder that now.

Evelyn took a step toward Abigail, her feet barely touching the carpet. "Well, Abigail, look at you. That dress does wonderful things for your eyes. You'll have all the single men pursuing you this evening." She elbowed Jeremiah. "Don't you think she's stunning?"

He cleared his throat. "Yes, she is."

There was only one man Abigail wanted, and she was careful not to glance at him. "Thanks, I'd better go find Clarissa," she said, turning and escaping on wobbly legs thankfully hidden beneath her full skirts.

As Jeremiah smiled at Evelyn seated in the buggy by his side, he stole a quick look at Abigail in the wagon behind them. If he hadn't seen it with his own eyes, he wouldn't have believed the transformation. Abigail looked like a different person. When he'd first spied her standing in the parlor, his heart had thumped against his ribs. Lust jolted him. Guilt flooded him when he turned and spotted Evelyn. How long had she been standing there? Had she noticed his fascination with Abigail?

He fastened his gaze on the winding road ahead, and promised that he'd be attentive to the woman by his side. He wound his arm around Evelyn's shoulder, and as she leaned into him, he tried not to compare the heavy scent of her perfume to the light fragrance he'd come to prefer.

As they pulled into Lowdown, the sound of fiddle music radiated from Buck's livery, which was lit with colorful paper lanterns hanging from the low branches of an old oak tree.

He hopped down from the surrey, tied the horse to the hitching post, and hurried to assist Evelyn. As he offered her his hand, he pressed a kiss on the inside of her wrist. "You're the prettiest gal here tonight."

She lighted onto the ground like a fairy princess, her smile incredible. "You're a lucky man, Jeremiah Dalton, and don't you forget it, either."

Jeremiah laughed. "How can I forget with you reminding me?"

She looped her arm under his elbow and as they entered the festive barn, heads turned. Pride washed over Jeremiah at being seen with Evelyn. Disappointment tried to creep in, but he'd have none of it. He was happy. Things were as they should be. He and Evelyn were the same, two peas in a pod. They'd have a wonderful life together. So why did he ache for someone else?

He felt a tug on his arm and looked into Evelyn's bewildered face. "Huh?"

"I said this is so quaint . . . and countrified."

"It is grand."

Numerous paper lanterns hung from the rafters. Vases of flowers sat in the center of each long table. Men and women dressed in their Sunday best clustered in small groups, the sounds of their voices and laughter blending with the fiddles warming up in the background. Jeremiah found a table for them. He was none too pleased to see Whip heading their way.

Whip touched a finger to the brim of his hat. "Evenin', ma'am, I was hoping you'll do me the honor of saving a dance for me."

Evelyn fluttered her floral fan in front of her face, her coy smile disappearing behind the paper arch. "Alfonso, if it's all right with Jeremiah, I'd be delighted."

Jeremiah shrugged. "We'll see."

Whip sauntered past them and sat at the same table, several seats away. Though he didn't outright stare at Evelyn, Jeremiah caught him stealing an occasional glance.

Jeremiah was about to sit down when someone grabbed his shoulder. "Son of a gun, hardly recognized you all duded up like a Texan."

Jeremiah swung around and introduced Buck Ridley to Evelyn. At first he couldn't understand the reason for the shock on Evelyn's face, which she instantly covered with a phony smile, but when he took another look at what Buck was wearing, he understood only too well.

A familiar Derby was angled on top of his head. The maroon silk vest with tiny golden triangles that Evelyn had given Jeremiah for his last birthday hung loosely over the old man's shoulders as he puffed out his chest like a proud peacock.

"You're looking dapper this evening, Mr. Ridley," Evelyn said, widening the old man's grin until it nearly split his face.

"Ma'am, you're a sight for sore eyes, yerself." He tipped his derby, and winked at Jeremiah as if to say their secret was safe with him.

Evelyn speared Jeremiah with a barbed look. "Seems to me, one of us is telling falsehoods to the other."

Jeremiah ran his finger inside his collar. "I know when my goose is cooked. I gave Buck the vest for some riding pointers."

Evelyn looked aghast. "Even the way you speak has changed."

"What are you talking about?"

"Your goose is cooked. Don't you think that sounds like someone who works with animals?"

Jeremiah shrugged. "I do work with animals."

"Yes, but you won't soon. Don't you think you should try to keep your old manner of speech for when you return to Boston and work in Daddy's bank? Sometimes, I wonder if you even want to go back. Sometimes, I even wonder if you still want us to be wed."

The words hung between them like a noose, and Jeremiah knew if he didn't choose his words carefully, he could lose his neck.

"Darling, I'll marry you the instant I step off the train if you'd like. But I told you the other day I'm not going back to the bank. You need to accept my decision. Surely, you remember my telling you."

Her lower lip wobbled, and she tapped at her forehead with a lace hankie she pulled from her pocket. "I heard every drunken word you said, but I never believed a one."

"Evelyn, I wasn't drunk, just hung over."

She raised her eyes heavenward and shook her head. "I couldn't believe that you'd imbibed, much less mean what you told me. What about Daddy? He'll be so disappointed. How shall I ever break the news to him?"

"I can send him a telegram if you'd like. Don't let this spoil our evening."

A pout formed and remained a few minutes. Evelyn's anger burst forth like a New England hurricane, but unlike the powerful storm, she weakened quickly. A few minutes later, her eyes lit, and she whispered, "I've been thinking about our forthcoming nuptials. Maybe we should get married now. Daddy will be angry, but he could give us a reception when we returned."

Now. Why did that word tighten his stomach? "Now? What about our plans? We don't want to disappoint our friends and family."

"Well, I guess not, only I hate waiting. You know how little patience I have, and where you're concerned, I have none."

He kissed her cheek. "We'll make up for lost time when we do get married." His grin made it clear what he had in mind.

The fan rose to conceal pink cheeks, fluttering beneath her deep brown eyes. "You're a hooligan, that's for sure."

Glad the subject was closed, Jeremiah breathed a sigh of relief. "Would you care to dance?"

"I would love to."

Evelyn drifted toward the dance floor, her hand on Jeremiah's arm. When she turned toward him, he reminded himself he was the luckiest man alive. No other compared to Evelyn. He only needed to glance at the other men's admiring glances to prove his point.

Evelyn rested her left hand on his shoulder, but when he tried to pull her against him, she stood her ground. "You know how I feel about carousing on the dance floor. We are human beings, not animals about to . . ." She blushed a deep crimson. "Well you know what I mean."

He knew, all right. Evelyn was prim and proper, a lady to the marrow of her bones. There was no denying that. "Honestly, Evelyn, if you can't allow yourself to speak freely to me now, I don't see how that'll change after we're wed."

She smiled coyly. "We aren't wed yet."

He was grateful for that. When that thought sprung into his head, he knew something was seriously wrong, but he refused to believe it. He and Evelyn were perfect for each other. They liked the same things, had the same friends; they belonged together.

Out of the corner of his eye, he spotted Abigail dancing with Whip, laughing at something he'd said. When Whip tightened his arms around Abigail's tiny waist, jealousy hit Jeremiah over the head. He bit back a curse. Whip was a louse, a philanderer, and a good for nothing. Abigail certainly didn't belong with someone like that. But then Jeremiah couldn't fathom Abigail with any man but himself.

And that was impossible.

Jeremiah intended to ignore Whip and Abigail. He twirled Evelyn around and swayed to the lively beat, making his way to the other side of the dance floor. He felt safer until someone tapped his shoulder.

He swung around and saw Whip's conniving grin aimed at him. "Let's switch partners."

Jeremiah knew by Abigail's startled expression, she wasn't prepared for this any more than he was. To make matters worse, when Jeremiah didn't answer right away, Evelyn took that as a yes, and she was already dancing away with Whip before Jeremiah found his tongue. He couldn't leave Abigail standing there by herself. And he wanted to hold her with a desperation that frightened him.

The song ended, followed by a slow mellow tune. When he opened his arms, Abigail stepped into them, but she kept a proper distance. He wanted to say something but found he couldn't speak. He felt connected to the woman he was holding, the mere touch of her fingers against his sending sparks up his arms. The music enveloped them and to Jeremiah they were the only couple on the dance floor.

223

When he looked at Abigail, he saw she kept her eyes focused downward, so he studied her nose, wanted to trace its freckled tip with his tongue. Her long auburn lashes fanned pale pink cheeks. "You look lovely tonight."

"Thanks." She smiled up at him, giving him a glimpse of emerald eyes that had attracted him since day one.

"You're getting better at accepting compliments."

She laughed, and he joined in, all of a sudden filled with happiness because she was close to him.

Her fiery curls were beautiful. He moved his hand up her back so he could feel the texture. Pure silk, he thought crushing a lock between his thumb and forefinger. He pictured those curls entwined over their naked bodies as they lay together. His thoughts ran rampant. And he didn't try to rein them in.

Instead, he pulled Abigail closer, not caring that someone might see, because he'd lost his mind, because his love had clouded his judgment. She stiffened and stepped back. He was sorry he'd embarrassed her but not sorry that he'd held her close.

When the twang of the last fiddle faded, Jeremiah forced himself to release Abigail. He stood there, speechless, drinking in the sight of her, storing her image in his mind where he could recall it whenever he chose.

Then Jeremiah forced himself to look away. He saw Evelyn walking toward him. At that moment, he knew what needed to be done. Evelyn deserved better. She deserved a man who loved her with all his heart and soul. He wasn't that man.

Tonight, after the dance, he'd tell Evelyn he couldn't marry her.

CHAPTER 22

On the way back to the ranch, Jeremiah was tormented with guilt. He'd asked for Evelyn's hand in marriage, and now he was about to break her heart—and his promise. He didn't want to hurt her, but he saw no other choice. He didn't love Evelyn.

He loved Abby.

"Jeremiah, do you always wear that Western hat?"

Feeling like a jerk, he smiled at her. "Yes, I like it better than my old Derby."

"It makes you look like an outlaw."

"Does it really?"

"Let me try it on. I want to know whether it'll make me look like a gunslinger, too."

"Evelyn, did you sip some hard cider tonight?"

"Of course not!"

Jeremiah laughed at the outrage in her voice.

As the moon slipped behind a cloud, he watched her pull a long hatpin from her hat. When he told her what was on his mind, he wouldn't blame her if she jabbed him with it.

A minute later she plunked his Stetson on her head. It fell over her forehead and landed on her nose. "What do you think?"

"I'd say you need a smaller size, but it's becoming. You should try wearing it the next time you go to the church social."

She didn't laugh as he'd expected. She pushed the brim of his hat away from her face and looked up at him a long time. He couldn't see her eyes but could feel their sadness. "Is something wrong, Jeremiah?"

He took a breath, let it out, and gazed at the starless sky. "Yes."

Evelyn allowed his hat to settle on her head. She stared at the blackened road, her face hidden beneath the wide brim.

Jeremiah glanced at her silhouette, barely recognizable in the pitch-black surroundings. He didn't want to do this, but he saw no other way. He reached for her hand and squeezed. "You know I care for you a lot."

"I know. If this is about you not working at Daddy's bank, I've already accepted that."

He heard the panic in her tone. Did Evelyn already suspect what he was going to say? She was a sharp lady, and maybe she'd seen the signs coming for a while.

He wrapped his arm around her shoulder, wanting to shield her from his painful words.

A gunshot blast rang out. Evelyn fell forward. If he hadn't grabbed her, she'd have fallen in the road.

Jeremiah struggled to slow the horse, spooked by the loud noise, running at a fast clip. He could barely manage to hold the reins and support Evelyn, slouched over his lap like a rag doll.

"Evelyn, can you hear me?"

His erratic heartbeat pounded in his ears. "Evelyn, answer me, dammit!"

He could smell her blood—and his fear.

She didn't move. She didn't speak. For all he knew she wasn't breathing. Jeremiah's heart plummeted.

The surrey careened on two wheels around the next corner, almost tipping over. "Whoa," Jeremiah shouted, pulling on the reins with one hand, his other hand gripping Evelyn's shoulder as the wagon bounced over the rutted road. He could feel her life's blood seeping through his fingers.

She'd die if he didn't get some help.

Was it already too late?

"No," he hollered into the night air, his voice echoing like an entity from Hell. He wouldn't allow Evelyn to die. This was his fault. That bullet had been intended for him. Guilt ripped him apart. If he hadn't allowed her to wear his hat . . .

He took a deep breath, tried to control his emotions. If he didn't get himself together, Evelyn would surely die. All because of him.

"Whoa, whoa," he repeated, trying to calm his voice, but failing. Thank God, the horse slowed. He yanked Evelyn back against the seat and checked for a wound. Her head rolled from side to side. Blood oozed from her chest. He cursed, and when Evelyn didn't correct him, he knew she was in bad shape.

He slapped the reins against the horse's back and prayed he wouldn't kill them both. As he urged the gelding forward, he tightened his hold on Evelyn's motionless form. When he reached the ranch house, he yanked the reins back and slowed the horse. Once the wagon stopped, he lifted Evelyn's limp body into his arms and ran into the kitchen.

Evelyn was pale. *Deathly pale.* Was she breathing?

"Come quickly," he shouted to no one in particular. He kicked his bedroom door open, gently set her down on the wide bed, and stared at the deep crimson stain spreading over the blankets beneath her.

When Abby ran into the room, Jeremiah looked down helplessly at Evelyn. "She's been shot. I think she's dying." The words came out rough and shaky. He brushed the back of his hand over his eyes. Jeremiah couldn't remember ever being this frightened. "Abby, you have to help her."

Abby hurried to Evelyn's side. "Let's get her dress off so we can see where the blood is coming from."

Jeremiah started to slide his arm beneath Evelyn's shoulders when Whip rushed into the room. "Evelyn," he said in a choked whisper, yanking a knife from his pocket. "There's no time to waste with buttons. Hold her still." He stuck the sharp point of the blade beneath Evelyn's collar and cut the satin fabric to her waist. As he parted the material, Jeremiah stared in horror at her blood-saturated chemise.

Whip glanced at Abby. "Get some clean bandages and hot water. We have to clean this wound and staunch the bleeding. And find Pedro, tell him to go get Doc and tell him to hurry!"

After Abby left, Whip took Evelyn's hand, brought it to his mouth. "Don't you dare die on me, lit' gal."

Jeremiah didn't care much for the way Whip stared down at Evelyn with love in his eyes, but right now, Jeremiah was too distraught to challenge him.

About an hour later, Jeremiah wrung his hands as the country doctor examined Evelyn. "It looks like the bullet went clear through. I reckon Miss DuBlois will be good as new in no time." Old Doc Carter rubbed the end of his bulbous nose and eyed the wound through thick glasses. When he straightened, the bones in his back creaked. He directed his gaze at Whip. "You did a right fine job of stopping the bleeding. You probably saved her life."

Jeremiah took a gander at the country doctor: wrinkled clothes, scraggly hair, and the habit of wiping a nose that resembled Hamlet's snout. Though he didn't like to judge a man by his appearance, he knew he couldn't be too particular where Evelyn was concerned. From what he could see, Evelyn didn't look any better. Did this man even know what he was doing? "Are you certain she'll recover?"

Two thick gray eyebrows meshed. "I been doctoring since before you were in knee pants. I seen many a gunshot injury. I'm telling you this one ain't bad. It's more of a flesh wound than anything." He glanced down for a moment. "She sure is a

228

pretty one but too fragile for these here parts."

"If she needs anything, money's no object," Jeremiah said.

The old man's back visibly stiffened. "This ain't a matter of money. I treat all my patients good, even them that can't pay."

Jeremiah combed his fingers through his hair. "I didn't mean to insult you, but this has been a harrowing experience."

Doc Carter bought his arm up to his face and brushed at his nose. "Don't you fret none. If I had myself a pretty gal like this one, I'd sure as shooting be keeping a close eye on her, too."

As the others left the room, Jeremiah sat on the bed and ran his fingers along the side of Evelyn's face.

"Evelyn, you have to pull out of this," he said and wondered if she could hear him. Frustration wreaked havoc with his nerves. When he thought of her wearing his hat and that bullet going through her shoulder, the last of his control snapped. He cursed long beneath his breath.

Evelyn's eyelids fluttered open and she whispered, "You've become a Texas hooligan."

Relief swept through him as he reached for her hand. "Thank God, you're awake. I've been worried about you."

"Jeremiah, promise you won't ever leave me."

His chest tightened with remorse. He couldn't break off their engagement after all she'd been through. He pressed his mouth to her forehead. "I'm here for you, and I will be always."

Four weeks later Abigail walked past Evelyn's room and was surprised to see her packing her bags. She tapped on the open door before entering. "Are you leaving?"

"Yes." Evelyn brushed an errant tear from her cheek and faced Abigail with a strained smile. "I'm going home to Boston."

"I saw Jeremiah this morning, and he never said a word about your leaving."

"I haven't told him yet, but I will shortly."

Abigail anchored a hand on her hip. "If anyone here has insulted you or done anything improper, I want you to tell me. You're welcome to stay here for as long as you like."

Evelyn shook her head, her gaze sauntering up and down Abigail. "I don't know what he sees in you."

"Who?"

"Don't play innocent with me. You stole my man. I don't know how, but I can clearly tell he's taken with you. I knew from the moment I set foot on this ranch that things between Jeremiah and I had changed."

Abigail was flabbergasted. "You're making a serious mistake. Jeremiah loves you. I saw the way he stood by you while you were recuperating."

Evelyn folded a pair of pantaloons and laid them in her trunk. "What you saw was a man of character, not a man in love."

"You're wrong."

"He's lost that gleam in his eyes when he looks at me. Can you tell me how you did it?"

"I did nothing."

Evelyn's lower lip wobbled. "I have my morals, and maybe if I'd been looser with them, I might have kept Jeremiah from straying."

Evelyn's words stung. Though in truth, they weren't meant to maim, Abigail didn't see it that way. She figured Evelyn was implying a woman with Abigail's reputation would readily lift her shirts, drop her drawers, and allow any man to have his way with her. With as much dignity as she could muster, Abigail swung on her heels and hurried from the room.

Evelyn sat on the porch rocker stiff as a statue when Jeremiah sauntered up the steps. "You're looking mighty fine today."

She fluttered her black silk fan beneath her nose. "I suspect I'm as good as new."

He settled next to her. "I'm glad to hear that. I don't think I could have gone on if you hadn't survived the gunshot wound."

"Jeremiah, you may be a hooligan, but you're also the most noble man I know. If you had lived during medieval times, you'd have made a wonderful knight."

He grinned and pressed his mouth against the smooth flesh of her palm. "And this knight is thinking my fair maiden is after something, perhaps?"

Though she laughed, her eyes held a sadness that tugged at his heart. "We need to have a serious talk, Jeremiah."

"About what?"

"I think you already know the answer to that." She took his hand. "You mustn't look so worried. I'm fine really, or I will be when this is over and behind me."

"I don't . . ."

She raised her hand to silence him. "I need to do this quickly, or I'll never be able to go through with it. Please let me finish."

She turned from him then and glanced across the farmyard before taking a deep shuddering breath. "My health has been back to normal for several days, but I couldn't face what I knew in my heart to be true." She glanced at him with tear-rimmed eyes. "What were you about to tell me the other night before that bullet tore into my shoulder?"

Jeremiah swallowed. What could he say? That he'd wanted to break off their engagement but had since changed his mind because of guilt. What kind of asinine logic was that? But he couldn't do this to Evelyn. He cared for her, and she'd make a wonderful wife. They had lots in common. Yes, lots in common, unlike his parents who rubbed each other the wrong way because of their differences. He would never marry Abigail, and even if he did, their marriage would never last. There was no reason not to go forward with his plans to marry Evelyn.

He rested his hand over her arm. "I was thinking about

something you'd said."

Suspicion clouded her eyes. "What was that?"

"About us getting married now and having the reception later in Boston. I'd really like that."

"I'd say that's a *damn* lie."

His jaw dropped open. It was a good thing he was sitting or he'd have fallen. He wondered what had gotten into Evelyn to use such language.

She raised her chin, daring him to comment. "I've always dreamed of having a grand wedding. When I suggested our getting married right away, I was desperate. I was willing to do anything to keep you from leaving me." She wove her fingers through his. "Even now, I have the urge to go along with this hoax and marry you anyway."

He opened his mouth to speak but closed it again because he didn't know what to say.

"No need to worry. I'm made of tougher fabric than you might think. I've always hated a clinging woman. One who didn't know when to let go. I'm not that sort of person. I've seen the way you look at Abigail, and I've seen the way she looks at you."

"Abigail and I have nothing in common. I admit I'm attracted to her, but I would never marry her. I'm willing to go through with our marriage. In time, my mind will clear of this idiocy. I think I can make you happy. If we marry, I'll be true to you."

Evelyn pulled away. "The nerve of you. To think I'd settle for mere leftovers. You should know me better than that. I've never settled for less than the best, and I'm not about to do so now. If I can't have all of you, then I don't want your paltry offering. I'd rather become a wrinkled old spinster than marry someone who doesn't worship the ground I walk on."

"Evelyn," he said in a soothing tone, reaching for her.

She slapped his hands away. "I promised myself I'd remain

dignified, but I've a couple of things I have to say. I'm the best there is, Jeremiah Dalton. You're making a grave mistake by brushing me aside."

"Evelyn, you're the one doing the brushing."

"Maybe so, but if I hadn't been shot, you'd have taken it upon yourself to do just that four weeks ago. That would have given me the opportunity to tell you what you're throwing away. What we had was good."

"Don't you think I know that?"

She stood, took a few steps across the porch, and tightened her fingers around the railing. "I loved you, Jeremiah, and I love you still, but I don't plan to let this get me down. I'm leaving this afternoon. I've already made arrangements with Alfonso to take me to the train station."

"You're leaving today?"

"There's no reason for me to stay any longer."

Jeremiah went to stand behind her, curving his hands over her shoulders. "I never meant to hurt you."

"I know that." When she turned, he took her in his arms and hugged her to him one last time. Slowly, she pulled away and opened the door before facing him. "You better watch your back, Jeremiah."

"I plan to."

"One more thing."

He expected her to say something sentimental.

A look akin to revenge streaked across her face. "Jeremiah, you're the laughingstock of Lowdown. Abigail's been collecting bets guessing when you'll fall flat on your face."

CHAPTER 23

Since Evelyn's departure, Jeremiah had kept his distance from Abigail. Abigail didn't rightly know why, but she guessed he didn't want her to get the wrong idea about them. He needn't worry about that. She'd never considered herself in the running for an honorable man like Jeremiah. It was impossible to forget what kind of woman she was with the uppity ladies of the community reminding her each chance they got.

If Abigail had been born a man, she could have had several lovers, and instead of people looking down their noses, they'd have clapped her on the back as if she'd accomplished a marvelous deed. Unfortunately, there were two sets of rules, one for men, and one for women. As a female, Abigail had taken the wrong path. She would pay for her mistake until the day she died. At least she had Clarissa, and for that she was thankful.

Evelyn had been weak and foolish to hightail it back to Boston. If Abigail had been in her place, she'd have stayed and fought for the man she loved. She'd been wrong about Jeremiah falling in love with her. Abigail only had to look at his face while he watched Evelyn recuperate to see the love blazing in his pewter eyes.

Jeremiah had kissed Abigail once, and she turned that moment over in her mind each night before she went to sleep. She'd always remember that kiss, the slight pressure from his mouth, his tongue tracing the seam of her lips, and the flames that roared deep in her belly. His kisses had driven Abigail to dream of things unsuitable for upstanding ladies, proving once more that she was no lady.

Yet she embraced those dreams, keeping her eyes closed when she awoke to remember every tantalizing detail. To Abigail, the kisses she'd shared with Jeremiah had been mind-boggling and everything a woman could want. Those kisses had sealed her fate. She'd fallen desperately in love, and the feeling tore at her soul every day and night. To Jeremiah, the kisses had been the mere touch of a lonely man who missed his home back East and his fiancée. To Jeremiah, those kisses had been a dalliance until someone better came along.

Shedding her foul mood the same way a snake sheds its skin, Abigail swung her legs out of bed, pasted a smile on her face, and prepared for another day.

She brushed her hair until the unruly curls almost behaved, and instead of shoving them atop her head any old way, she fastened a ribbon at her nape and knotted the thick skein where it came to rest on her crown. Several long curls bounced freely along the sides of her face. She still didn't like the brassy color, but she'd decided to make the most of what she had. Besides, according to Evelyn, women back East spent large sums to curl their hair, and here was Abigail taking such a thing for granted.

She'd decided before Evelyn's arrival that she was through imitating the ways of men. There was no longer a need because soon she'd have her own place and people working for her.

It was high time she showed her daughter how to act. Until now, Abigail had set a poor example, but no more. She was through trying to impress Jeremiah. Today when Abigail slipped into a shirt made of soft calico with a tiny buttercup print, she did it for herself and Clarissa.

"Damn the entire male population," she mumbled under her

breath as she swung her bedroom door shut and went in search of breakfast.

Jeremiah almost choked on a swallow of coffee when he caught a glimpse of Abigail. Breathtaking best described the woman standing before him now, the same woman he'd dreamed about last night, and here she was, her small breasts evident beneath the soft material covering her chest. The top button of her collar was undone, emphasizing her slender neck. As she sat in the chair by his side, the sunlight coming though the window streaked across her hair and turned her curls a deep burnished gold. She wore a riding skirt, the denim material hugging her hips and falling gently to her ankles concealed in shiny boots.

"Morning, Jeremiah," she said, her maple syrup voice sliding over his senses.

He nodded and hid behind his coffee mug, taking a long swallow. It irked him like the devil to think she'd collected bets about how long he'd last. She'd probably laughed at him behind his back along with half of Lowdown. Abigail had always struck him as a direct person, the kind of woman who said what she meant. But this other surprised him. She hadn't struck him as the type who'd bet behind a man's back, waiting as Evelyn had put it for him to fall on his face. Lately, nothing surprised him. He'd already concluded women were as unpredictable as the weather.

"Boss, what are your plans for today?" he asked, trying to keep the rancor from his voice.

"We start rounding up the cattle."

Her smile had the same effect as a punch to his gut because it took away his breath. He wanted this woman, but unlike his father, he wasn't going to act on his yearnings. Lust surged through his system like a forest fire, and he knew if they'd been alone, he'd have crushed her to him, pressed his mouth to hers, and if she'd allowed, he'd take what he had no business taking. Jeremiah had to be sure they weren't alone. He didn't trust himself.

Her emerald eyes held his. Was she thinking similar thoughts? She licked her lower lip. His undoing. Without realizing, he looked down and found his hand covering hers. He felt like a dope and made light of his action by tapping her hand. "Would you mind passing the biscuits?"

She blinked. "Oh, yes, sure." She handed him the basket of rolls and he grabbed two, his throat all of a sudden too thick to swallow the tiniest bite.

"Thanks," he replied, his voice foreign to his ears.

Jeremiah glanced away and noticed Whip had reverted to his old self. His shirt was wrinkled, his face unshaven. He'd taken Evelyn's absence worse than Jeremiah had. Whip's attraction to Evelyn bordered on insanity. The thought of Evelyn married to Whip and raising little Texas ruffians made Jeremiah smile. Had he been alone in his room, he would have laughed aloud.

Whip's mustache twitched, his lips stretching into a wide grin. "Jeremiah, today, we start to make a real cowboy out of you. Chances are your ass will be kissing the ground more than it does the saddle."

Pedro and Mort roared with laughter.

A few minutes later Mort leaned forward in his chair. "Don't fret none. The ladies 'round here like a man with hoof prints on his forehead."

A pair of chaps covered his denims. Spurs jingled when he walked. A black Stetson sat on his head, and the wide silver belt buckle engraved with a mustang all proclaimed Jeremiah was already a cowboy. Then why did a twinge of worry tighten the muscles between his shoulder blades? He'd be expected to rope a longhorn from atop a horse, that's why. No man with half a brain would look forward to such a task. Jeremiah nonchalantly slipped his hands into his leather gloves and held the rope in his palm. He stood in a relaxed stance, hoping to fool anyone watching.

Abigail nodded toward his hand. "We're going to practice roping that hitching post over yonder."

He took a gander across the expanse of ground between him and the post, at least ten feet away. Unless he could persuade a small bird to grab the other end of the braided rope, it was doubtful it'd be circling anything. And this was simple compared to the real thing—the fence post wasn't bearing down on him with long horns sticking out from the sides of its head. And he wasn't riding a horse. He took a breath and forced an easy smile.

"It'll take a little practice, but with my help, I expect you'll be catching on right quick."

And the moon is really a big circle of cheese. "Is that so?" He wanted to clear the air between them because it bothered him that she'd collected those bets, making him feel like a fool for wanting her so much it hurt.

"Yup, now watch me."

As if she needed to remind him.

"This small loop is called the honda. Pull about three feet of the lasso through, then lift the rope in the air, and rotate it over your head." The lasso swished above Abigail before snagging the fence post. "Now you try."

"Looks easy enough," he said, thinking the opposite. He glanced at his hands, which had sprouted thumbs where there had once been fingers, and yanked at the rope, managed to pull out thirty or so inches, held it over his head, directed a grin at Abigail before whipping his arm in a wide circle and lassoing his own hat to the ground.

At least Abigail had the decency to fake a cough and hide her taunting grin, but when she saw him watching, her laughter rang out. "Sorry," she said, her eyes lit with amusement. "I can't seem to help myself."

He reached for his Stetson, slapped it across his leg, and plunked it on his head. "You'd think you'd never seen a man lasso a hat before now."

She sobered a little, her cheeks pink, her eyes bright. "Sorry." He heard another low chuckle as she brought her hand to her mouth. "Maybe you need to try that again."

He'd missed hearing Abby's laughter. He'd missed her, period. He pulled the rope through the honda and held it the way she'd instructed, brought it over his head, and swung. The lasso landed a few feet short of the hitching post, but at least his hat remained intact. He tried several more times. And each time the lariat missed the target a warning bell rang in his brain, hinting he didn't belong in Texas. Each time his heart ached more than before for the woman he could never have.

He'd been practicing for forty minutes when by a stroke of sheer luck, the lasso circled the post and landed on the ground. Abigail whooped with delight. He dropped the other end of the rope, and forgetting his earlier decision to keep his distance, he grabbed her by the waist and twirled her around, the two of them laughing. He set her down, and she glanced up, her eyes melting his irritation about the betting. He stood there, his hands around her waist, their gazes locked, and time stood still. He'd have kissed her if the pounding of approaching feet hadn't driven some sense into him.

They both pulled away at the same instant.

"Hi, Maw, hi, Mr. Dalton." Clarissa skipped toward them with Caesar and Hamlet at her heels.

The goat and pig scurried to Jeremiah's side, looking for a treat. He reached in his pocket and handed the two animals a lemon drop each. Then he extended a small bag toward Abby and Clarissa. "Would you like one?"

Clarissa grabbed a piece of candy and dropped it in her mouth. "Thanks."

Abigail hesitated, then smiled. "Thanks, just the same, but I have my own." She reached into her shirt pocket and pulled out a lemon drop. "They're my favorite, you know."

"Yes, a small bird told me." In that instant he knew she'd found him out, but he didn't let on. He inclined his head. "Did you get yours at Bufford's?"

"My neighbor left them on my pillow."

"You can thank the little bird for that."

Clarissa took a loud suck on the candy. "You mind if I watch?"

Abigail gave her daughter a hug. "Only if you sit quietly, and don't say anything."

Jeremiah didn't like the idea of any female eyeing him, but he couldn't object. He lifted the lasso, tried again, and missed the post.

"Mr. Dalton, you're holding the rope too tight."

"Clarissa, what did I tell you?"

Clarissa ignored her mother and plunked herself down beside Hamlet. She patted the pig's head. "Hamlet, you better sit and be quiet or we'll both have to leave."

The pig lowered its bulk to the ground and stretched out next to the child, but it kept an eye focused on Jeremiah for fear of missing a bite of food.

Jeremiah twirled his arm in the air and was about to let go of the rope, but Clarissa made him lose his concentration. The wide loop fell at his feet.

"Hamlet, you're a good bastard pig."

Abigail gasped. She marched over to Clarissa, who seemed unaware of her mother's shock. "Where did you ever hear such a thing?"

"Tommy Jenkins told me about bastards at the dance. He

said I was a bastard child 'cause I don't got a paw." Clarissa's eyes were wide with innocence.

"Damn that Tommy Jenkins!" Abigail planted her hand on her hip and stared down.

Clarissa gave her mother a look of disgust. "Maw, you said you weren't gonna say swear words no more."

Abby got down on one knee and rested an arm around the child's shoulders, panic streaking across her face. "I'm sorry. It's just you caught me by surprise."

Jeremiah feared her past was catching up with her, and the need to protect her overwhelmed him. Though he didn't know the story, he doubted Clarissa's father was the hero she'd been led to believe.

"You mustn't use that horrible word."

"But if I don't have a paw, then I'm a bastard. Tommy Jenkins says so."

"You most certainly are not. You had a paw that loved you very much. You should be proud of the man who fathered you. Never believe anything else. You hear?"

Clarissa shrugged off her mother's arm and stood. "Can me and Hamlet and Caesar have a cookie now?"

Abby gave a nervous laugh and patted her daughter's behind. "Sure, you go ahead."

Clarissa rounded the corner. Jeremiah moved close to Abby. When she leaned into him, he wrapped his arms around her waist and pretended she'd be his always. As he held her, his heart drummed an unsteady beat. "Abby, would you care to talk about it?"

She heaved a weary sigh and shook her head. "All the talk in the world won't make a lick of difference. I'm a terrible mother."

"You may be the most ornery, stubborn woman I've ever set eyes on, Abigail Wilcox, but you're a great mother, probably the best there is. I knew that the first day when you stomped on my foot and warned me to watch my language in the presence of your daughter."

She giggled. "Sorry about that."

"You surprised me."

"You thought I was a man."

"Definitely not a man."

She looked confused. "What, then?"

"A boy with just the slightest bit of whiskers on his face," he said with a wink, curling his forefinger under her chin.

She frowned, but a laugh tumbled from her mouth. "You're lucky I don't stomp on your other foot for that."

CHAPTER 24

As Abigail tried to help Jeremiah with roping techniques, her heart still pounded, and the word *bastard* rang in her head. She'd known the time would come when she'd need to have a serious talk with Clarissa, but the child was too young to understand such things. Abby had hoped to protect her daughter, but now she saw that she couldn't.

Jeremiah's voice cut into her thoughts. "Well, what do you think?"

She looked up and even in her troubled state laughed aloud. Jeremiah had lassoed Hamlet. "I hope that was deliberate."

"Of course." His incredulous expression lightened her heart.

"I think you're ready for the real thing."

"Meaning?"

"Whip put a couple longhorns in the corral for you to practice on. I figure you should try your skills on them."

When Jeremiah took her hand, it seemed natural. His touch lightened her worries, and the strangest feeling took hold—the need to share her burden with someone she loved. Abigail didn't realize what she was going to say until the words were out. "Let's go for a walk first."

They strolled past the corral, past the cacti with lush crimson blooms, and followed the stream that crisscrossed the ranch. The air was alive with the scent of fresh flowers. Birds sang and water rippled. In the distance sunshine danced along the fertile field and gilded the lush meadow.

Jeremiah picked several buttercups along the path and stuck them in her hatband.

Abby's heart overflowed with love. "Have you ever considered staying on and running the ranch?"

When he glanced down at her, she had her answer before he said the words. "I won't lie to you, Abby. I can't stay."

"Oh." The word caught in the back of her throat. "Why's that?"

"I don't belong here." He escorted her to an old tree stump where she sat, and he followed suit. He pulled her to him, and she went willingly. "Have you ever seen the Atlantic?"

She shook her head. "I've never been more than twenty-five miles from this ranch."

"The ocean is a sight to behold. Water as far as the eye can see."

Abby closed her eyes and tried to imagine such a thing. She'd heard about the wild waves and the large ships.

"I own a shipping company back East. My partner is keeping an eye on things until I return." He gave a low laugh. "That's if the men who work the docks haven't quit before I get back."

She leaned her head against his shoulder. "Why do you say that?"

"Joel, my partner, isn't diplomatic, but he's a great guy. He prefers doing the bookwork, which is fine with me because I don't like being cooped up in an office all day."

"I thought you worked in a bank."

"I did for a while, but I've come to realize that's not for me."

He smelled like lemons, leather, and bay rum. She could feel his pulse beneath her ear. "Have you ridden in a boat?"

"I own a small sloop, and when the water isn't too rough, I take her out. Abby, there's nothing as exhilarating as sailing on the ocean," he said, his voice ringing with excitement.

Abby's heart drummed with disappointment. The imaginary

chasm between them widened.

"I think I'd be frightened of the large waves."

He hugged her closer. "The waves aren't always large. I'd love to give you a ride on my boat. Would you ever consider coming to Boston?"

For Jeremiah she'd do almost anything. Almost. "I'd be an oddity there. Me and my country ways and clothes. People would surely laugh."

"I wouldn't let them."

"You couldn't stop them. Look at the things Clarissa is hearing. I can't control that."

"I guess you're right." His disappointed tone mirrored the hollow ache in her chest. Maybe she could change. Maybe if she talked and dressed differently, learned to flutter a fan, wear fancy hats and dainty white gloves. Then she'd be a phony, and she still wouldn't fit in.

"Would you like to tell me about Clarissa's father? Maybe I can help."

"You'll think poorly of me, that's if you don't already."

He tucked a finger under her chin and gazed into her eyes. "I'd never think poorly of you. You're a fine woman."

"There are some who'd disagree."

"That's because they don't know you like I do."

"I shamed my family. I shamed myself. Now that shame will be passed on to Clarissa."

"Clarissa is a strong kid. But she needs to hear about her father from you before someone else enlightens her."

Abigail's hands shook at the thought of telling her daughter the truth. "You may be right, but I don't know what to tell her. I'm afraid Clarissa will look at me the way my paw did before he turned me out."

Jeremiah couldn't believe his ears. "Your father sent you away?"

She gave a slight nod. "Noah took me in when no one else would. I was out of money, and I'd have done anything for food and shelter. My belly was out to here when your father first set eyes on me." She raised her hand several inches above her abdomen. Shaking her head, she continued, "If he hadn't come to my rescue, I don't know what would have happened to me and my daughter."

Jeremiah understood now what had turned Abigail into the hardened woman he'd first met. "I was raised to believe my old man was a son of a bitch." Even now, the thought knotted his stomach.

She straightened, looked at him as if he'd sprouted a horn on his forehead. "That's a horrible thing for you to say."

"Maybe so, but it's the truth. My mother carried her hatred for Noah to her grave. Unfortunately, she took it upon herself to fill my head with every mean thing my father ever did. I suspect most of it was exaggerated, but as a young boy, I never doubted a word she said. As I grew, I adored my mother, and because Noah never bothered to answer my letters, I figured Noah didn't care."

"Your father wrote many letters. He sent gifts, too. No one ever acknowledged either, and after a while, he gave up. It wasn't until he became sick about a year ago that he wrote one last letter, begging you to come for a visit."

Jeremiah slid his hat from his head and set it on the ground beside them. As a kid, one of his father's letters would have meant the world to him. "I never received a one," he said, aware of the tremor in his voice.

"Well, letters were sent."

He ran his fingers through his hair. "I believe you. When I saw the box my father had saved over the years with the photographs and the tiny pair of boots, I knew he wasn't the sort of person to abandon his son. My mother, God bless her soul, must have hidden his letters from me."

He stared unseeingly across the meadow and remembered a small boy waiting for a birthday gift or a single word that his father loved him. He uttered a frustrated sigh. "My mother lied to me. It's hard for me to forgive her for that, though I know I must. Otherwise I'll become a bitter man." He paused and chose his words carefully. "Your lies to Clarissa are well intended, but they're lies just the same. You need to tell her the truth before she learns it by other means."

Abby stiffened and angled her head. "What do you suggest I say? Clarissa, by the way, your mother's a trollop."

"You aren't any such thing. You could tell your daughter you made a mistake. Surely, she wouldn't hold that against you."

"Oh, I made a mistake all right." The look that crossed her features tugged at his heart.

"Abby, do you want to tell me about him?"

She blew out a slow breath. "His name is Frank. He was a slick-talking traveling salesman who could sell boots to a rattlesnake and dentures to chickens. He talked his way into my britches. Before I knew it, I was with child and he'd hightailed it for parts unknown."

"Did he know you were pregnant?"

"When I told him, he whooped, swung me around, and sounded as if he was the happiest man in the world. Told me to pack my bags and we'd be married by the first preacher we came to. By the next day, Frank was long gone. I was forced to face my paw, who told me never to step foot in his house again."

A shiver racked her body, and Jeremiah tightened his hold, running his hand up and down the length of her arm.

"The following day before my sister and mother awoke, my father dropped me off on the outskirts of town and left me there to make my own way. I had several pieces of bread in a knapsack, one change of clothes, and enough money for two days' lodging. I was fifteen and lost and frightened. If Noah hadn't taken me in, I might have died."

Jeremiah curled his finger under Abby's chin, lifted her face, and looked into her emerald eyes brimming with tears. "I'm glad my father was here for you. You have nothing to be ashamed of. Long ago, when you were barely more than a child, you made a mistake. It's time you forgave yourself."

Maybe if she hadn't looked so vulnerable, maybe if he hadn't brushed that one tear from her right cheek, maybe if he hadn't loved her so damn much, he wouldn't have lowered his mouth and nibbled her lower lip.

He'd planned a light touch. A brief touch, but intense heat shot through him and pooled in his groin. She sighed, the sound muffled by his kiss. The last of his common sense evaporated like a drop of rain in the Texas sun. Unlike the first time they'd kissed, her mouth opened willingly; her tongue reached for his. He touched, tasted, and went out of his mind with longing. Desire surged through his bloodstream, and he knew he'd never forget this woman.

He pulled her onto his lap, her arms wrapping around his neck as he molded her body to his. Unknowingly, she wiggled against his erection, driving him to the brink. He moaned and deepened the kiss, slid his fingers over her breasts, and felt her beaded nipple beneath the layers of clothing.

She was all he wanted in a woman and everything he couldn't have. She was warm, loving and beautiful. But she was as different from him as night was to day. If he followed his heart, they'd destroy each other. He had to do what he knew was right.

Besides, another man had abandoned Abby. She was vulnerable, and he didn't want to hurt her. Jeremiah couldn't make love to Abby knowing he intended to leave. It took several minutes before he could lighten the kiss, another few minutes before he removed his hands from her breasts. Finally, when he'd taken a deep breath and allowed the oxygen to penetrate his brain, he unwound her arms from his neck and gave her a sheepish grin. "If we don't stop now, I won't be responsible for what happens."

"Jeremiah, I trust you."

He knuckled her jaw. "That's a mistake."

Arms entwined and in no particular hurry, they started back to the ranch. They'd reached the corral where Jeremiah was supposed to practice lassoing the longhorns when they saw Sheriff Clark crossing the yard.

The sheriff nodded. "I come to say I've no more news about the shooting. The day after Evelyn was wounded, I looked all around, but because of the dance, everyone was in town that night. Hoof prints were everywhere. Finding those of the intended killer's horse is impossible. I've kept my ears open and asked my sources in the saloon to do the same. But no one's heard a whisper about who's responsible. Between the shooting and Blue's accident, and the fact that someone cut the strap on Jeremiah's saddle, I've put two and two together, and concluded the killer is someone who knows the two of you."

Jeremiah ran a finger along the brim of his hat. "That's pretty much what I thought."

Worry streaked across Abby's face. "Who'd do such a thing?"

"Who'd benefit from Jeremiah's death?" The sheriff took a cheroot out of his pocket and struck a match on the sole of his shoe.

Abigail didn't say a word, and Jeremiah wondered whether she knew someone he didn't. She was about the only person he didn't suspect.

Jeremiah had his suspicions but nothing concrete. "Sheriff, I don't want to point a finger at anyone without proof."

"If you have any idea who might be responsible, I want to know."

"I'll tell you as soon as I'm certain."

The sheriff lit his cigar and took a deep pull before blowing out a ring of smoke. "By then you might be dead."

As Sheriff Clark swung onto his horse and rode away, Jeremiah turned to Abigail. "I saw the look on your face. Do you know something I don't?"

She chewed her lower lip. "I can't believe anyone on this ranch would try to kill you. But the day the cinch strap to your saddle broke, I saw Pedro in town. When I asked him what he was doing there, he said he'd gone into Lowdown for salt. There was a large bag of salt in the storeroom before I left. Pedro lied." Her forehead creased with worry. "But Pedro would never hurt anyone."

"I don't want to stake my life on that. Another possibility is Whip."

"Whip's a moody son of a gun, but he's not a killer."

Jeremiah calculated the distance between the horns of the animal he was expected to rope. Would he ever be able to lasso a longhorn? "Think of it. Whip has the most to gain. If something happens to me, he inherits part of the ranch, and he's free to pursue Evelyn. Surely, you noticed his preoccupation with her."

"Whip is a surly man, and I'd be the first to admit he scowls more than he smiles, but that doesn't make a person a killer. So you better be looking elsewhere."

Jeremiah climbed onto the fence and took the rope from the post. He swung the lasso in wide circles above his head, released it, and snagged one horn of a mean-looking animal glaring back at him. He was about to hop over when Whip's voice rang out.

"I don't think you should do that, or you might find yourself impaled like a side of beef on a spit." Whip sauntered over and leaned a hip on the fence. "Of course, if you've a mind to entertain me, go right ahead." He said this with a wink and a nod that bespoke friendship.

Jeremiah yanked on the rope and when the giant beast neared, he was able to pull his lasso free. He hopped down and stood next to Abby. "Thanks for the warning," he said, figuring he owed Whip.

"Think nothing of it." There was a considerable pause before he continued, "Are you planning to look up Evelyn when you return to Boston?"

"I expect to see her, if that's what you mean."

"Will you be trying to win her back?"

"There's not a chance of that. I expect she'll have men flocking to take my place, and that's as it should be. I was very fond of the lady, but I didn't love her. She was wise enough to realize that before we both made a mistake."

"Then you don't mind if I write her?"

"What Evelyn does is no longer any of my business."

Whip brought two fingers to the brim of his hat. "I just wanted to be certain before I make my move." As he turned to leave, Jeremiah saw the start of a grin.

"See what I mean," Abby said. "The man has scruples. He doesn't want to infringe on another man's territory. Does that strike you as the trait of a killer? You better be looking elsewhere for your man."

"Of course, there's one other possibility."

"What's that?"

"The killer could be one of the hotheaded cowboys who bet on the date I'll be falling on my face." Evelyn had delivered her parting blow with that statement, and he could still feel its force when he said the words.

Color climbed her neck. "You know about that?"

"Yes." He folded his arms over his chest and tried to see what was going on beneath the brim of her wide hat.

"Oh." The reply was barely audible.

"What do you have to say for yourself? I hear this was your idea."

Her chin shot up. "It most certainly was not."

"You needn't act so uppity. I'm told you collected the bets."

"Well, yes, but I didn't want to. I made it clear I didn't approve."

Just looking at her upturned face, he could tell she was sincere. Some of the anger slipped away. "I'm glad you didn't bet."

The corners of her mouth dropped.

"You placed a bet?"

"But I didn't want to."

"Did someone hold a gun to your head?"

She was silent a moment. "No, they didn't, but what they did was just as threatening."

"What would that be?"

"They implied I was smitten with you. I didn't want anyone to know, so I put down my wager."

Instead of anger, warmth spread through his middle. "And did you bet that I'd make it though the six months?"

"That would have been like shooting myself in the foot. But I guessed you'd last longer than anyone else did. I've already won. So unless you suspect me as the killer, you've come up empty again."

Chapter 25

I was certain Evelyn would wrap Jeremiah around her little finger and persuade him to head East. But she failed. And I did, too. If the moon hadn't slipped behind a cloud when I took aim, I might have seen Jeremiah's silhouette, but all I saw was the outline of his hat. I have a little treat in mind for Jeremiah. Next time, I won't miss.

After supper, Abigail asked Clarissa to meet her in her bedroom, and while she waited for her daughter to arrive, she paced nervously. For years shame had festered like a boil. Humiliation consumed her when she thought of what she'd done all those years ago. She'd disgraced her family. If she lived to be a hundred, Abigail would never forget the look of disappointment on her father's face when she'd confessed her sin. And now, Abigail needed to admit to Clarissa that she had never been married. Her stomach tightened, and she felt sick when she heard the light tap on the door and her daughter's voice. "Maw, can I come in?"

"Yes." She forced the word through her constricted throat.

"Is something wrong, Maw? I did my chores like you told me."

Abigail sat on the feather mattress and patted the space beside her. "Stop fretting. I just want to discuss something important with you."

Clarissa hopped onto the bed, her legs swinging with the restless energy of a young child. "Phew, I'm glad I'm not in trouble again."

Abigail wondered how to begin. She considered putting off the talk and preventing Clarissa from going into town. But that would be unfair to her daughter.

"Is this talk gonna take long?"

"No, why? Do you have plans?"

"I was gonna help Jeremiah with his roping."

"That's nice of you."

"He says he'll buy me the biggest bag of candy I ever seen if I can show him how to rope as good as I do. I reckon I can teach him if I really try. And I aim to try real hard so I can get my candy."

Abigail barely heard a word. "I need to tell you something about your birth."

"You mean about my paw being a hero."

"No." Abigail glanced across the room. "I was never married to your paw."

"You wasn't? I thought only married ladies grew babies in their bellies."

"That's the proper way, but it's possible to grow a baby without being hitched."

Clarissa bit the inside of her cheek and studied her mother's face. "But I thought you said . . ."

"I told you I was married because you were too little to understand. Now that you're a big girl, I reckoned it's time you knew the truth."

"Was paw still a hero?"

"Yes, and handsome, too."

"But if you wasn't married, how come I growed in your belly?"

"You've seen animals mate." She gave her words time to sink in. "When a man plants his seed in a woman, it's love that makes the seed grow into a baby. You grew into a very special child because of all the love from both me and your father."

At fifteen, she was sure she loved Frank. Since then, she'd wondered if her father's stern upbringing might have sent her looking for affection elsewhere.

"Did Paw die before he could marry you?"

"No, I don't rightly know what happened to your paw. He might still be alive. He was a traveling man, so he could be anywhere."

"Then why didn't Paw marry you?"

"I don't think he loved me as much I loved him. That happens sometimes, but he gave me a special gift. Without him, I wouldn't have you for my daughter."

Clarissa was silent for a minute. Abigail wiped her sweaty palms against the bedspread.

"Can I go now?" Clarissa asked.

Abigail knew her daughter didn't fully comprehend what she'd been told, but there'd be other talks and more understanding as she grew older. One more thing needed to be settled. "In a minute. Earlier today, I told you never to say the word *bastard.*"

"And I won't."

"I'm glad, but I want you to understand what it means. When an unmarried woman has a baby, those who don't know better call that child a bastard. It's a mean thing to say, and they're wrong because no baby should be held accountable for its mother's mistake. If someone says the word, you should ignore them because it doesn't pertain to you, understand?"

"Yup."

Relieved to have this behind her, Abigail kissed her daughter's cheek.

"Maw, did Paw know you had a baby growing in your belly when he left?"

When Abigail glanced into Clarissa's wide eyes, her heart

spilled over with love. "If he had known, don't you think he would have stuck around?"

A week later Jeremiah was standing in the corral with his rope circling a steer's horns when he heard approaching footsteps. The sweet scent of roses mingled with soap and fresh air, and he knew without glancing it was Abigail.

"Morning, Jeremiah."

"Yes, it is," he said, realizing how much the day had improved with her presence. Rather than worry about his attraction toward her, he decided to enjoy Abigail's company. And enjoy it he did, but with some reservations. He held her hand, gave it a gentle squeeze, releasing her fingers and resting his palm over her shoulder.

She'd plaited her hair, but wild strands had escaped, teasing her neck and the sides of her face, adding to her femininity and his desire to taste the delicate patch of flesh beneath her ear. Tucked into the waistband of tight-fitting Levis was a plaid shirt with tiny ruffles around the neck and sleeves. Abigail's transition reminded him of a caterpillar emerging into a beautiful butterfly.

"Well, what do you think?" He nodded toward the roped steer and took a few steps to retrieve his lasso.

"You're ready for the real thing."

He loved the way she looked at him, her eyes alight with admiration and something more frightening. He widened his stance and with practiced ease, twirled the rope over his head, released, and snagged another longhorn.

She cheered and clapped. "Jeremiah, I can't believe all you've accomplished this week."

Pride surged through him at her compliment. What Abby thought about him mattered. Jeremiah enjoyed the challenge of roping. He was beginning to think he might like ranching.

Two hours later he discovered that roping a calf from the ground was different from doing it atop a moving horse. His rope was suspended from the saddle horn, and without glancing down he was suppose to grab it with his right hand and lasso runaway steers as Whip and Pedro cut the animals that needed branding from the herd. Then he and Abby needed to guide the steers into the branding pen, which in theory sounded easy, but the cussed critters had other ideas. When one took off, it was Jeremiah's job to retrieve it with his rope. At the start he missed more than he caught, but Abby always gave him an encouraging smile. "You're doing fine," she said, often leaning over to pat his arm with affection.

A thick layer of dust coated everything, Jeremiah's clothing, his arms, and his lungs. He'd yanked a bandanna over his nose, but his nostrils still tickled, and his throat was parched. He could taste the dirt on his tongue. He couldn't see unless he squinted into the rising dust cloud. The smell of sweat and manure permeated the air. The sounds of hooves and baying longhorns rang out along with the shouts of men trying to get the animals to move.

A calf took off. Jeremiah threw his rope in the air, came up empty, and watched Abby charge in and catch the animal. Determined to get the next one, he fingered the rope that he'd just looped over the saddle horn. Out of the corner of his eye, he spotted one breaking from the pack, so he took off and nearly shouted victoriously when the rope slid over the critter's neck.

As the beast tugged with all its might, pain speared through Jeremiah's thumb caught between the rope and the saddle horn. He struggled to free himself, sweat beading his forehead. His palms dampened. His thumb throbbed and felt as if it were being ripped off. He tried to ease the gloved fingers of his left hand beneath the loop of rope without success.

He heard the lash of a whip and felt the pressure ease. The

257

end of a long whip circled the animal's horn, and with effort, Whip pulled back on the steer.

Jeremiah freed his thumb and blew on it, trying to curb the pain. Whip wheeled his mount around and rode beside him. "Are you all right?"

"Yes. Thanks."

Whip tapped two fingers to the brim of his hat. "Think nothin' of it."

As Jeremiah rejoined Abby, she reached for his hand. "Maybe we should have the Doc take a look."

"I don't think that'll be necessary. The color is starting to return already." He paused to look at the sea of animals around him and knew without a doubt this wasn't how he wanted to spend the rest of his life.

They broke for lunch, son-of-a-bitch stew, which Jeremiah gulped down with the speed of a starving man. He wiped the juice in the bowl with the thick, crusty piece of bread. "This is really good."

Abigail tapped her lips with her handkerchief. "Working with cattle builds an appetite."

"I expect it does."

"Adele's agreed to stay on until the branding is done. She made the stew so Pedro could give us a hand. If Pedro had made it, he'd have put jalapeño peppers in it."

"Somehow, that doesn't surprise me." He took a swallow of coffee. "Was Adele involved with my father?"

"They were lovers for a while. Adele loved your father, but there was only one woman for Noah. He loved your mother until the very end. He told me as much before you arrived."

"If he felt that way, why didn't he come to Boston and persuade her to return?"

"He was a prideful man, stubborn, too. Do you think your

mother would have come back if he had showed up on her doorstep?"

"Probably not."

"Noah loved your mother with all his heart."

"Sometimes love isn't enough. And they were from opposite ends of the earth," he said, the ache in his heart intensifying.

Jeremiah ran a hand over his face. When he glanced at the creases between his fingers, he noticed the dirt that had turned his flesh a dull gray. Back in Boston he'd have scrubbed the small crevices with a brush, but out here, it seemed like a waste of time. He ate two bowls of cobbler for dessert before he heard the call to mount up. Jeremiah was weary to the bone. He'd worked long hours on the docks, but unloading heavy crates was child's play compared to coercing a stubborn animal to do his bidding.

As they walked toward the branding pen the ranch hands had built for this purpose, Abigail gave him the good news. "We're changing positions. Since you need to learn everything about the cattle, it's imperative you work every station."

He was so happy, he caught Abby around the waist and gave her a hug, pressing his mouth to her dusty forehead.

"What's that for?"

"It seemed like a good idea, and because I'd rather do anything than catch strays."

"I hope you still feel that way come nightfall."

The look on her face worried him, but he shrugged good-naturedly. "With you for company, I'd enjoy anything I did."

From inside the pen, the sickening smell of burning hide and hair filled the air along with the painful cries of the animals being forced onto their sides. Jeremiah did his best to ignore the stench and instead focused on Abby.

She adjusted her hat. "I want you to observe for a while. When the steer comes through the fence, the ropers snake out a loop, and catch the critter's hind legs. They then drag the calf to the flankers who turn the steer onto its side. It looks harder than it is."

"You've wrestled a steer to the ground?" Abby must have weighed one hundred pounds soaking wet. He couldn't fathom her doing this type of work.

"I've worked as a flanker if that's what you mean. But I've never tried to wrestle a calf, or I'd have lost. There's a technique that makes the task possible. Watch how Whip and Mort work together."

Jeremiah had begun to wish he were back on his horse catching strays. He tried to memorize each move. First Whip grabbed the rope, Mort the tail. The animal wailed and fell on its side. Jeremiah couldn't see what Mort was doing under the animal, but he did see him slice the ear. "What in the hell is he doing that for?"

Abby shrugged. "He's marking the ear. It's easier to see at a distance than the brand."

The putrid air clogged Jeremiah's throat. He glanced at Abby and saw she was oblivious to the smells. No amount of time would do that for him.

Whip and Mort branded about a dozen steers before Whip waved for Abby and Jeremiah to join in the fun. Jeremiah wished he'd skipped the stew and cobbler. As he ambled toward the two men, Abby held his hand. Jeremiah tried to concentrate on her touch, the shade of the sky, the dirt under his fingernail. He tried to concentrate on anything but what he was about to do. Burning an imprint on an animal's hide looked painful, and from the looks of the calf's eyes rolling in its head, it was. The smell flung his stomach around like a wind-tossed ship.

Jeremiah dabbed the sweat on his face with his arm and waited for the next steer to cross his path.

Whip stepped forward. "For the next few minutes you and I

are going to work together. We'll grab the rope around the legs, flip the animal over on its side, and press a knee on its neck. That'll allow Mort to do his thing. Pedro has the irons heating, and he'll brand the calf. It'll be over in no time, and though the animal fusses, it doesn't hurt near as much as it looks."

Jeremiah wondered where he'd gotten his information. If someone were to take a branding iron to Whip, would he still feel the same way? The sun glinted on the sharp knife in Mort's hand, and by his grin, Jeremiah deduced the man enjoyed this work.

All too soon, the ropers snagged the legs of a calf. "Now," Whip shouted above the din, grabbing the rope. Jeremiah had his hands on the rope when the calf went down, but he didn't think he helped much. To his left Mort was busy, but Jeremiah looked away as rank smells surrounded him, sinking into his pores. He tried not to breathe, but the odors lingered.

When the tenth steer landed on its side, Jeremiah was surprised to see Whip standing behind him with his arms over his chest. "You done good, for a greenhorn."

For the next three hours, Jeremiah knocked calves onto their sides, shoved his knee onto their necks, and ignored everything else going on around him.

Some time later Whip whistled through his fingers. "Time to switch."

Jeremiah found himself standing at the tail end of an animal. Mort shoved a sharp knife in his hand. "This here's the fun part," he said with a dry chuckle.

Jeremiah watched the old man reach down, cut off the tip of the animal's scrotum, yanked out the testicles, and cut them off, heaving them into a nearby jar. It was all Jeremiah could do not to holler out in pain. As he squeezed his knees together, his crotch aching in sympathy for the poor beast.

Jeremiah didn't see how he could do this. When the next

unsuspecting victim arrived, Mort nodded, "Your turn."

Jeremiah broke out in a cold sweat. He'd been through a lot in the last few months, and if he didn't castrate the animal, all his efforts would be in vain. He'd come too far to back out now. Taking a deep breath, his stomach roiling inside, he tightened his fingers around the handle of the knife. He grabbed hold of the scrotum and sliced—the testicles fell in his opened palm. As if they were hot coals, he jerked his hands back and watched the glistening orbs land in the dirt at his feet.

Mort scooped them up, blew away a grain of sand, and dropped them into the jar. Jeremiah wondered why he went to all that trouble, but he felt too sick to ask.

Some time later after his stomach had settled beneath his rib cage, Jeremiah splashed water on his face and sat on the ground with his back against a rock. He bent one knee and extended his other leg and watched Abby leaning over the stream, her heart-shaped behind toward him. Lust roared through his veins, turning him hard. His mind erased all the day's unpleasant experiences and focused on the woman before him. He imagined her naked, him creeping up behind her and sinking into her soft flesh. He suppressed a groan.

When she stood and turned, rivulets of water ran down her face. He wanted to lick the drops with the tip of his tongue. "You did a good day's work, Jeremiah. It'll get easier in time."

"I'll never eat another piece of beef without thinking what some poor beast went through."

She laughed and dropped down next to him. "I told Clarissa about my past, and it didn't seem to bother her. I feel better not having to lie to her any more."

"I'm glad things went well. I expect there'll be questions later on."

"I know that, but this way she'll be coming to me for the

answers instead of someone else."

She removed her hat, setting free a riot of red curls that begged for a man's touch. His touch. He wanted to thread his fingers through the silken strands. The sunrays filtered through the leafy canopy overhead, dappling her face with light and shadow like a fine painting in a museum.

She seemed unaware that he grew hard each time he inhaled her scent. No woman had ever smelled any better. No woman ever would.

She leaned closer. "I promised to take Clarissa on a picnic tomorrow. Come morning, we're packing a lunch and going wherever the urge strikes us. Would you like to come along?"

He couldn't think of anything more appealing than being with Abby. "It sounds good to me."

She yawned and stretched her arms to her sides. "It's been a long day. I think I'll be turning in early."

He wanted to lie down next to her, to take her mouth in a searing kiss, to claim her as his own. But he had no right. He'd be leaving in another six weeks.

He stood and helped her up. "I think I'll call it a day, too."

He walked her into the house and as he passed the kitchen, he heard laughter and loud voices. Whip stuck his head around the doorframe. "Jeremiah, join us for a beer."

"Be with you guys in a minute," he replied, pleased that they'd invited him. He walked Abby down the hall and paused at her bedroom. He wanted to kiss her so much it hurt. Instead, he rested his hand on her shoulder the way one might a sister. "Goodnight, Abby."

She stretched on tiptoes and pressed her mouth to his cheek. "Goodnight, Jeremiah."

He wouldn't sleep much with her in the room next to his. He scowled down at her and growled. "Be sure to shove that chair beneath the doorknob."

Abby turned around and stepped into the room. She had started to shut the door when a shy smile claimed her face. "I haven't wedged a chair under the doorknob for some time." Color climbed her neck as the door clicked shut.

Was that merely a statement of fact or an invitation? Jeremiah didn't know what to make of it, but he sure as hell wasn't going to complicate his life by charging headlong through the adjoining door like a bull in heat. All the more reason to join the men for a beer and try to put the matter out of his mind.

Jeremiah sauntered down the hall, entered the kitchen, and sat next to Whip.

"Jeremiah, do you like oysters?" Mort asked with a deep laugh.

Jeremiah couldn't hide his excitement or his disbelief. "Why, do you have any?"

Whip took a swig of beer and wiped the foam from his mouth. "Yeah, lots."

Jeremiah hadn't expected to find such a delicacy so far from home. They took a little getting used to, but after the first one had slithered down his throat, he'd been hooked. "I love oysters," he said, his mouth watering.

Blue moistened his lower lip with his tongue. "After eating a dozen or so, I feel like moseying into town to git myself a woman."

"You wouldn't know what to do with her once you found one," someone pointed out.

Blue absently ran his hand over his injured leg. "I may be old, but I ain't dead."

"It takes me only three *calf fries* to make me horny as hell," another ranch hand added.

"You're horny from sunup to sundown. Can't blame the oysters for that," came the comment from across the table.

Blue slapped his hand on the table. "Trouble is, you young

whippersnappers think with yer dicks, and it's all over before the real fireworks begin. An old geezer like me moves slow. Real slow. I could teach you fellers a thing or two. But I ain't divulging none of my secrets or no gal 'round here would be safe."

Jeers and foot stomping ensued.

Whip handed Jeremiah a beer. "You're in for a real treat."

"Are you serving the oysters on a half shell?"

Whip's mustache twitched. "I don't reckon. Pedro fries them up in a spicy batter. In Texas we call them Rocky Mountain Oysters."

Jeremiah uncapped the bottle of beer. "I've never had oysters prepared that way, but I'm game to try them if you are." He didn't think to question the wide grins on the men's faces.

CHAPTER 26

After a restless night, Abigail awoke to the sound of rain tapping the windowpane. Clarissa would be disappointed about the picnic.

Abigail climbed out of bed, and as she slipped on her clothes, she heard a familiar knock on the door. "Maw, can I come in?"

"Yes, sweetheart."

Clarissa entered, closed the door behind her, and pointed to the drapes. "Did you look out there? It's raining like the dickens."

"I've no control over the weather." *Or the fact that Jeremiah would be leaving in six weeks.* Abigail felt as though her entire life was spinning out of control. She'd never intended to fall in love, and especially not with someone who'd be leaving. Jeremiah wanted her, and she suspected he cared some, but not enough. Otherwise, why would he hightail it back to Boston the instant his six months were up?

Clarissa slid open the drapes, knelt, plunked her elbows on the sill, and rested her chin on her upturned palms. "It sure don't look like it's gonna stop any time soon."

"We can go next week instead."

Her small shoulders drooped. "But I wanted to go today."

When they left Abigail's bedroom, Clarissa was walking with her head down, and she bumped into Jeremiah. He steadied her and placed his hands over her shoulders. "What's the matter with you?"

Clarissa glanced up. "It's raining."

"And that's why your chin's dragging on the floor?" Jeremiah winked at Abigail.

Her stomach somersaulted several times. She took a moment to admire him, tall build, shirt stretched across broad shoulders, the leather vest she'd given him hugging an impressive chest, and a mustache that haunted her dreams.

"Now we can't go on a picnic," Clarissa mumbled as if the rain had sapped her strength.

"Says who?"

Clarissa's head snapped up. "But it's raining."

"Are you afraid you're going to melt if a few raindrops fall on your head?"

Inside, warmth spread through Abigail's limbs. Not only was Jeremiah a good-looking son of a gun, he was kind. Special. And he'd *never* be hers.

"Of course, I'm not gonna melt." Clarissa giggled. "But everyone knows you can't have a picnic in the rain."

Jeremiah tweaked Clarissa's nose. "I'm not letting a little rain ruin my day. I'm going on a picnic anyway. Is anyone else joining me?"

Abigail figured it was plumb crazy to head out in a downpour, but she wasn't going to be left behind. "I'll come," she replied after Clarissa was through shouting and jumping up and down.

"Mr. Dalton," Clarissa asked, tugging on his sleeve, "what was all the ruckus about in the kitchen last night?"

"Just me and the men kicking up our heels." He ruffled Clarissa's hair and turned to Abigail. "I hope I didn't keep you awake last night."

Since thoughts of him kept her awake every night, she decided to ignore the question. "Did you have a good time?"

"I sure did. But you know, I was really surprised to find oysters so far from the ocean."

"Yuck," Clarissa said, sticking her tongue out. "Those oysters don't come from the ocean, they come from a bull's . . ."

"Clarissa, that'll be enough." Abigail's sharp voice stopped her cold.

Jeremiah glanced from one to the other. Abigail knew the instant he realized what he'd eaten because his face turned a pale shade of green.

Pedro packed their picnic lunch in a wicker basket; fried chicken, fresh greens with dressing, cornmeal bread, and pie for dessert. Clarissa took out her colored pencils and made place cards for each of them. When Abigail arrived some time later, she found her daughter humming.

"Are you ready?"

"Yup. I've been ready ever since Mr. Dalton said we were going on the picnic."

Abigail grabbed the food basket. They donned their raingear and went in search of Jeremiah, whom they found in the barn hooking up the wagon to Old Red. "Morning, ladies, it's a fine day for a picnic."

Clarissa giggled. "It's raining buckets out there."

He turned to Abigail, his gray eyes holding her captive. "Ma'am, what's your opinion on the matter?"

She cocked her head and listened to the water drumming the roof. "It's a good day for bathing."

"We could do that, too." His roughened voice brought gooseflesh to her arms.

He took the basket from her and swung it under the wagon seat. As Clarissa leaped aboard, Jeremiah held Abigail's hand and helped her climb up.

"I hope we don't have far to go," she whispered in his ear, not wanting to ruin her daughter's excitement.

"Time will tell," he replied.

She met his wide grin with one of her own.

Jeremiah climbed onto the wagon seat and picked up the reins. "I have blankets for you two ladies to cover yourselves. We have a mighty long trek ahead of us."

The second the wagon exited the barn, driving rain pelted her face. Abigail heaved a sigh. Was he out of his mind? And more important, was she? She pulled her hat down low and wrapped a thick blanket over her shoulders and was surprised when a moment later Jeremiah shouted, "Whoa."

"We're here, already," he said, as if they'd journeyed a long distance. "Only goes to show how quickly the time goes when surrounded by good company."

As Clarissa hopped down and entered the crude shelter, Jeremiah reached for the basket beneath the seat and escorted Abigail under the hammered boards covered with tarpaper.

Abigail sat on the blanket he'd stretched out on the ground. "You could have saved yourself some time if we had walked here, and we could have used the porch."

"That would have ruined the spirit of things, and this is more fun, right, Clarissa?"

"Right, Mr. Dalton. This is gonna be a grand picnic."

Abigail had loved Jeremiah long before this picnic, but when she saw how he treated her daughter, that love multiplied. Feelings bubbled inside her chest like water in a hot kettle, filling her with a desperate need to win his heart. Six weeks, so little time left.

They sat and talked awhile. Jeremiah amused them with tales of city life, boat rides on the wild surf and climbing the granite cliffs of New England. Abigail could tell Clarissa was captivated by what he said, but to Abigail each word reminded her of the inevitable. He'd be leaving soon. Too soon. One hundred years would be too soon.

Jeremiah insisted a picnic wasn't a picnic without games.

They ran barefooted in the rain, playing tag, and hide-and-go-seek. Abigail treasured their time together, and whenever Jeremiah touched her hand or reached for her shoulder, she tucked the memory away in a special part of her heart. Their clothing was pasted to their bodies by the time they stopped to eat. Though they were already drenched to the bone, they ran toward the shelter, holding hands and laughing like school children.

Jeremiah stopped suddenly and jerked Clarissa and Abigail back. "Abby, you two wait here."

At the sound of his harsh tone, fear gripped Abigail. She watched him run toward the shelter. From where she stood, she saw Hamlet laying on his side near the wicker hamper, the pig's head cocked at an unnatural angle.

Clarissa stretched on tiptoes. "Hamlet," she wailed, tearing free of Abigail's grasp and running toward her pig.

Jeremiah caught Clarissa in his arms and crushed her to him. "Honey, I'm sorry, but there's nothing we can do."

Clarissa's loud sobs rent the air.

Abigail ran past her daughter and Jeremiah. She stood beneath the shelter staring down at the animal that had wedged open the picnic basket and had paid for the mischief with its life. Abigail had seen animals die and had always felt a sense of loss, but this was a senseless death. Though she had no way of proving what had caused Hamlet's demise, the hog had been healthy earlier that morning. She reached the only plausible conclusion.

Someone had poisoned the food.

She turned and gazed at Jeremiah still calming her daughter and realized how close they'd come to dying.

Distraught, Clarissa cried herself to sleep in Abigail arms. Abigail carried her to the sofa, laid her down, and tiptoed outside where Sheriff Clark was slapping handcuffs around Pedro's wrists.

"Señorita Wilcox, I did not do this. Please tell them I am innocent."

Abigail ignored his pleas and accepted Jeremiah's offer of a shoulder to lean on. For years, she'd considered herself a strong woman, but at the moment she felt as weak as a newborn kitten. "I never thought Pedro could do such a thing."

Jeremiah hugged her tight. A cold shiver raced down her spine despite the heat radiating from his body.

"Pedro tried to kill me so he could inherit a share of the ranch. With me gone, he'd get substantial acreage. If both of us had died, he'd have been a rich man."

"Yes, but not Pedro. He's always been so nice to me."

"I suspect greed twisted his mind. I don't think his intent was to hurt you, just me, but when his bullet struck Evelyn, he got desperate. He knew time was running out."

"Maybe Hamlet was sick."

"I thought of that, but when I showed the sheriff the picnic basket, he recognized the leaf from a poke plant in the dish along with traces of dried particles, which could have been foxglove. Pedro was determined not to fail this time. Hamlet was poisoned. Sheriff Clark is certain, and so am I."

As Abigail lay in the dark, her fingers meshed over her chest, staring at the ceiling, she thought of their close call. Panic gripped her. If Hamlet hadn't eaten the food, all three of them would have died.

Chilled to the bone, she pulled the quilt up to her face and hugged the blankets close to her. When Jeremiah had first suggested playing games, Abigail declined, saying she preferred to observe. If she had remained on the blanket, she might have been tempted to eat. Clarissa would have returned a short while later to find her mother dead. Who would care for her daughter if something happened to her?

Life was precious. She needed to embrace each day, live life to the fullest, stop worrying about the consequences.

The tap on the door was so light she thought she'd imagined it. But her heart lurched at the slightly louder knock on the adjoining door.

Her heart felt as if it were going to leap from her chest. She stared into the dark, her fingers cutting off the circulation in her hands.

"Abby, mind if I come in?"

Did she mind? She'd dreamed of this almost every night, but dreaming and reality were two different things. Joy and fear fought for control. She didn't answer. She couldn't. She wanted him to go away and prayed that he wouldn't.

The door inched open.

"Abby, are you awake?"

"Yes." She managed one word through trembling lips.

He froze in the doorway.

Her pulse pounded in her ears. Unable to breathe, she stared at his silhouette illuminated by the glow of a lantern in his room. He was naked to the waist and barefooted. She couldn't see his face but knew his pewter eyes were directed at her. She felt his need, hers too.

Abigail knew that if she allowed him to enter her room, she'd affirm her bad reputation. She battled with her conscience—being with Jeremiah was wrong—yet it seemed so right.

He took a step.

Don't come closer, she cried without issuing a sound.

As he moved toward the bed, her lungs burned from the lack of oxygen.

Jeremiah was a good man. He'd leave if she asked him. One word would stop him in his tracks.

No.

Say it, you damn fool.

But she couldn't say the words. She wanted him. Needed him. And if she had nothing else, at least she'd have tonight.

One night to make up for an entire lifetime.

Then he was standing by her bed, looking down at her. She was tempted to pull the covers over her head—or to jump into his arms and hold him tight.

"Abby," he said, his voice rough and gentle at the same time.

That one word spoke volumes. He was asking her for permission. Deep in her heart, she knew this was her last opportunity to say no. A small voice in her head again shouted this was wrong.

She reached one hand out to him. Their fingers connected, intertwined. Their hands meshed, became one. Heat radiated from her palm, continued down her arm, and settled low in her belly where embers flared.

He pulled back the blankets. The mattress dipped from his weight. He settled in next to her, his rough denims abrading her legs.

"I shouldn't be here," he said. "But I couldn't stay away. I need to be with you."

She couldn't speak, just hugged him, reveling in the feel of his muscled arms beneath her fingertips.

"I won't lie to you. You need to know I'll be leaving when the time comes. I can't live here. I want to, but this existence would eventually drive me crazy and tear us apart."

She nodded against his chest and pretended, just for tonight, that he wasn't going anywhere. "Don't worry none. I know what I'm doing." She sounded a great deal tougher than she felt. Inside she trembled with fear—and longing.

He kissed her.

She deepened the kiss and enjoyed hearing him moan when

she slipped her tongue between his lips.

"You make my blood boil," he whispered, kissing the corner of her mouth, then trailing a heated path from her earlobe down to her neck.

When his hand rested on her breast, she thought her heart would explode. When he bent to suckle the turgid tip through the cotton fabric of her nightgown, a small cry tore from her throat.

He pulled away and reached for something beside the bed. She didn't know what he was doing until he struck a match and lifted the glass dome on the lantern.

Panic surged though her. "What are you doing?"

He lowered the wick until the smallest glimmer remained, stood, and reached for the top button on his pants. "I want to see you, Abby. I want to memorize every inch of your beautiful body."

The warmth in his eyes set her limbs ablaze. Heat pooled at the juncture of her thighs. No man had ever seen her naked, and the thought both frightened and excited her.

As Jeremiah undid his fly, Abigail became fascinated with the V that widened each time he released a button. The hair that circled his navel dipped down, directing her eyes to that part of him that strained for freedom. She'd never seen a naked male, not even a baby, and the thought tightened her nerves. Her stomach grew jittery. She fought the urge to squeeze her eyes shut, but instead fastened her gaze on a spot across the room. Out of the corner of her eye, she caught a glimpse of him.

But one glimpse didn't satisfy her curiosity, so she dared another glance. He caught her looking, and heat rose to her cheeks. He considered her an experienced woman, but she'd done this only one other time, in total darkness, an episode that had lasted all of five minutes with her eyes closed.

Would she disappoint him? What did he expect of her? As she

recalled, all she had to do was lie there and wait. She dreaded this part—hated it, in fact. But the need to be with him transcended her fears. She remembered pain, and blood, and afterwards embarrassment. For a moment she regretted having allowed Jeremiah in her bedroom but quickly dismissed the thought as nonsense.

He was magnificent. His chest was bronzed from the sun, emphasized that part of him that wasn't. His erection sprung forth like a divining rod in search of water. Without touching, she could feel its heat, smell its musky scent. Her senses reeled.

Then memories surfaced. Fear consumed her. She knew what came next. Knowing the moment was fast approaching, she squeezed her eyes shut and waited. Her knuckles turned white as she grabbed handfuls of the bed sheets by her side.

The bed creaked. Jeremiah's breath caressed the side of her face. One gentle finger stroked her brow, her neck, then dallied at her breasts until Abigail's breath quickened.

She opened her eyes and found him looking down at her. "I don't want you to fear me," he said, his eyes filled with concern.

"Of course I'm not frightened," she replied, her voice a squeak.

He smiled and kissed the tip of her nose, the fine hairs of his mustache tickling, teasing. "I'm glad to hear that. I guess I was mistaken."

He stroked the side of her face and increased the pressure of his mouth. Her fears started to melt away. Her hands released their desperate hold on the covers. She curled her fingers around his neck and traced the corded muscles. His hair, like silk, brushed her fingertips. She took a moment to explore his face, stroking his strong chin, freshly shaved and smelling of mint. She burrowed her face in his neck and tasted him, felt her heart rate leap with excitement as he pulled her onto her side, his hands lingering on the small of her back. For an instant a tremor of apprehension skittered down her spine, but he kissed away her concerns, and instead of pulling away, she leaned into him.

His erection pressed against her belly—hard, hot, and insistent. With the fear came satisfaction. She'd done this to him. Were it proper, she'd have run her fingertips along its length.

He toyed with the buttons of her nightgown, and she not only allowed it, but assisted him. She feared her evil ways had surfaced because she wanted to lie naked in his arms. Again, indecision tugged at her mind when he wedged the nightgown open, reached inside, and fondled a breast. But the feeling disappeared, replaced with a certainty that she not only wanted this but also looked forward to it.

He tugged her nightgown over her head and tossed it to the floor, then pulled away enough to look at her. "I've dreamed of this for a long time. You're more beautiful than I'd imagined."

Instead of embarrassment, she felt pleasure.

When he pulled her to him, there was no hesitation, no fear, and no indecision, for she knew this was where she belonged. He claimed her breasts, suckled until she grew dizzy and continued down to her navel, kissing a heated path before making his way back up again.

He claimed her mouth; his tongue mated with hers.

She ran her hand down to his waist, lingered a moment before reaching for that part of him that intrigued her. Her fingers stroked quickly and fled, certain he'd think poorly of her.

"I want you to touch me," he whispered against her lips, his hoarse tone giving her courage and the freedom to explore.

With a boldness she didn't think she possessed, she took him in her hand and ran questing fingers along the length and breadth of him—silk and steel, heat and power.

A ragged sound tore from his throat.

When he rolled her onto her back, she curved her legs around his waist and relished the feel of his mouth on hers and the touch of his erection between her thighs. He slid inside of her in one steady thrust. Instead of pain, pleasure radiated inward and grew. As the friction from their union increased, a new strange feeling took hold. Her breath faltered; her heart soared, and as the last of her control slipped away, she whispered, "I love you Jeremiah. I always will."

CHAPTER 27

Before dawn Jeremiah kissed Abigail's forehead. Without waking her, he tiptoed from the bedroom. Though his heart sang with joy, a small part of him regretted having made love. He'd been wrong to bed Abigail when he knew he'd be returning to Boston.

But last night, wrong had felt so right.

He hadn't known what to expect of Abby, but his suspicions had been right all along. Though she'd shared another man's bed, Abby had never made love until last night. It pleased him to be the first. Unfortunately, he couldn't continue to tutor her in such matters, although nothing in this world would have pleasured him more.

Too restless to sleep, Jeremiah decided to check on Moonbeam. He dressed and went outside. As he stepped off the porch, a voice startled him.

"Where are you sneaking off to this time of morning?"

"Adele, you scared the hell out of me. Why are you up so early?"

She uttered a low laugh. "I asked first."

Jeremiah adjusted his hat. "I couldn't sleep, so I decided to go for a walk."

"I haven't had a good night's sleep since Noah passed on."

"I suspect you miss him a lot."

"He died too soon. We had some unsettled business that needed to be addressed."

Jeremiah didn't want to appear rude, but he moved back, hoping she'd drop the conversation. "That's too bad."

When he took another step, she stood.

"If you don't mind, I'll join you on that walk. It'll allow me to clear my head before I need to start breakfast."

What could he say? "Sure, if you'd like."

As they strolled across the yard, she rested her hand on his arm and glanced at the stars. "Do you think Noah is up there?" she asked, her tone filled with pain.

"He could be watching you right now."

"If he's up there, he's probably too damn busy carousing with your mother to spare me a glance."

Stunned, Jeremiah remained silent.

"Crumbs, that's all I ever got from your father. Lord knows I was good to him. When you and your mother went back East, I comforted him. Then ten years ago my husband passed away, and I spent considerable time trying to win Noah's heart. I treated him like a king. But he never noticed. My son and I never mattered. Crumbs. All we got were crumbs."

Jeremiah tried to steer the conversation away from his father. "I'm told your husband was a banker, a well liked man in the community."

"Banking was Eb's life. He always wanted everything just so. Life isn't like a neat row of numbers that always tally up."

Having had his fill of the depressing conversation, Jeremiah's thoughts strayed to Abby. Was she still lying on her stomach, her arms hugging the pillow? Would she regret having shared her bed when she awoke? He wished he were beside her now so he could wake her and . . .

"When I didn't measure up, he beat me."

Jeremiah didn't know what to say to that.

They'd just passed the door to the barn when she stopped.

"Aren't you going inside to visit that horse you're so taken with?"

"You mean Moonbeam?"

She laughed. "Not much gets past me. Since I can't sleep, I'm aware of the goings on around here. I'm impressed with the progress you've made with that beast. You actually rode him around the barn," she said, surprising Jeremiah. "Whip was never able to get within two feet of that white devil."

"I think I'll visit Moonbeam later."

She looked up at him and patted his arm. "Good, then let's walk to the stream. The rippling of the water always eases my thoughts." She blew out a breath. "You're a determined man, Jeremiah. In that respect, you're a lot like your father."

"Thanks," he said, shocked that she'd been watching him.

"Having determination can be good. But there comes a time to give up, don't you think? Your father never did." In a low voice, she continued, "Crumbs, that's what we got. Whip and me got crumbs."

Her cold tone stirred the hairs at the base of Jeremiah's neck. "When I go back East, I'll be taking Moonbeam with me."

She waved her finger in front of his face. "I'm onto you. You're trying to change the subject. Your father used to do that, too, but I'm getting this off my chest or I'll go crazy."

Although Jeremiah felt compassion for Adele, he didn't want to encourage the conversation. He figured he'd cut the walk short and head back to the ranch, maybe awaken Abby, and kiss her good morning. He didn't want Abby to think he'd taken last night lightly. He wanted her to know she meant a great deal to him. He loved her, but he couldn't tell her that.

Jeremiah glanced up. "It'll be dawn soon. Maybe we should head back. You have work to do, and so do I."

"There's still plenty of time. We'll leave shortly. I'd like you to sit with me by the stream. Surely, you can spare me a few minutes."

He hesitated, and then sat on a rock at the water's edge.

She leaned against a tree trunk to his left. "I'm sorry for carrying on so. I didn't mean to rant and rave the way I did."

He stretched his legs in front of him. "I understand that you're grieving." The gurgling brook did soothe his nerves. Adele's voice had calmed, so he figured the trek had done her some good until she started to pace behind him.

He decided to wait another few minutes and start back with or without her.

"If Noah were here right now, you know what I'd do?"

"I can't say for sure, but I'm guessing you'd hold him close."

Her cold laughter echoed over the water. "I'd shoot him."

Jeremiah jumped to his feet. "You need help, Adele," he said, jerking around and staring at the barrel of a Colt 45 aimed at him.

"You're the one who needs help, Jeremiah. Any last words before you meet your maker?"

He cussed long and hard.

She nodded toward heaven. "If that's your idea of a prayer, you'll be burning in Hell."

Why hadn't he worn his guns? His mind had been preoccupied. "Why are you doing this? I've never done anything to you."

"You've been a burr on my backside ever since my son was born."

"What does Whip have to do with this?"

"He's Noah's son, too. I'm seeing to it he finally gets what's coming to him."

"Whip's my brother?" Things finally added up: the surly glances, the gray eyes much like his, the hatred for no apparent reason.

"Noah had his mind set on you and your mother coming back. My son and I didn't matter." She aimed at his chest. "I'm tired of crumbs. It's about time I sliced myself a thick piece of cake."

If the bullet struck him at close range, it would rip him apart. The tree to his right and a rock behind him blocked his escape. His best bet would be to drop to the ground and roll. Even then, his chances were slim.

She waved the gun. "Don't even think of it. I have time to get off more than one shot. And one's all I need."

"You'll get caught."

"You won't be around to find out."

Jeremiah tossed Adele a sincere look. "I'll give Whip a share of the ranch."

"You think I'm going to fall for that?"

"I've always wanted a brother," Jeremiah said truthfully. He pondered trying to wrestle the weapon from her hand. At least ten feet separated them, and if he lunged forward, she'd shoot him before he'd covered half the distance.

Jeremiah figured he'd leap to his left. With luck, he'd escape the first bullet, and he refused to think beyond that point.

As if in slow motion, prepared to drop to the ground, he watched her thumb pull back the hammer and sight down the gun barrel.

When Abigail entered the kitchen and saw no one had started breakfast, she wondered if Adele might be ill. Figuring she'd check Adele's bedroom, she turned and collided with Whip.

He surveyed the kitchen. "Where's my mother?" He tightened his fingers around the small book in his hands. His knuckles turned white. His upper lip disappeared beneath his mustache.

Abigail had never seen Whip this disturbed. Her heart turned over with fear. "I don't know. I was about to check her room."

"Don't bother. I just came from there."

"What's wrong?"

"Have you seen Jeremiah this morning?"

"No, why?"

"He's not in his room either."

"You're frightening me. What is this about?"

"I was hoping you'd sent him on an errand."

The worry in his voice increased her concern. "No, I didn't."

"Pray that I'm wrong," he said and slammed the book on the table, then grabbed his hat and gun and charged out the door.

As Abigail thumbed through the pages of the book, she realized it was Adele's diary. Words blurred before her eyes. Abigail cursed her stupidity. The answers she needed were on these written pages, but she couldn't read worth a damn. Trying to calm herself, she shut her eyes for a moment, took a deep breath, and then scanned the last few entries. Her hands shook, and the pages fluttered. Her heart pounded. Two words popped out among the rest.

Kill Jeremiah.

Abigail ran outside, hoping she wasn't too late. She rushed to the barn. When she saw Old Red in his stall, she knew Jeremiah and Adele had gone on foot. Not sure which direction to take, she hurried from the building and tripped over a root from a nearby tree. She scrambled to her feet, took off toward the stream, and prayed her intuition was right.

After a few minutes, sweat ran down Abigail's face and neck. Her throat clogged. Time was running out. Might have already run out. *Jeremiah, please be all right.* He had to be alive.

At the sound of Adele's wild laughter, Abigail's blood ran cold. She froze and listened.

"It's about time I reverse the odds in our favor. Whip's been good to Noah. He helped him a lot, and I was sure his kindness would pay off. But then you sashay into Lowdown, ready to grab everything away from my boy." Adele's sick laughter turned Abigail's stomach as she crept closer to Jeremiah with her gun drawn.

"You should have stayed back East where you belonged."

"You'll go to jail," Jeremiah pointed out.

"They won't find your body. You and me are the only ones who know what I'm about to do, and you won't be around to tell."

Abigail took in the situation. Adele's gun was pointed at Jeremiah trapped between a tree and a boulder. His only chance of escape was to his left.

Abigail's hands shook. If she fired, would the bullet strike Adele's arm before she could kill Jeremiah? Abigail had prepared herself for Jeremiah leaving, but not this way. The ache deep inside intensified.

Trying to get Adele into her sights, Abigail tiptoed around a large tree. A branch snapped beneath her foot. Its sound announced Abby's arrival.

Adele's head jerked up. Her crazed eyes held Abigail captive. "Glad you could join us. Now drop that gun or Jeremiah won't take another breath."

"Run, Abby," Jeremiah shouted over his shoulder. They shared a glance, her heart tripping over itself. She could feel his love pouring over her.

He turned back to Adele. "Let her go. I'm the one you want. Abby hasn't done anything to you."

Abigail considered shooting, but if she missed—Jeremiah would die. Adele slipped behind a tree. "Abby, it's your decision. If you don't throw down your weapon by the count of. three, I'll fire. One, two . . ."

"Don't!" Abigail heaved her weapon into the clearing, close to Jeremiah in hopes that he might be able to retrieve the weapon, but all hopes disappeared when Adele kicked it away.

The gun skittered under a bush.

"Get over here where I can see you."

Abigail joined Jeremiah. When he pulled her against his side, she felt safe despite their predicament. "I'm sorry you got involved."

Adele sneered. "Very touching."

Twigs snapped and branches rustled behind them. Adele glanced away for a split second, but quickly turned back. "Whip, get out of here," she shouted. "This don't concern you."

"Maw, this isn't right."

"You're wrong about that. You deserved more than a few horses. You know what was in that chest Noah willed me? A bunch of sentimental gibberish and a few pieces of jewelry. I'm tired of us always coming in last."

"I don't want the ranch, not this way. If you do this, they'll send you away."

"Never you mind. I don't plan to leave behind any evidence. No one will know."

"I'll know, Maw."

"Go back to the ranch and start breakfast. I'll be along as soon as I've cleaned up here."

"Maw, can't I change your mind?"

"I've been planning this for some time."

"I know. I read your diary. You planted the pitchfork in the hay."

Adele nodded. "How was I to know that old fool would leap, too? Served him right. A man should act his age."

"You shot Evelyn."

"That bullet wasn't meant for her."

Whip stepped forward, his hand extended. "Give me the gun. You and I can go back to the ranch and we'll talk about this."

"I talked myself blue when Noah was alive. It didn't make a

bit of difference. You talking to me now won't either. I've made up my mind. I'm evening the score in our favor."

He took another step. "Give me the gun."

"Come any closer and I'll shoot them. You want that on your conscience?"

When Whip turned and started to walk away, Abigail's heart dropped.

Deep laughter rose from Adele's throat. "Alone again, just the three of us."

In slow motion, her finger squeezed the trigger. Before Abigail could react, Jeremiah pushed her to his left and threw himself over her. The air whooshed from her lungs as his weight pinned her to the ground.

A gun blast exploded. Abigail wondered whether Jeremiah had been hit, and she prepared herself for the next shot.

When Jeremiah sprang to his feet and rested his hands on Abigail's shoulders, relief lightened her head and turned her legs to mush. "You're safe now, thanks to Whip." Abigail stood and saw Whip cradling his mother in his arms. On the ground lay a discarded whip still lashed around the barrel of Adele's gun. She figured Whip had circled back and snagged the weapon from his mother's hands.

Jeremiah pulled Abigail to him. "I hope I didn't hurt you."

She tightened her arms around his chest and nodded. "I'm all right now." And she would be until he left.

Then Abigail's world would crumble all around her.

Five weeks later Jeremiah was outside leading Moonbeam around by the halter when he spotted Sam Burns approaching. "You're just the man I wanted to see," he told the lawyer.

The attorney doffed his hat. "That makes us even, because I wanted to see you, too."

Jeremiah tied the horse to the hitching post and led Sam into

Noah's study. "Can I offer you a drink?" he asked with a wave, indicating the generous liquor supply.

Sam nodded. "Don't mind if I do."

Jeremiah splashed the amber liquid into two glasses, then sat in the chair behind his father's desk. "I'm assuming you're here to check up on my performance."

"I've been keeping close tabs on you from the start. You've done better here than anyone imagined." He took a long gulp. "Why don't you stay here and run this ranch? It's in your blood."

"I was born here, but this is no longer my home. I've missed smelling the salty sea air. I have another business to attend to in Boston."

Sam set down his glass. "So I've been told. What is it you want me to do for you?"

"I want you to make out two deeds for this property. I'm giving the house and half of Noah's land to Abigail. I want the rest to go to my brother, Whip."

The attorney's brows rose. "That's mighty generous of you. Are you sure this is wise?"

Jeremiah pondered the question a moment. "Whip worked this spread most of his life. He's Noah's flesh and blood as much as I am."

Sam nodded. "I'm aware of that. But he wasn't Noah's legitimate son."

"Does that make a difference?"

The lawyer shrugged. "It's your ranch. You can do with it whatever you choose. I'll draw up the papers."

As Sam Burns ambled toward the door, Jeremiah wished he could offer Abigail a life as his wife. Since he couldn't give her a piece of himself, he'd instead give her a share of the ranch. Though the two weren't equal, he hoped it made up for his abandoning her.

CHAPTER 28

Abigail cradled her head in her hands and took a breath to settle the growing queasiness. A fine sheen of perspiration dotted her upper lip as she stood and made her way on wobbly legs to the washbasin. She grabbed the bureau with one hand and with the other hand splashed cool water over her face and neck.

Even as her vision steadied, her stomach churned and threatened to spill its contents. Sagging into a nearby chair she glanced at her flushed reflection in the mirror. Had something she'd eaten not settled well? Was she ill?

She grasped at any explanation but the obvious.

Surely, the beef she'd eaten for supper was spoiled. Or her symptoms were due to a bad case of the grippe. That had to be it. Just last week Mort was ill. Often, illnesses spread like wildfire. In a couple of days, she'd be back to normal. But as she glanced in the mirror, she recognized the terror in her eyes. Mort had been hung over. Abigail didn't drink. Her last sip of hard liquor had been over two years ago. She was running out of options.

She sighed wearily, tears burning behind her eyelids. She'd felt this way one other time—when she was with child.

She was pregnant.

She'd allowed her heart to overrule her good judgment. Her tears fell freely as she indulged herself for a brief moment, knowing there would be no time for such foolishness later. She cried for her unborn child who would never know its father.

She cried for their love, hers and Jeremiah's, that never stood a chance.

Yet Abigail wanted this baby, their child, conceived in love. Though Jeremiah would leave for Boston in three days, she'd always cherish this part of him.

As Jeremiah threw his clothing into the valise, he could see Abby watching him from the doorway. He wanted to hold her. He wanted to dump the contents of his boxes onto the floor and stay in Lowdown for the rest of his days. But he dredged up the image of himself as a young boy, waiting for mail from his old man. He and Abby were too much like his parents. They were opposites. They didn't stand a chance.

Or did they?

He attributed his doubts to weakness. And need.

And he hated the longhorns. The dumb beasts stank, and he couldn't picture himself living in the middle of Texas for the rest of his life. With a heavy heart, he nodded. "Is Whip getting the wagon ready?"

She glanced over her shoulder. Her arm brushed her face. He was breaking her heart—his, too. Better to end this now than to prolong the inevitable. "Will you be okay?"

"Of course I will," she replied, her shoulders stiffening.

He grabbed two suitcases and started across the room. A few steps seemed like such a long distance. He pretended he didn't see her pain-filled eyes, mirroring what brewed in his heart. He'd never hold her again, never see her smile, and for as long as he lived, he'd remember today. He'd remember every moment they'd spent together.

"Maybe I'll come back for a visit," he said, knowing he wouldn't because it would be too painful. He missed her already, and he hadn't even left.

The urge to hold her overwhelmed him, and against his better judgment, he lowered his bags and raised his arms. She collapsed against him, and he relished the feel of her against the length of him. He memorized the way she smelled, roses and fresh air. He'd forever remember their one night of passion. Even when he grew old, his memories would keep him warm.

"Won't you come with me?" he asked, because he was too weak to let her go.

She gulped a breath, turned tear-rimmed eyes toward him. "I'd be an oddity back East. Everyone would laugh at me."

"I wouldn't let them."

She was right, but he wouldn't admit it. Like a man dying of thirst, he drank in the sight of her, the emerald eyes, the unruly red hair, and the chin jutting at a stubborn angle he'd grown to admire.

"That would be beyond your control."

He kissed her forehead because he knew he might never leave if he tasted her lips.

He released her, grabbed his bags, and left without a backward glance. As he climbed into the wagon, out of the corner of his eye, he saw Abby waiting for a final wave or a friendly gesture. He kept his arms by his side, directed his gaze away from the woman he loved and the ranch that had been his home for six months. It was time to sever their ties, and if he so much as spared her another glance, he wouldn't be able to leave. As the wagon rumbled along the rutted road to the train that would take him home, the hollow ache in his chest swelled.

Though Jeremiah was finally going back to Boston, his heart would forever remain in Texas.

Six months later Abigail maneuvered her bulky stomach around the kitchen table and leaned against the counter. Her back ached. Her legs had ballooned to twice their normal size. Sweat beaded her brow. The baby in her belly rolled and stretched, kicking the breath from her lungs. She rested her hands over her abdomen and imagined herself cradling her son in her arms. Though some called her ridiculous, she was certain she was carrying a boy. Just thinking of him filled her heart with warmth. At night before going to sleep, she'd picture his gray eyes much like his father's.

Abigail had stopped going into town because of the wagging tongues and disapproving glances. Though she'd held her head high, she'd felt shame. For her baby's sake, she'd bought a gold band that she wore on the ring finger of her left hand. She wasn't fooling anyone, but it looked respectable.

On good days, she thought of Jeremiah and how much she loved him. On bad days, she cussed his memory and called herself an idiot for making the same mistake twice in one lifetime. She didn't care that much about her reputation, but this baby would be shunned.

He'd be called a *bastard*.

Whenever Abigail thought of that vile word, her fists clenched. Worst, she provided a poor example for Clarissa. How could she teach her daughter morals when she had none? How could she expect her daughter to become a lady while she was shunned by the townspeople?

Abigail had been abandoned again. Even when she reminded herself that Jeremiah didn't know about the baby, she pushed that thought aside, because anger was easier to deal with than the pain clawing at her heart.

She heard the sound of approaching hooves and glanced out the window, grabbed hold of the counter for support. Her hands trembled, and for a moment she squeezed her eyes shut. Was she dreaming? Surely, she was mistaken. But when she again looked outside, she knew this wasn't a dream.

It was a nightmare.

About twenty feet away stood Jeremiah hitching Moonbeam

to a fence post. Why was he here? How long was he staying? When would he leave again?

No longer able to stand, she collapsed in the chair and hid her girth beneath the wooden table. She waited to see the man who had caused her so much misery.

The door opened and shut. "Abby, are you home?"

At the sound of his voice in the hallway, her heart thudded. She cursed herself for being so weak. She still loved him, always would.

"Abby?"

She didn't answer. She couldn't.

"Abby, are you home?"

She willed her voice not to waver "I'm in the kitchen," she finally said, as if no one in particular had come calling.

When he entered the room and leaned against the door casing, all her memories came flooding back. She remembered how good he'd made her feel, how his mouth had traveled over hers. She remembered laughter but she focused on the tears. She forced herself to remember his leaving, how he'd abandoned her and their unborn child. She glanced at the marred tabletop and traced a deep groove with a trembling fingertip.

"What do you want?" she asked, her tone harsh. She saw the disappointment on his face, ignored it, and continued, "How long will you being staying this time?"

He smiled. "You're looking good. You're face seems a little rounder, a little rosier. You're beautiful as always."

If he thought he could sashay in here, take up where they'd left off, and then leave again, he was sadly mistaken. She twisted the golden band around her finger and tried not to cry. Because of the pregnancy, her emotions were always close to the surface. She couldn't look at a squashed ant without bawling. She prayed he'd leave before her tears flooded the kitchen, before she threw away her pride and begged him to stay.

As she twisted the wedding band around her finger, she saw him look down at her left hand. The light died in his eyes. He moved toward the table and sat in the chair opposite her. So close, yet so far away. How many nights had she prayed for his return? And now she was sending him away. She couldn't live with another rejection. She couldn't chance having him around for only a short while.

He reached for her hand, fingered the gold band. His pain-filled eyes met hers. "What's this?" he asked, his voice thick and rough.

She couldn't answer right away, but when she did her voice was strong. "Isn't it obvious?"

He swallowed. His mouth thinned. "Oh." He took her hand, squeezed until it almost hurt.

Tears surfaced, and she blinked them away.

He held on tight, their lifeline to each other a fragile link. Abigail knew when he went out the door, she'd never see him again. "How's Boston?"

"The day I left here, I met a man with land for sale along the coast of eastern Texas. When I saw his property, I knew I'd found the perfect solution . . ." His voice broke, and he waved away the rest of what he'd started to say. "Well, it doesn't matter now. I'd better be going."

When he stood and started across the kitchen, he paused and studied her for a long time. "I can't leave without hugging you. Just a hug, and then I'll go."

Before she could reply, he rounded the table and pulled her to her feet. He yanked her to him and just as quickly pushed her away and looked down in disbelief.

Jeremiah stared at Abigail's distended belly. He'd been shocked to discover she'd married in his absence. When he saw she was carrying another man's child, the hurt inside threatened to rip him apart. "It looks as though congratulations are in order."

She didn't meet his eyes, but instead nodded. Tears ran down her cheeks. He lifted her chin with his forefinger and kissed the tip of her nose. Still she avoided his gaze. It was then that he did the math, read the truth in her eyes.

He turned from her and braced his hands against the counter. His shoulders slouched. He stared unseeingly out the window.

"This is my child, isn't it?"

"Yes."

He faced her, the pain in his chest wrenching him apart. "Why didn't you tell me?"

"I wanted you to stay because you loved me, not because you had to."

"You should have told me." And because of his stupidity, she'd run off and married another man who'd be father to his son or daughter.

"You kept saying you didn't belong in Texas. I allowed you to leave because you wanted to."

"You denied me the opportunity to become acquainted with my own child."

Guilt darkened her green eyes. "I didn't want our son to grow up feeling he was responsible for trapping his father into marrying his mother. And don't go standing there shaking your head. Your restlessness would have eventually shown."

She slipped into the chair. Her shoulders shook. "You didn't love me enough to stay. Now I want you to go and leave us alone."

He left her sitting there, looking so vulnerable that he wanted to comfort her, but he didn't have a right. She belonged to someone else. "Who is he?" he asked, needing to know and not wanting to in the same instant.

Looking confused, she met his gaze. "Huh? Oh."

Hope speared through him. "Abby," he said stepping forward. "Are you married?" He stood one foot away from her, praying he still had a chance. When she looked down and shook her head, he dropped to his knees and rested his hands on her narrow lap. "I was a fool to leave. I didn't think we stood a chance together. But I've come to realize it wasn't my parent's differences that kept them apart, but their inability to compromise."

When she reached down and traced the side of his face with her fingertips, he felt he stood a chance of winning her back.

"Tell me about east Texas," she said between sniffs.

"My partner is taking over the Boston branch of our company, and I'll manage the Texas division. I've already sent two shipments of beef back East. I expect my partner and his crew are unloading the crates onto the dock about now. I've bought a small spread and I plan to raise horses. I've bought piglets for Clarissa. I figured . . . that is . . . I'd hoped you and Clarissa would join me."

When she threaded her fingers through his hair and whispered, "I love you, Jeremiah. I always will," joy surged through him.

He rested his head on her belly, holding his child and the woman he loved. His baby kicked him, hard, knocking some sense into him.

Jeremiah laughed, his tear-filled eyes meeting hers. "Marry me, Abby, and I'll spend the rest of our lives making sure you never regret the decision." When she didn't answer right away, he realized he'd forgotten the most important part.

"I love you, and I have for a long, long time."

CHAPTER 29

"Maw, I think I'm gonna call this one Hamlet." Clarissa hugged a piglet to her chest.

Abigail smiled at her daughter. "What are you going to name the other two?"

"I haven't decided yet."

Bracing her hands on the arms of the oak rocker, Abigail lowered her bulky frame onto the sturdy chair. As the baby tumbled inside, she rested her fingers over her distended belly and watched Clarissa kiss the top of Hamlet's head and set the piglet in the pen Jeremiah had built next to the porch.

Clarissa sat on a bench near Abigail. "I'm getting mighty tired of waiting for my brother to be born."

The baby kicked the breath from Abigail's lungs. "I look forward to seeing him, too."

"How can you be sure I'm gonna have a brother instead of a sister?"

"I just know. When I carried you, you weren't always jumping around the way he does. It's a boy. I'm sure of it."

"I'd rather have a sister, but I guess a brother will have to do."

Abigail ruffled her daughter's hair. "It's too late to do anything about that now."

"I guess so."

"Maybe the next baby will be a girl."

Clarissa's lower lip jutted out. "I sure hope so. I want a sister to play with."

"You can play with your brother."

"Yeah, but that won't be the same."

Abigail rocked gently.

Clarissa glanced toward her pets inside the pen. "I finally have a paw all my own. No one can ever call me that bad word again."

She squeezed her daughter's hand. Abigail had escaped her past, too. She could now hold her head high and look everyone in the eye without being ashamed. She had a new life with a husband who loved her.

"Maw, I like it here, don't you?"

She looped an arm over her daughter's shoulder. "Yes, dear, I do."

Their two-story house stood on a rise overlooking the Gulf of Mexico. As Abigail lifted her eyes toward the horizon and admired the aqua-tinted water shimmering in the sunlight, a sense of peace settled over her. She almost had to pinch herself to believe all that had happened during the last two weeks. She was now Jeremiah's wife, lived in a new home, and had the respectability she had always craved.

Jeremiah refused to sell her share of the ranch, insisting that it be kept for their children. He was a fine man with a generous heart. He was *her husband. Her lover.* A shiver raced down her spine whenever she thought of him that way. She'd never expected a decent man would be willing to marry her, yet according to Jeremiah whatever happened before they met didn't matter to him. And she loved him even more for being able to overlook her past.

Clarissa cupped her hand over her eyes. "I see someone coming."

Abigail peered toward the winding road that led to their home. "I expect it's Jeremiah."

Clarissa jumped to her feet. "He said he had a surprise for us."

Abigail slowly pushed herself to her feet and peered into the distance. She'd been dying of curiosity since before dawn, when Jeremiah kissed her goodbye and said he had an errand to run. No amount of prodding did any good. He'd winked, promising to return shortly. She aimed a pillow at his arrogant smirk, but he caught it midair, blew a kiss, and left without giving her a single clue.

Clarissa jumped up and down. "He's got someone with him."

A woman sat on the seat beside Jeremiah. Boxes filled their wagon, piled two and three high.

As the wagon approached, Abigail braced her hands over the porch railing, unable to move, unable to believe her eyes.

Jeremiah leaped off the wagon, ran to her side, and escorted her down the two steps. "Abby, we have company."

Tears pouring down her face, Abigail hugged the woman and held on tight. "Maw, I've missed you so very much."

Eight weeks later Abigail leaned against Jeremiah as they sat atop Moonbeam. "I don't like leaving the baby."

"Emma will be fine with your mother and her big sister caring for her." He kissed the back of her neck and nibbled a warm path to her ear. "Tonight I want you all to myself."

"I was so sure the baby would be a boy."

"Clarissa's convinced you chose a sister just for her."

"You aren't disappointed."

"As long as I can be part of our children's lives, it doesn't matter to me whether they're boys or girls." A deep laugh rumbled from his throat. "And I'm especially glad Emma has your flame-red hair."

Abigail rolled her eyes. "Poor little thing, chances are she'll be covered with freckles, too."

"I hope so," he replied and traced her earlobe with his tongue. "Where are we going?"

"You'll see." His right hand held the reins, but the fingers of his left hand cupped her breast.

"I love you," she whispered with a sigh, wiggling her bottom against that part of him that hardened on contact.

He groaned. "You're a wicked woman, Abigail Dalton."

"I can't believe we're really married."

"Believe it. I aim to have my way with my wife this evening."

Her face flushed, and she laughed. "Maybe."

"There's no maybe about it, Mrs. Dalton." His hoarse whisper ignited the embers deep inside.

Abigail didn't think it was possible to love a man more than she did Jeremiah, and she was looking forward to making love with her husband.

As they wound their way along the narrow path leading to the ocean, she saw a sailboat docked in the harbor. The faint scent of salt drifted toward them. A few minutes later he pulled on the reins and assisted her down from the large stallion. "Have you ever slept on a boat, Abby?"

"No."

He winked. "You won't be sleeping on this one either." He pulled her to him for a hungry kiss. They held each other for a long time, tasting, touching, and reveling in the feelings bursting inside.

Finally, Jeremiah pulled away, his breathing fast and unsteady. "Wait here for a moment. While I'm busy getting things ready, check out the transom."

"The what?"

"The back of the boat. I've named her after you."

He ran along the wooden dock and leaped aboard his sailboat, disappearing down the narrow stairway that led to the cabin.

Pleased that he'd named his boat after her, Abigail meandered down the dock. In the dimming sunlight, she stared in disbelief at the gold lettering, *Freckle Face*.

A moment later Jeremiah joined her.

"I hate my freckles," she said.

"I love your freckles. I'll prove it to you very shortly. I aim to kiss every last one."

He escorted her into the cabin where wavering candlelight bathed the mahogany interior in a golden hue. They kissed their way past the small table and benches, past the round portholes, and ended up in the small cubicle with a narrow bed covered with bluebonnet petals.

Jeremiah tumbled Abby onto the bed of flowers, his own senses reeling. He captured her mouth in a sizzling kiss that set their course for the night.

"I love you, Jeremiah," she whispered in his ear.

"I love you, and Clarissa, and Emma, and the babies yet to come." He looked into her emerald eyes and whispered, "I'll never leave you, ever again."

He sealed his promise with one kiss, and then another, and another . . .

ABOUT THE AUTHOR

Diane Amos lives with her husband, Dave, in a small town north of Portland, Maine. They have four grown children, five grandchildren, a mischievous kitten named Milly and an energetic miniature Dachshund named Molly. Diane is an established Maine artist. Her paintings are in private collections across the United States. She is a Golden Heart finalist and winner of the Maggie Award for Excellence. For more information about Diane and her books, check out her Website at www.dianeamos.com.